· BOOK 3 ·

SKYBORN

PHOENIX FLIGHT

LINDEN

THELANTIS

THRAILLE

ROBIN CLAN

CANYON

WOODPECKER CLAN

THE CLANDOMS

THE TRUTH WILL SHINE IN GOLDEN EYES

PHOENIX PALACE

CYRITH

BEACH CAMP

GARDEN OF STATUES

BEREL MANOR

ICARA'S HOUSE

VESTRA

THE EMBERS

SOUTHERN JUNGLES

MAY A PHOENIX RISE

FROM ASH ALONE

· BOOK 3 ·

SKYBORN

PHOENIX FLIGHT

JESSICA KHOURY

Scholastic Press / New York

All rights reserved. Published by Scholastic Press, an imprint of Scholastic Inc.,
Publishers since 1920. SCHOLASTIC, SCHOLASTIC PRESS, and associated logos are
trademarks and/or registered trademarks of Scholastic Inc.

The publisher does not have any control over and does not assume
any responsibility for author or third-party websites or their content.

This book is a work of fiction. Names, characters, places, and incidents are either
the product of the author's imagination or are used fictitiously, and any resemblance
to actual persons, living or dead, business establishments, events, or locales
is entirely coincidental.

Library of Congress Cataloging-in-Publication Data available

ISBN 978-1-338-65246-8

1 2022

First edition, August 2022
Printed in the U.S.A. 23

Book design by Maeve Norton

FOR JUNIPER, WHO BURST INTO THE
WORLD WITH ELLIE, AND WHOSE EYES
ARE FULL OF THE SKY

CHAPTER ONE
· THE HUNTER ·

Stone made for an unforgiving pillow. As he woke, the Hunter groaned and turned his head, feeling as though his skull had been split by a sledgehammer. The hard rock beneath him was cold and indifferent to the pain thrumming through his body. When he peeled his eyes open, he saw nothing but muddy shades of gray all around. He was in some kind of crumbling palace, walls of great stone blocks that were half collapsed, dead vines clinging to everything. Beyond that was nothing but mist.

A sudden burst of pain in his leg made him squeeze his eyes shut again.

He struggled to recall what had happened.

His last memory was of his quarry—the smug little Crow and his Sparrow friend. The Hunter had been about to set to work, his fingers tingling with anticipation of their screams, when . . .

I was attacked!

A burly high clanner had come out of nowhere, wielding a sword. They'd tussled, and the Hunter's thigh had been cut. He'd taken off, vowing vengeance, swearing to make them suffer for his pain as none of his past victims had suffered before.

Then what?

Vague memories skittered just out of reach: gray skies, rolling fields drenched in thorns, and . . .

Grrrrnnnch.

The Hunter's reverie was broken by the sound of grinding stone.

He wasn't alone.

He opened his eyes again, hissing through his teeth. Perhaps that was his prey now! Perhaps they thought to sneak up on the Hunter, to finish him off . . .

All at once, he sprang up, or tried to, anyway. The pain in his sliced thigh cut through his abdomen, and he gasped and fell back.

Then he saw them.

Not the Crow, nor the Sparrow, nor the high clanner who'd cut him. He saw *gargols*.

Dozens. Scores. Gargols of every shape and size, with snouts and tails and horns and spines and claws. The grinding sound was the noise their heavy bodies made as they shifted their weight, dragged a leg, lowered a head to peer at him. Each one had a pair of glowing blue eyes, which the Hunter realized must be the *skystones* the king was always going on about. What had he said of them? That they were filled with evil magic, yes. The Hunter hadn't paid much attention.

Now he wished he had.

He lay very, very still, as still as the stone slab upon which he was sprawled, and felt, for the first time in his life, true terror. Like an animal in a trap, like one of his own pathetic victims, he was immobilized with fear. It burned on his tongue. It knotted in his throat until he couldn't breathe.

Suddenly, the gargols shifted, moving aside to make space for someone, ducking their heads and tucking their tails.

What sort of creature made *gargols* recoil like beaten dogs?

No part of the Hunter moved except his eyes, which rolled in his head, looking for escape, for a weapon, for *anything* that might end this nightmare, as a man stepped through the crowd of gargols.

At least, the thing was *shaped* like a man. The features were all there—a heavy brow, clean-shaven jaw, long hair that hung over each shoulder. He had his hands tucked into opposite sleeves, held before him in a dignified manner, as the Hunter had seen many of the hateful courtiers walk in the king's court. This one had such a look—aristocratic and scornful. Which was odd. His wings were too short and round to be those of a high clan courtier.

Also unlike the courtiers, he was made entirely of marble.

Even his clothes were carved from the same cold gray stone as his skin. He should have been standing on a pedestal in a garden, perhaps holding up a basin of water in a fountain, a proper statue. His feathers were flat gray, their barbs as hard as a porcupine's quills. What clan he was, the Hunter could not tell, for there was no color to his wings, no defining patterns or markings.

He should *not* have been moving around as if made of flesh and bone. But there he was, leaning over the Hunter and gazing with eyes of brilliant blue skystone.

"Vermin," hissed the gargol man. That had to be what he was—some kind of gargol.

The Hunter flinched upon hearing the creature speak. Sweat rolled down his neck, cold as melting snow. "What are you?" he rasped.

The man looked him over as if he hadn't heard. He moved as the gargols did, grinding and slow, living stone.

"Trespasser," he spat, with even more venom. "You think to invade *my* sky? You think to violate my decrees?"

"The Hunter goes where he likes," the Hunter snarled, but his voice wobbled, which filled him with fury. If he hated to be made a fool of, he hated even more to feel afraid. Whatever this . . . creature was, how *dare* he treat the Hunter as if he were prey? "Freak! I will split your stony skull and drink from it!"

He lunged up again, this time pushing through the spasm of pain, and reached for the man.

A gargol pounced with phenomenal speed, swatting a claw and striking the Hunter on the chest. He screamed as he was tossed through the air, landing hard on the cobblestone floor. Scrambling up, he put all his weight on his uninjured leg and looked around in horror as gargols crept toward him from every side.

Spreading his wings, the Hunter crouched, preparing to launch himself into flight.

But when he thrust up, his feet did not leave the ground.

Instead, the soles of his shoes seemed to congeal to the stones. He jerked his legs, to no avail. He may as well have stepped in wet tar; he was stuck fast.

"What the—" His head snapped up, his eyes finding the stone man. "What are you doing to me?"

The stone man's eyes glowed brighter. He held out his hands, palms toward the Hunter. "I see you have grown bold in your ignorance," he said harshly. "Is a thousand years so long a time that the Skyborn should forget my warnings?"

The Hunter yelped as his shoes began to turn to stone, his ankles hardening as if stuck in drying clay. "What—what is this?"

"I issued but this one decree: That you should crawl the earth until the end of time, like cockroaches. That if you dared spread wing in my skies again, my fury would wipe you from existence. And yet you heed me not? You think to try my might again? You think I have not seen your kind sneaking through my islands, creep-creeping through my cities, stealing what is not theirs?"

"I don't even know you!" howled the Hunter. He beat his wings furiously, but he could not pull himself free from the man's spell. Staring down in terror, he watched as his legs turned grayer, changing to stone beneath him. The magic rose slowly, consuming his thighs, his hips. He lost all feeling below the waist, even the pain of his wound erased—replaced by terrible numbness.

"Then know me now!" roared the stone man. "The clans will pay dearly for their trespassing, and this time . . . I will not be so merciful."

He thrust his hands forward, and the magic accelerated. The Hunter could only scream as his torso, then his arms, turned to stone. His hands froze in the air, outstretched, reaching for a sky in which he would never again soar. His head was the last to turn, his mouth open in a howl, his eyes wide with terror—until the light in them faded and his gaze turned as blank as the mist.

CHAPTER TWO
· NOX ·

Warm flames danced over Nox's feathers, playful, bright, a bit ticklish.

He shivered, sick to his stomach.

The sea rushed and bubbled just inches from his feet. He stared at it so he wouldn't have to look at his wings, but they were always in the corners of his eyes, too bright to be ignored.

They sparked with fire—*real* fire, flames curling and flickering over feathers, burning without fuel or smoke. Not that it hurt Nox. He'd been immune to fire before his death, and he'd stayed immune even after.

His death.

He had died.

He'd been *dead.*

And then . . .

A clatter of falling wood startled him. Instinctively his wings shot open. The flames flared along their length, growing brighter and larger.

"Agh!" Twig shouted, stumbling back from the driftwood he'd just dumped on the sand. "Watch it!"

Nox gasped and retracted his wings at once, the blood draining from his face.

"Sorry!" he said.

Twig patted out a flame that had caught his sleeve. "It's no problem!"

he said quickly. "I shouldn't have sneaked up on you like that."

Nox's eyes ran guiltily over Twig's clothes, which were covered in singed holes and burned patches. This hadn't been the first time he'd gotten too close to Nox.

"It's fine," Twig said again. He watched Nox's face, looking anxious. "I'm not hurt."

Yet.

Always the unspoken *yet.*

How many times would Nox *almost* set his friends on fire before he finally *did*?

And it had been only one day and one night since he'd woken to his new wings.

"Are you . . . feeling okay?" asked Twig.

Nox swallowed and said nothing. He resumed staring at the sea, at the sweet, icy water that rushed softly over the sand.

When he'd first woken to find himself surrounded by a torrent of flames, he'd thought for sure he was dead. That even if he was still *slightly* alive, he wouldn't be for long. Though he'd been immune to fire all his life, there was just *so much* of it that surely even his flame-proof skin wouldn't withstand the heat.

Instead, he'd stumbled out of the fire, gasping, in terrible pain . . . and completely naked.

In front of both Ellie and Twig.

That was one memory he couldn't relive without wanting to bury himself in the sand. But even his embarrassing state had quickly been forgotten once he'd seen his wings—no longer Crow black, but gold. And not dark brownish–gold like the Eagle clan, but the bright gold of the morning sun, feathers shifting from orange to yellow to red in an endless shimmer. And that was nothing compared to the flames— real, hot flames that twisted and danced over his wings.

Phoenix clan wings.

Nox had screamed until he choked, then run straight into the sea, plunging himself into the waves. Underwater, the flames had extinguished, but the moment he came up, his wings caught fire again. It had taken Ellie and Twig nearly an hour to convince him to come out of the water. Even then, his heart had been racing and his chest pounded with panic and confusion.

A day later, and nothing had changed. He'd listened mutely while Ellie told him how she'd brought him back to life by literally setting him on fire. The words had washed over him like the waves, a dash of cold before receding. It made no sense to him, that he could be dead one minute and then alive again the next.

When Ellie returned to their little beach camp, carrying an armload of clothes she'd scavenged from skies knew where, Nox hadn't moved from the same spot he'd been in when she'd left. That had been two hours ago.

He was having trouble looking at Ellie.

"Found these in an old fisherman's cottage south of here," she said, tossing the clothes to Nox. "Looked like nobody had been there in years, so it *wasn't* stealing."

There was a white linen shirt, much too large for him but surprisingly clean; a pair of boots that were nearly the perfect size; and brown trousers he had to tie up with the horse halter Twig handed him. He dressed in silence behind a rock, then sat again by the fire.

"Everything okay?" the Sparrow girl asked Twig. She limped as she walked. Her left leg had been shattered by a gargol's claws just weeks ago.

"Um . . . yeah." Twig sounded anything other than okay. None of them were okay. Ellie had to know that.

Skies, yesterday morning they'd been standing on a gallows

in Thelantis, about to be hanged in front of the whole city. Now here they were on some random strip of beach, with Ellie and Twig tiptoeing around Nox like he was a tightly strung crossbow—nocked with a flaming bolt.

"We can't stay here," Ellie said. It was the fifth time she'd said it since morning. "The Goldwings will be looking everywhere. I think I saw one on my way back, but I can't be sure. Could've been a gargol."

Nox didn't even glance up. The sky was an endless sheet of gray cloud. An occasional drizzly rain fell, but it wasn't enough to put out the flames on his wings.

"Nox," Ellie said.

He flinched at her direct address.

"Nox, it's not safe here."

"Then where *is*?" Nox snapped back, answering her for the first time. Before he half knew what he was doing, he'd leaped to his feet and turned to face her. He glared at Ellie, his wings spreading of their own accord.

"Do you think I can hide like this, Ellie? Do you think I can blend in like *this*?"

Deep within Nox, something hot and vicious growled, a beast of shadow and flame. It lunged, as if trying to take control of him from the inside, and all at once, the fire on his wings blazed brighter, snapping and curling.

Ellie screamed and fell backward.

The heat washed over Nox's skin. With a yelp, he frantically flapped his wings, trying to put out the fire, but the rush of wind only stoked the flames higher.

"Nox!" Ellie shouted. "Get in the water!"

He sprinted into the surf and dove under the waves, relishing the cold bite of the sea. His feathers went dark again, and he stayed below the surface for as long as he could hold his breath.

What had happened?

He searched his mind in confusion and terror, until something . . . *wriggled.* The beast was still there, lurking somewhere inside him, like a pair of eyes in the dark. When Nox focused his attention on it, it snarled, flames curling through his thoughts.

Nox went up for air, gasping, and blinked hard until the vision of the creature cleared.

Ellie and Twig stood on the shoreline, eyes wide.

"Well, that was new," said Twig.

"Nox . . . it happened because you got angry," said Ellie.

"You think?" The cold was knifing through him now; his teeth chattered. Still he made no move to leave the water. "What's *wrong* with me?"

"You're a Phoenix," said Ellie, spreading her hands. "Maybe your fire is tied to your emotions somehow. Maybe if you just—"

He groaned and again pulled his head underwater, where he couldn't hear her. Couldn't hear anything but the roar of the ocean.

But he couldn't hold his breath forever.

He came up again eventually, shaking water from his hair.

When he was done wringing out his new clothes, he walked past them to the small campfire and sat stiffly.

"I hate this," he whispered, hearing them approach cautiously from behind.

"We'll figure it out," said Ellie.

"I nearly set you on fire. Again."

"But you didn't. And you won't. There has to be a way to control it, Nox. We just have to . . ."

She went on, but he stopped listening, choosing instead to press his face into the rough linen of his sleeve. His wings hung heavy on his back, so much heavier than his old Crow wings had been.

These new Phoenix wings were longer and thicker, a high clanner's wings. They felt *wrong*, even without the flaming feathers.

Skies. He didn't like to admit it, but Ellie was right.

He *was* a Phoenix. How many times had he denied it, refused to even consider it might be true? And how many times had she tried to convince him?

Well, she'd won in the end. Ellie usually did.

He was descended from the Phoenix clan, the long-lost rulers of the islands in the sky. What that meant, he couldn't begin to comprehend, but he knew he hated it. All of it. The wings, the fire, the strange ancient clan that were his ancestors. It was all *wrong* for him.

He might have a Phoenix's wings, but he had a Crow's heart still.

". . . have to go to Thraille," Ellie was saying. The word caught his ear, and he turned his head just enough to listen. "It's the only clue we have."

"What's Thraille?" asked Twig.

"It's the clan seat of the Crows," Ellie replied. "Or *was*, before the Eagles destroyed it. They must know about the Phoenix clan, and that some of their descendants survived and intermingled with the Crows."

"Do you think there are more Crows like Nox?"

"No. My guess is the place is empty. But Nox's grandmother set out to find some secret buried there, something about their family's history and why they got on the wrong side of Eagle clan. I mean, it pretty much *has* to be about their Phoenix bloodline, right?"

Leave it to Ellie to have a plan.

Nox was torn. He wanted to shut everything out and pretend he was the same person he'd been yesterday . . . but he knew that was impossible. He'd never go back to being a common Crow thief.

So what did that leave him?

Maybe Ellie was right. Maybe he needed to learn how to control his wings. Anyway, it wasn't like he could hide like he usually did when trouble arose. He'd spent his life blending into the crowd. But now, glancing at his golden wings, he bit back a curse. There'd be no hiding those, no matter what he did. Even if he cloaked them, the glow of the flames would shine through—if they didn't set the cloth on fire altogether.

"If you'd just done what I asked and buried me at sea," he said hoarsely, drawing Ellie's and Twig's attention, "we wouldn't be talking about this."

"If I'd done what you asked," Ellie replied, "you'd be *dead*."

He shrugged.

Ellie dropped to one knee in front of him.

He flinched, sitting up. "No! You're too close—"

She grabbed his shoulders, despite the slight leap in the flames on his wings. She had to feel the heat rolling off his feathers, but she didn't let go. Instead she looked him dead in the eyes.

"You're alive," she said. "You're alive, and I'd save you again and again and again if I had to. Because you're *alive* and that means we have hope."

"This is about your plan," he said. "To use me to lead everyone back to the islands in the sky, to cure wingrot and—"

"*No*." Ellie's fingers tightened on his skin. "This is about you, Nox. None of the rest of it matters until we make sure you're okay. Got it? Tirelas can wait. Wingrot can wait. All I care about right now is *you*."

He stared at her, speechless.

Ellie had changed.

Days ago, she'd been willing to do anything to save the world, even if it meant destroying their friendship.

But now?

Was she really willing to put all that aside to help him?

Or was he just another step in her ultimate plan?

He wasn't sure, but he did know she'd never talked this way before. Ellie Meadows was a lot of things he didn't care for, but *devious* wasn't one of them. If she was lying or trying to trick him, he'd know.

She was a terrible liar.

"Okay," he said quietly. "We'll go to Thraille."

Letting out a breath of relief, Ellie finally let go of him and danced backward, shaking her hands with a rueful grin. "No offense, but you're like a walking bonfire."

"Yeah. I noticed." He shook out his strange wings, watching the flames dance over them in response.

CHAPTER THREE
· ELLIE ·

Exhaustion dragged at Ellie's bones. This was the third night in a row she'd been unable to sleep, and it was getting to her. She lay by the warm embers of the campfire, watching Nox and worrying.

He was fast asleep, at least. His resurrection seemed to have left him drained, and he'd had no trouble dropping off. Ellie envied his deep slumber. Twig too was out cold, a few beach creatures nuzzled against his skin. Wherever he went, animals were drawn to him and his innate ability to understand them. Tonight he was joined by a few crabs, a snail, and a silvery sea snake that curled just under the skin of the sand. But there was a certain ball of fluff missing; Lirri, Twig's faithful pronged marten, had gone missing when he'd been captured by Goldwings two weeks ago. It was strange to see Twig without the marten's pale white horns peeping from his pocket.

They'd all lost things over the past months.

Ellie had lost her home, her clan, all her belongings, including the hooked lockstave she'd wielded for a weapon. And then there was her leg—crushed and twisted, paining her with every step she took, though she'd learned to hide it. Ellie couldn't take the looks of pity the others gave her when they saw her cringing.

Nox had lost his gang of thieves back in Thelantis; his mentor, the Talon; and now his Crow identity.

And Twig . . . Lirri wasn't the only thing he'd lost. He was now flightless after his battle with wingrot, the terrible disease that withered wings and sometimes even claimed lives. Ellie still relived that horrible night in her memory, when she'd first seen his feathers piled on the floor, his back bandaged, the doctor standing over him with a bone saw.

And then there was the loss none of them could talk about: the empty gap stretching between her and Twig, the spot that would have usually been filled by the dark skin and striped wings of Gussie of the Falcon clan.

But Gussie had betrayed them in Thelantis, nearly to their deaths. They hadn't seen her since.

Thinking about *her* made Ellie want to punch things.

Stretching out on her back, her freckled brown wings spread just enough to curl up and over her chest, Ellie stared at the cloudy sky and tried instead to think of what they'd *gained*. Of the one all-important, world-changing thing they'd learned.

She had been right.

Nox was a Phoenix.

He was the key to their return to Tirelas, the world of floating islands from which their people had been living in exile for generations. His ancestors had ruled those islands as kings and queens. The Eagles—who ruled the Skyborn on the ground—had done their best to stamp them out of existence. Yet here Nox was, proof that the ancient royal bloodline lived on.

And they *had* to return to Thelantis. It was the only way they'd be safe from wingrot for good, up in the sky, where they'd be close to the floating, magic skystones that held up the islands, and which were the only true cure for the disease. If they didn't return soon, Ellie feared the worst: that the Skyborn would become earthbound, losing their wings forever.

Nox was the key to their salvation, of that she was sure. He could show the Skyborn the truth about their past, how they belonged in the sky. He could lead them all home, where they belonged. And it was Ellie's job to help him.

You will carry a flame through the darkness, went the prophecy she'd been given. *But if you drop it, or if the flame goes out . . . the sky will fall.*

But Nox was in no position to help anyone yet, and she wasn't sure how to help *him*.

He was worrying her.

Nox stared at the sea too much and talked too little. It was a bit like the way he'd been after his mother's death, but different. Back then, she'd at least known what was going through his head. This time, she had no clue. Was he truly angry with her for saving his life, or was he just scared what that life might mean for him now? Did he really wish she'd left him to the sea, cold and lifeless?

As it turned out, saving him from death might have been the easy part.

How did she save him from himself?

In the morning, they left their little beach camp behind and began walking, their backs to the sea. The clouds had cleared at last. The early sun cast the world in bronze, a monochrome landscape of golden dune grass, pale sand, and yellow skies. Fog rolled off the land and sank into the ocean, as if to reveal the path before them. But the clear sky only made Ellie shiver.

"The Goldwings will be out in full force now," she said.

Nox nodded but didn't look overly concerned. He still had the same numb expression he'd worn since he'd come back to life. If the king's knights did show up, Ellie wondered if he'd even try to fight, or if he'd just stand there mutely and let them take him.

Her leg ached from walking, but she bit back complaints. The doctor who'd tended her after it had been crushed told her she would never run again. She was lucky to be walking at all, even if her gait was slow and pained. She could have just as easily lost her life to that gargol. She should be grateful her leg was the only thing it had taken . . . but still, some days even Ellie's fierce determination wasn't enough. Some days, she just wanted to howl her anger to the skies and it took all her self-control to hold it back.

After several hours of monotonous pine forest, the ground suddenly opened up into a deep gulch clotted with spiky trees and sharp rocks. On the other side, the land stretched in a flat, featureless plain of sandy soil and pale grass.

Ellie leaned over and peered down, her shoe kicking loose a clump of pine needles.

"Too wide to jump," she muttered. "See anywhere we can cross?"

Nox shook his head while Twig's face fell.

"You two should go on," Twig said softly. "I'm holding you back."

Ellie winced; she'd been secretly ruing that very fact but would never have said so aloud. Twig's lack of wings would slow them enormously, and they had a lot of ground to cover if they were going to reach Thraille.

"It's fine," she said, forcing lightness into her voice. "We'll just carry you across."

He looked doubtful but let Ellie hook her arms under his. She pushed into the air, wings straining, only to barely lift Twig more than an inch before she was forced to drop him.

"When did you get so heavy?" she panted. "Nox, help me."

Nox gave her an aghast look. "And set you both on fire? No way!"

"You can do this, Nox! I trust you. Twig trusts you too, right, Twig?"

"Uh . . ." Twig blanched.

"It'll be *fine*," Ellie said emphatically, shooting Twig a hard look. "Look, *I'm* not scared to touch—"

She reached for Nox's hand only to have him jump back. "No! Don't!"

His wings opened, and flames leaped from his feathers, scorching the trees behind him. The dry needles caught fire at once. Nox gasped, closing his wings again, as Ellie bounded toward the flames, trying to stamp them out. But a villainous wind rushed in from the grass plain, and at its touch, the fire roared up. The dry pines were the perfect kindling.

"Get back!" Nox said. "Ellie!"

She stumbled away, coughing on the rising smoke. It had only taken seconds, but already the fire was too big to put out. Worse, it was spreading behind them, blocking the way. If they didn't cross the gulch soon, the fire would be on them.

Nox lifted into the air. "I'll look for a place Twig can jump across, or maybe there's a . . ."

His voice trailed away as his eyes fixed on something in the distance.

"What?" Ellie asked. "What is it?"

With a curse, Nox dropped to the ground and folded his wings. "Goldwings. Two of them."

Ellie's heart tumbled. "You're sure they're Goldwings?"

"Only knights glint like that. It's the armor. They must have seen the smoke, and now they're coming to investigate."

Her chest tightening, Ellie looked from the rising wall of flames to the gulch. "We have to cross. *Now.* We can deal with the knights on the other side."

"Where we'll be as obvious as three rats in a pot," Nox pointed out.

"Got any better ideas?" Ellie's voice pitched upward as she swept a hand toward the flames. "Grab hold of Twig and *let's fly!*"

Finally, he relented, taking Twig by his armpits while Ellie grabbed his ankles. They flew awkwardly, Ellie's wingbeats hampered by Nox flying above her. His wings were betraying his emotions, crackling with more flames, but she gritted her teeth and tried to ignore the heat.

Thankfully it wasn't a long flight, and in seconds, they reached the other side. Nox dropped Twig roughly and pitched away before the fire in his wings could do more damage. Twig and Ellie rolled, coughing and groaning. Pain shot through Ellie's bad leg.

Struggling up to her feet, Ellie scanned the sky and caught sight of the two fliers. Sure enough, there was no mistaking the glint of their armor. Their pursuers had caught up to them—thanks to the raging beacon fire Nox had set.

And now she, Nox, and Twig were on the other side of the gulch, with only prairie before them and nowhere to hide.

"Just *fly*!" Twig urged them.

Ellie shook her head. That wasn't an option, now or ever. She wouldn't leave him to be captured again.

She was pretty sure the Goldwings hadn't spotted them yet. They were still flying at a leisurely pace, more curious about the fire than they were suspicious of its origins, she guessed. But that luck wouldn't hold long. As Nox had pointed out, they were pretty unmissable in this open grass. Open, *dry* grass, Ellie noted with a wince. If Nox set that on fire too, the smoke alone . . .

"That's it!" Ellie shouted. "Nox, light up the grass!"

"What?"

"Do it!"

He glanced at the knights in the distance, then his eyes widened as he caught on. Spreading his wings, he lowered them to the ground.

"Get ready to run," he warned.

Run? If only. Her bad leg spasmed at the mere thought.

Instead, Ellie grabbed Twig's hand and took off, flying into the wind. Twig stumbled after her, legs churning as fast as they could go. She tried to fly as slowly as she could, matching his pace. Hearing a sudden crackling roar, she looked back to see Nox had brushed his feathers through the grass—and a line of fire shot upward.

"Go go *go!*" he yelled.

With Nox behind them, lighting more of the grass as he ran, Ellie towed Twig along. Every few steps, his feet left the ground entirely and she pulled him through the air like an out-of-control kite. They were a pathetic group, she thought: Nox setting wildfires with his wings, her unable to run, Twig unable to fly.

The Goldwings had to have spotted the grass fire, but her hope was that the black smoke rising behind her would be enough to hide the three of them from view. The knights would think the fire had spread from the woods.

Finally, she spotted something in the distance—a barn? A rock? She wasn't sure, but whatever it was, maybe it could hide them.

The thing she'd spotted turned out to be an abandoned shack, its roof half fallen in and the door rotted away. She clambered through the gaps in the wooden slat walls, pulling Twig in after her. Nox came last, hesitantly, trying to squeeze through so his wings wouldn't touch the dry wood.

They were all panting, their clothes sooty.

"The wind's blowing the flames away from us," Ellie gasped out. "We're safe here, as long as the Goldwings don't come searching."

"And if they do?"

Ellie glanced at his wings, then quickly averted her eyes—but he saw the look anyway.

"I'm not setting people on fire," he said flatly. "Not even them."

"I didn't . . ." She bit back the lie. She *had* thought it and felt ashamed. "Of course not, Nox."

He peered out at the fires still raging across the grass. The smoke was thick and black as a thunderhead, darkening the sky.

"They probably turned back," Ellie said. "Nobody could fly in all that smoke."

But he looked ill, his wings tightening. "I could just as easily have killed you and Twig if that wind had turned against us."

"Well, you didn't. You *saved* us."

"You both would be better off without me and you know it."

"That's not true, Nox! We need you! You can't run from this."

He gave her a sour look. "Let's face it: I'm a disaster waiting to happen. Sooner or later, I'm going to start a fire that will be too big to escape."

That's just it, Ellie thought. That's exactly what they needed him to do, to *be*. A fire that couldn't be stamped out. A fire that would be seen across the whole of the Clandoms, the whole of the world. A fire of hope and change.

But anyone who looked at Nox right now wouldn't see hope. They'd just see a kid terrified of himself, desperate to escape the burning feathers anchored to his back.

Ellie wouldn't convince anyone to believe in Nox until he first learned to believe in himself.

CHAPTER FOUR
· NOX ·

"There *has* to be some way to control your wings," Ellie muttered. "The Phoenix clan couldn't have just gone around setting everything on fire, right? There must be a trick to it."

It was nearly nightfall. They'd evaded the pair of Goldwings, who must have changed their course due to the smoke—thankfully taking them away from the shack where Ellie, Nox, and Twig had hidden for the afternoon.

Now they were walking again, through countryside that was greener than the pine forest and thus, hopefully, less flammable.

Nox was miserable, thinking of the destruction he'd left behind him. Sure, the fire had saved their feathers, but that was only because of luck. If the Goldwings had turned toward them, if the wind had changed direction, if they'd been just a little slower in outrunning the flames . . .

Nox shuddered and tried to turn his thoughts away. "Got any ideas?"

He was ready to try anything. Even one of Ellie's wild schemes.

She tapped her lip. "Hmm. You know, I think I do."

"Just *breathe*," Ellie called out. "Empty your brain!"

Nox stood barefoot in a babbling creek, wings spread, eyes shut, hands turned palms up, while Ellie called out instructions from the bank. They'd found the creek tumbling through a green cow pasture, a few old willow trees leaning over the water. It was a nice spot, he supposed, if you were a farmer or something. To him, it reeked of cow dung and mud, and the air was clotted with gnats. Why couldn't they be on the run in some nice, crowded city, where at least the stinks were familiar ones?

"I *am* breathing!" he retorted.

"You need to calm your thoughts," Ellie said. "Like the Restless do, remember?"

Fat chance. Nox had never been able to sit still long enough to go into the meditative state achieved by the members of the Restless Order. The reclusive hermits lived in the Aeries Mountains and had sheltered his gang after the first time they'd fled Thelantis.

"Twig, you tell him how it's done," Ellie said.

The boy looked up from the creek eddy where he'd been watching a crayfish. "Huh?"

"You used to meditate with the Restless. How'd you do it?"

"Oh. Um." Twig stood up, flinching his shoulders as if to shake out his wings—an involuntary instinct, Nox knew. As usual, the reminder of his lost wings sent a flash of pain across Twig's face. But he blinked it away and focused on Nox.

"When I meditated, I just thought really hard about something, until I couldn't think about anything else. That's what the Restless told me to do. Think about the most peaceful feeling you ever had."

"What did you think of?" Ellie asked.

"Well, uh . . ."

"C'mon, Twig!" She gave him an encouraging smile. "Nox needs our help. If we can get him to calm his mind, maybe it'll calm his wings too. What did you meditate on? What was the most peaceful you ever felt?"

Twig swallowed. "If you insist, then. I, uh . . . I thought about this time when, uh . . . I'd eaten a ton of cheese, see, because I was starving and then I stole this big old wheel of cheese from a shop and . . . Well, *that* turned out to be a mistake, see, because cheese and me, we don't get on too good. And then for, like, a week I couldn't . . . uh . . . Well, my stomach hurt pretty bad. But then *finally* . . . Um."

"*Uggghhh!*" Ellie groaned, catching on.

"I remember that," Nox said, grinning. "You were in the outhouse behind the Chivalrous Toad for an hour. Winster said he'd have to burn the whole thing down and build a new one, the smell was so—"

"*Enough!*" Ellie cried out.

Twig beamed. "I'm just saying, I felt pretty peaceful after that."

"I hate you both," she moaned.

Nox laughed, but it turned to a yelp when his wings responded with a flurry of flames. He held very still, watching his feathers anxiously. "For some reason, I don't think meditating on Twig's reaction to cheese will help me control my wings."

"Forget the whole thing," sighed Ellie. "We'll try something else. And if that fails, we'll think of another idea."

"That's our Ellie," Twig said wryly. "Always with the ideas."

"It's a waste of time." Despair clouded Nox's mind again. This all suddenly felt very stupid and futile. Who was he kidding? Leaping to the bank, he kicked a rotting branch, shattering it into pieces. "I'm not going to learn to control these wings. How can I? They aren't *my* wings. They belong to a clan out of ancient history!"

Ellie stepped closer, raising a hand. "If you'll just let me help you—"

"Don't *touch* me!" he warned.

"I'm just saying, you're not alone, Nox."

"But that's just it, Ellie! I *am* alone. I'm the most alone I've ever been." He flung his arms wide. "In case you haven't noticed, I'm literally the *only* one of my kind in the world!"

She pressed her lips together. "Maybe that's true, but you don't have to figure this out on your own. We're a clan, remember?"

He looked at the moss under his shoes, turning over a clump with his toe. "Yeah, well," he muttered. "We're not *really*, are we? You're a Sparrow, and I'm . . . whatever this is. You don't understand, Ellie. You *can't*."

She crossed her arms, her jaw jutting stubbornly. "*You* are the one who doesn't understand. You can push me away all you like, but as long as I'm alive, you'll never be alone. Nothing can change that. Not your wings, not the king or his Goldwings, not even with the whole sky between us. We're clan, and nothing is stronger than clan."

"You only say that because of your stupid ideas about destiny."

Ellie stiffened. "I say it because I'm your *friend*! Why can't you just believe that?"

"If nothing is stronger than clan," he snapped back, "then why are you here, and not at home with the other Sparrows?"

She gasped, and Twig shot him a horrified look.

Feeling rotten, Nox shook his head and turned away. "I didn't mean—I'm sorry."

She drew a deep breath and let it out shakily. "*Apart* isn't the same as *alone*, you know. My strength comes from my clan, and I carry my clan in my heart. No matter how far away I am, they are with me. Just like me and Twig are with you, whatever happens. Whatever it takes."

Nox swallowed hard, wishing he had her confidence. But for all her talk, she couldn't possibly understand what he was feeling. No one could.

"I know you mean it," he said, "but the truth is, as long as I have these wings, I won't fit in anywhere or with anyone."

"Maybe it's not your *wings* that are the problem."

"What?"

"Nox, you've been fighting the truth ever since I first told you I thought you might be a Phoenix. Of course you can't control your fire. You won't even *accept* it."

He scowled, looking down at his bare toes in the water.

Ellie tapped her chin, studying him for a long moment. Then she said, "Let it burn."

"Huh?"

"*Let it burn*, Nox. Stop fighting it. Stop trying to control it."

"I don't think that's a good—"

"Just try it. What are you so afraid of?"

He thought of the fiery creature lurking inside him, of its angry eyes and its snarls, and wrenched his mind away again before it could rear its head. "Oh, I don't know. Maybe that I'll burn down the whole world and everyone in it?"

"You won't do that."

"How do you *know*?"

"Because I trust you."

"Well, *I* don't trust me."

"Like I said. It's not your wings that are the problem." Before he could stop her, she grabbed hold of his arms.

"Ellie, stop!" He twisted, trying to break free, but she held him too tightly. His wings began to dance with flame as he panicked. "I'll hurt you!"

"You won't. *I trust you.*"

Deep inside him, the creature showed its fangs, as if awakened by her touch.

"*Get back!*" His breath came in hot, stabbing gasps as he struggled to pull away from her. Hotter and brighter the flames burned, until the air shimmered with heat. Still Ellie stood firm, locking gazes with him, her expression calm. Teeth snarled in his chest; the creature seemed about to lunge. And he knew he would be powerless to stop it.

"I can't control it!" he cried. "Ellie!"

"Stop fighting it! I'm not afraid. You shouldn't be either. This is who you are. Isn't it time you trusted yourself?"

"No, it's not! I'm not a Phoenix, Ellie. I'm not what you want me to be. I can't control these wings, I can't be your hero, I can't do *any of it!*"

The creature leaped up, and its roar flooded Nox's head.

Flames shot from his wings in all directions, a crackling inferno.

"No!" Nox yelled.

Ellie screamed as flames devoured her arm and licked her face. With a shout, Nox started to grab for her, but the look she gave him was one of complete terror.

"Stop!" she screamed, stumbling out of his reach.

"Stay back!" Twig shouted, sliding between them. "Nox, get away!"

His stomach tightening into a knot, Nox could only stand by helplessly and watch as Twig pulled off Ellie's sash, dunked it in the creek, and used it to wrap her flaming sleeve. She dropped to her knees and sobbed with pain.

When Twig pulled the wet cloth away, Nox saw the burns on Ellie's skin. Red and already blistering, they made his own skin tingle with phantom pain. The marks spread up her arm, neck, and the side of her face.

He had done that to her.

"Nox . . ." Ellie whispered, her face streaked with tears. "Nox, it's okay. I'm okay."

"You're not," he said hoarsely. "Look at you."

"I'll heal. I will. Anyway, the whole thing was my idea—so really, I have only myself to blame."

"I hate this!" he yelled. "I never wanted it! You don't understand, Ellie. You don't understand this . . . this *thing* that's inside me!" How could she possibly know? How could he make her see that something dark and dangerous and *angry* was trapped inside him, waiting to be set free so it could destroy and devour?

"That thing inside you," Ellie said, "is your power."

"NO!" He recoiled. "All I do is hurt you and destroy stuff!"

"You didn't mean to hurt me."

It didn't matter whether he'd meant it or not. He'd *done* it. She was still crying, looking dizzy with pain.

And here she was trying to comfort *him*?

No.

He couldn't keep putting Ellie and Twig in danger—and not just from himself. He was a walking beacon. Every knight in the Clandoms would be drawn to his wings like beetles to a fire.

Walking away from them, he crouched by the stream and put his head in his hands, grappling with the snarling, living thing inside him. He wrestled it back, pushed against it with all his will, trying to silence it, smother it, anything to make it *stop*.

Ellie would never give up on him, even if it hurt her. She believed in a Nox who simply didn't exist. He didn't know how to become what she wanted him to be. Maybe she thought they were clan, but all Nox felt was alone. Desperately, impossibly alone.

He knew what he had to do.

CHAPTER FIVE
· ELLIE ·

Something wet, prickly, and smelly smacked Ellie's cheek, waking her. She sat up, spluttering, as a long black tongue planted another lick on her forehead.

"Ugh! Gross!"

She fended off the animal—a fat brown cow with doleful dark eyes—and struggled to roll out of the haystack in which she'd fallen asleep. A spasm of pain reminded her of the rash of burns on her arm and neck. She lay gasping for a long moment on the ground, tears squeezing from her eyes.

"What'd you expect?" came Twig's voice. "This *is* a cow pasture."

Ellie stood queasily and shook hay from her wings, squinting in the dawn light. A whole herd of cows had converged on their camp, blinking at them curiously.

"Nox, you could have warned us at least!" she said, pushing away the cow's head as it came in for a sniff. She gritted her teeth against the pain of her burns. "You had last watch, didn't you see . . . ?"

She looked around. "Where is he?"

Twig was sitting cross-legged in the grass, happily accepting nuzzles from several adoring calves. "Huh?"

Ellie fluttered into the air, surveying the landscape. A cluster of farm buildings lay to the west, distant enough that she wasn't worried about its residents spotting her. There were no other buildings in sight. The pastures rolled over a series of hills, dotted with strips of hardwood trees and cut by several small creeks. Fog lay heavy in the depressions between the hills.

"Nox!" she called out.

She'd woken him hours ago for his watch, before falling asleep herself. Last she'd seen him, he was perched on a fence post, his wings gleaming like embers.

But now the fence post was empty.

And Nox was nowhere.

Ellie's heart skipped a beat. She flew to Twig's side, scattering calves. They lowed indignantly, trotting back to their mothers.

"Twig, have you seen Nox?"

"I was busy with these." He held up a handful of burrs wrapped in cow hair. "The poor creatures were covered in them."

"Where is Nox?"

Twig frowned. He brushed away the burrs and stood up. "He shouldn't be hard to find. He glows like a campfire."

"Exactly. So where is he?"

A cold sweat broke out on Ellie's neck. She launched into the air again and flew in a wide loop, eyes scanning every inch of the ground below. It was hard to see through the film of pain in her eyes; she needed more than just cold mud and water on her burns, but her worry over Nox was greater. Had Goldwings taken him? A gargol? The sky was clear, but that was no reassurance; ever since she and Nox had first landed on one of the islands in the sky, invading the gargols' own territory, the attacks had grown more frequent. Now the monsters were known to strike out of clear skies, a thing unheard of before.

"Um . . . Ellie?" Twig waved, and she landed beside him.

Wordlessly, he pointed to the fence post where Nox had been sitting. Carved there was a single word:

Sorry.

Ellie's stomach dropped.

Nox hadn't been taken at all.

He'd *left.*

The only other sign of him was a single golden feather, lying dejectedly in the mud. She picked it up by the quill and found it warm as a candle. When she twirled it, little flames curled over the barbs.

Ellie touched the sash wrapped around her burned arm. Guilt churned in her stomach. Why hadn't she seen this coming? All evening Nox had been acting weird, unable to meet her eyes, glancing at the sky every moment . . . as if looking for an escape.

If he'd left not long after Ellie fell asleep, he could be anywhere, miles and miles away.

"Stupid, selfish Crow!" Ellie shouted, kicking what she thought was a rock but which turned out to be a pile of cow dung. Gagging, she wiped her shoe in the grass. "He left us, Twig! He just—*left!*"

Twig stared at her, then the sky, his eyes growing larger. "Where do you think he went? To Thraille?"

She shook her head, her eyes blurring with angry tears. "He doesn't care about Thraille, or Phoenix clan, or controlling his wings. He did what Nox does best when things get hard—he *ran away*. He could be anywhere at all."

Twig shrank back, watching her rage and limp around the pasture.

"Who does this help, Nox?" she shouted at the sky. "What about Tirelas? What about your destiny? You can't just *run away* from that!"

The cattle lowed and shifted around her, eyes rolling. Her shouting was upsetting them, but Ellie didn't care. Her chest throbbed with fury and panic.

"Featherbrained, thieving, selfish *lump*," Ellie muttered.

She was angry, yes, but she was also afraid. Nox was a beacon, and who knew what dangers he'd bring flocking his way like ants to honey? What would he do without Ellie and Twig to protect him? Sure, he'd taken care of himself for years, but that was *before*. Everything had changed that morning on the beach, and he needed her more than ever. Didn't he see that?

Brushing away her tears, Ellie picked up her newly acquired staff—a sturdy length of oak she'd found the day before—and turned to Twig.

"Are you . . . going after him?" Twig asked hesitantly.

You, he'd said. Not *we*. If she were going to catch up to Nox, she'd never do it on foot. She would have to leave Twig behind.

For a moment, she wavered, her heart thudding. Nox could be anywhere by now. He'd had several hours' head start, and she had no idea what direction he'd flown in.

Carefully, Ellie wrapped Nox's golden feather in damp hay and put it in her pocket. She'd have to remember to keep it wet, or it might set her clothes on fire.

"Remember that homestead we saw last night, toward the west?"

Twig nodded.

"Let's head there and then decide. We can't get far without supplies, anyway."

Maybe someone had seen what direction Nox took. Surely he'd be hard to miss, flying at night, glowing like a beacon. At the least, they could have something to soothe the fiery burns on Ellie's arm and neck.

Giving Twig what she hoped was a reassuring smile—but which probably came off more like a grimace—she put her unburned arm around his shoulders. They walked slowly, her leaning on him for support more than she wanted to admit, though the pain in her leg dimmed compared to that of the burns. Grinding her teeth, she forced step after step. Whenever Twig glanced up at her in concern, she forced another smile. She had to stay strong. She had to find Nox.

She hadn't saved his life just to lose him.

The homestead was in ruins, as it turned out. They'd flown past it the day before, but too distantly to realize the state it was in. Her heart sank at the sight.

Ellie and Twig approached cautiously, looking for signs of trouble, but all they found was an old woman sitting on an overturned barrel, with a few silent, staring fledglings gathered around her. They were hollow-eyed and gaunt, not even bothering to shoo away the flies that buzzed all around them.

"Hello?" Ellie waved, and one of the fledglings, a boy whose wings were still puffy with down, glanced at her. But no one spoke.

"I'm Ellie, and this is Twig. Are . . . are you okay?"

The house looked like a toy that had been smashed in a fit of temper. Even the wooden furniture inside had been pulverized to splinters.

"Gargols," whispered Ellie. She spotted two freshly dug graves by the house. Looking from them to the old woman and the children, she could guess at what had happened. "I'm so sorry. Is there anything we can do?"

Finally, the old woman lifted her gaze. Her face looked like a shriveled apple, wrinkled and dry. She said nothing, only stared at Ellie as if seeing right through her to the empty plain beyond.

The other fledgling, a girl who looked twin to the boy, was holding a leather ball. She dropped it and it rolled toward Twig, who picked it up and handed it back. Instead of taking it, she retreated behind the old woman and hid.

Twig looked at Ellie, his face twisting with pain. Walking back to her, he whispered, "Not gargols. Goldwings were here."

Ellie's eyes widened. She gripped her burned arm, the damp bandage creasing under her fingers. *"What?"*

He tilted his head, as if listening. Ellie knew he was using what she called his *inner ear*, a special, strange sense that let him read the emotions and desires of both animals and people. He'd been getting better at it, almost scarily good. Sometimes Ellie wondered if he could read thoughts as easily as if they were signposts. "That's all I can get. It's been a while since I held a skystone, so my ability is getting weaker again. But I know this was done by Goldwings."

Ellie looked at the old woman. "Why would the king's knights do this?"

The old woman spat in the dust. Ellie jumped.

"Was his own fool fault," she said. "Erran wouldn't stop going on about the islands in the sky . . . Nothing but smoke and dreams, I told him, but he couldn't keep his mouth shut."

Ellie's heart dropped. "The Goldwings killed him for talking about Tirelas?"

She glanced at Twig, who was watching the woman closely. When he returned her look with a small nod, she knew she was right.

"I'm so sorry," Ellie said.

The old woman scoffed. "Weren't any of your doing, girl."

Except that it was. After all, Ellie was the one who'd spread the story of Tirelas through the Clandoms. She was the one who'd insisted they hand out skystones. And the Goldwings had come soon after, arresting or executing anyone who repeated her stories.

"I want to help you," Ellie said at last. "What can I do? Find food? Take you somewhere—a town, to another family?"

The old woman shot her a look that was pure venom. "What can you do, scrawny little Sparrow? Can you reattach my son's head to his shoulders? Can you bring back his wife? Can you undo all the wrong that's been done here?"

Ellie felt rooted to the ground, unable to speak.

"Little fool." The old woman turned away. "You are nothing. You can do nothing."

"That's not true!" Ellie retorted. "I'm doing everything I can! We don't have to live like this. We can fight back. We—we can—"

Twig pulled at Ellie's sleeve. "We should go."

"But—"

"She won't accept our help," he said. "Anyway, she's right. We can't help here."

Ellie looked at him, then abruptly began walking, turning away from the grieving old woman and the dirty, silent fledglings. She limped away with her head down and her wings drooping. The pain from her burns seemed to pulse, spams of fire lancing through her.

You are nothing.

You can do nothing.

No. The old woman was wrong. She had to be wrong.

Doing something was what Ellie lived for. There was always a plan, always a next step, always something she hadn't tried yet. For as long as she'd been alive, she'd had hope, and nobody could take that from her.

"She didn't mean it like that," Twig said softly.

Ellie shot him a glare, knowing he'd been reading her emotions, and he looked away apologetically. "Sorry. I can't always turn it off, after I've used it."

"It's fine," she sighed. "I'm fine."

But she wasn't fine. She couldn't shake the old woman's bitter words from her head, no matter how far she walked.

You are nothing.
You can do nothing.
Nothing.
Nothing.
Nothing.

CHAPTER SIX
· NOX ·

Curse that they were, Nox's new wings were *fast*. Far faster than his old Crow wings, especially since one of them had been clipped. The land sped below in a dizzying blur as his feathers caressed the air. It took several hours to find a new rhythm with them. No longer did he need to flutter, flutter, soar, as he had all his life. Instead, his wingbeats were longer and slower and much more powerful, a few pumps sending him into a heady soar that melted away the miles.

Was this how it felt to fly as a high clanner?

That thought startled him a little, and his stomach soured. All his life he'd hated the high clans because they'd so clearly hated *him*. Now here he was, not much different from one of them. Wings long and tapered, shaped for speed and power . . . It was just more proof how wrong these Phoenix wings were on his body.

But at least he had one comfort: At this pace, Ellie would never catch up to him. She was fast, true—faster than most fliers he'd ever seen. But her smaller, rounder wings needed rest often. While she might beat him at a sprint, his new wings were clearly better suited for long, sustained distances.

And Ellie *would* come after him. He had no doubt about that.

Nox would have to be far out of her reach by nightfall. He might be faster, but he suspected she was more stubborn. She wouldn't give up after one day. She might *never* give up. He knew what she thought of him—what she wanted him to be.

Only he knew the truth: Nox was no hero. He'd been telling her that since the day he'd met her, and she never seemed to believe him. Well, maybe this would finally prove his point. He would fly so far and so fast that even Ellie Meadows would stop believing in him.

His course was set vaguely west, taking him away from the coast and over the midlands of the Clandoms. He'd always heard the midlands were nothing but flat, featureless fields, and the stories seemed to be true. He saw buildings here and there, clusters of farms that barely passed for towns. It reminded him a little of Ellie's hometown, Linden, where he'd first met her. But where Linden had been awash in fields of golden sunflowers, these fields were mostly grass dotted with sheep and cows, or rows of pumpkins and other crops. Much of it wasn't settled at all, and he tried to stick to areas like that, with less danger of being spotted. His wings took him high, where he'd be no more than a speck to anyone watching from below, his clan indistinguishable. Hopefully the flames shimmering on his feathers would be mistaken for a trick of the sun.

It was nearing noon when Nox began to tire; even his new wings, with all their strength, couldn't fly all day. He swooped lower, banking against the shifting winds, and looked for a place to land. A dirt road wound through the fields below, but no one traveled on it and there were no buildings nearby. He figured that would be as good a place to rest as any, and better than the dry grass where his wings might start another wildfire.

But just before he could land, he heard a scream.

Nox pulled up, his wings whipping up a cloud of dust. His senses went on high alert, wondering if it had all been in his mind.

But then he heard more screaming—from his left, in a hayfield. It sounded like a child.

Nox grimaced.

Not his problem, right? Whoever they were, they were a stranger. And his showing up to help would probably just make things worse.

Still, he couldn't help lifting higher into the air, enough to peer over the field and see . . .

A gargol.

It was skimming over the top of the wheat, searching for someone hiding below. The sight made Nox's heart curdle.

He'd met more than his share of gargols over the past few months. In fact, he'd landed smack in the middle of their own city, where thousands of them had been perched. And still the sight of one struck him cold with fear.

This one was lizard-like in shape, its stone wings nearly soundless, the downstrokes flattening the wheat. It flew in a sinuous pattern, hissing, claws extended.

Another scream rang out.

And then Nox saw them—a man and a little boy, running through the wheat with their hands clasped tight. They were low clanners— Nox guessed Robin by their gray wings with hints of orange in the coverts. The man, who looked like the boy's father, was smart not to take to the air, even against instinct. If they did, they were done for.

Still, it was only a matter of seconds before the gargol would close in on them. Then they'd have no hope left.

No hope but Nox.

He flew without thinking, reckless, yelling at the top of his lungs. His new wings shot wide and clawed at the air, propelling him forward like a stone from a sling.

Nox swooped over the wheat and intercepted the gargol just before it could dig its claws into the Robin clanners. He kicked its head, hard, enough to draw its attention to himself.

Which was undoubtedly one of the most stupid things he'd done in his life.

The gargol screeched—a sound like a thousand iron swords scraping rock—and swatted at Nox, but it didn't change course. It was still focused on the Robin clanners below.

The pair stumbled onto the dirt road, where the man fell hard and cried out, his leg injured. The boy, who looked no older than three or four, wailed and tried to pull the man up. His fledgling wings fluttered, too underdeveloped to fly.

The gargol dove toward their unprotected forms.

But Nox landed between them, spreading his wings to their full span.

"Stop!" he shouted, knowing it was useless. Nothing, not even a dozen Goldwings with spears, could convince a gargol to turn aside.

But when he shouted, his wings suddenly flared. The shadowy creature inside him howled and raged to life, clawing at his skull. In response, fire leaped from his feathers, spreading outward, crackling and hissing. His heart stopped, and all he could see was the face of the irate gargol bearing down on him. Its eyes shone blue, each one a skystone.

Instinctively, Nox beat his wings.

The fire generated by his feathers gushed forward in a blazing, searing torrent that washed over the gargol and knocked it backward. The monster tumbled away with a sound like splintering rock.

Nox gaped. It didn't just sound like splintering rock—it *was* splintering. A web of cracks spread over the gargol's wings, and the creature reeled, seemingly as astonished as Nox. Chunks of stone rained from its body. The gargol howled in a way Nox had never heard one howl before, a screech not of fury or violence, but of *pain*. He would not have guessed gargols could feel pain at all, but the sound was like that of a wounded cat, or rather, a *thousand* wounded cats.

It crashed into the wheat, stumbled a few times, then fell to the ground, where it writhed and screamed and then—before Nox's startled eyes—it *shattered* with a sound like cracking glass. Pieces of smoking, scorched rock flew everywhere.

The gargol was gone entirely, splintered into a thousand bits.

But Nox couldn't stand gaping for long. The gargol wasn't the only thing his flames had scorched. The wheat field had caught fire too, and now a wall of flames crackled before him. The stony remains of the monster were soon lost in the inferno. He watched, eyes wide with horror, as the crop went up in smoke.

"You—you *killed* it," whispered a voice.

With a start, Nox remembered the Robin clanners behind him. He whirled, retracting his wings.

The man was still sitting in the dirt, his ankle swelling where he'd tripped over a stone. He and the boy both stared at Nox with wide, wondering eyes, the light of the flames flickering over them.

Nox took a hasty step backward. All he could think of was how lucky they were that the torrent of flames hadn't consumed *them*.

Only their crop. Perhaps their entire livelihood.

"You killed a gargol," said the man hoarsely.

Nox's mouth was suddenly dry.

"My grandfather used to tell me stories," the man continued. "Tales of a fire-winged clan . . . But I thought they were just myth."

"You have to get out of here!" Nox said. The flames jumped the road, sparks landing in the field opposite and catching the stalks aflame. "It isn't safe!"

The Robin clanner heaved himself up, looking around as if suddenly aware of the terrible danger they were in. Coughing, he leaned on his son. The sky above blackened with smoke.

"I—I should go." Nox took a few more steps backward and spread his wings. The longer he stayed, the more damage he did.

"Phoenix!" said the man, with a snap of his fingers. "That's the word! Phoenix clan. That's what you are."

Nox's heart twisted. The last thing he needed was for word to reach King Garion that he'd sprouted flaming wings. The man hated him enough already. What lengths would he go to to kill Nox if he knew this latest development? What would he do to Ellie, to Twig, to anyone he thought might have information on Nox? "I'm nobody. Please, forget you saw me!"

With that, he launched himself upward, leaving a scorch mark on the road.

Heart hammering, Nox fled into the sky and didn't look back.

CHAPTER SEVEN
· ELLIE ·

"That's the last of them!" declared the farrier, stepping back to wipe his hands on his apron. He stared in amazement at Twig, who was holding the halter of the black horse he had been shoeing. "How'd you do it, lad? I've been trying to shoe this demon animal for days, but there wasn't a body in Robinsgate that could get near him!"

Ellie leaned in the doorway of the farrier's barn as Twig calmed the horse, clutching the fresh bandage on her burned arm. The cooling salve she'd found at the local healer's shop had helped soften the pain, or at least take the edge off. The burns on her neck and face were not as bad, but still they stung whenever she moved.

Now, while waiting for Twig to finish helping the farrier, she watched an old man hunched in the dirt across the street, begging for coins in front of the grain shop. His wings were twisted and gray, gnarled uselessly against his back. *Wingrot.* Ellie knotted her hands into fists, hating how helpless and guilty she felt. If she'd only had a skystone . . . But their supply was long gone, either given away or lost or crushed by the Goldwings.

They'd reached Robinsgate—clan seat of the Robins—that morning, after days of walking through endless plains. The town had appeared on the horizon like an oasis in a desert, and it had taken everything in Ellie to keep walking with Twig, rather than flying ahead.

"He's not a *demon animal*," Twig said testily. "He's just upset because he's got a stomachache. Someone's been feeding him too many oats."

The farrier blinked, then reddened. "I *told* that daughter of mine to stop sneaking in here to— Wait, how in the blazing skies do you know a thing like that?"

Twig shrugged. "He told me."

"*Told* you?" The farrier frowned.

"He also told me that he does not like his new stall, that the old one was much warmer and—"

"Almost done in there?" Ellie said hastily.

"Look," the farrier said to Twig, "if you want to stick around, kid, I've got a big shoeing order coming up. Could use those magic hands of yours."

Ellie decided it was time to intervene.

"Glad he could help out," she said, swooping between them and smiling broadly. She waited pointedly until the farrier grumbled and handed her several copper coins. Pocketing them, she thanked him and waved to Twig. He patted the horse, and they headed out into the street.

"Watch the skies!" she called back to the farrier, and he nodded in return.

It had taken them all day to scrounge enough odd jobs around Robinsgate to pay for the supplies they needed, not to mention paying the healer for the salve and bandages, but Ellie thought they might finally have enough for a knapsack, some food, a waterskin, and blankets. The nights were getting colder, with winter creeping ever closer. Ellie was looking forward to sleeping without shivering all night. Her wings could only keep her so warm, and poor Twig had none to wrap around himself.

But then she glanced again at the old beggar, her heart pinching.

She dumped the handful of coins they'd just earned into his little clay bowl. Then, her guilt unassuaged, she dug out the rest of their coins and added those too.

He looked up in astonishment.

"Watch the skies," Ellie murmured.

"Watch the skies, child," he replied, still shocked. "Are you sure—"

Turning quickly away, before she could second-guess her act of charity, Ellie limped down the street, toward a small crowd gathered outside a row of shops.

Twig jogged to catch up. "Was that *all* our money?"

She nodded.

"Oh." Twig looked back at the man, then sighed. "All right, then."

"We'll figure something else out," she assured him.

He raised one eyebrow—a habit she was pretty sure he'd picked up from Nox.

"Something that's *not* stealing," she added firmly. "What's over there, anyway? Some kind of market?"

But as they neared the small crowd, she saw no stalls or wares for sale. The people had gathered around a haycart and the pair of Robin clanners standing atop it.

"I'm telling you the truth!" said the Robin man, his wings spread wide. His leg was in a splint, and beside him stood a small boy, perhaps his son. "If you don't believe me, come closer—and I'll show you proof."

They were all straining to look at something in his cart, covered by a burlap sack. Ellie could practically hear Nox whispering how this would be a perfect chance to pick some pockets, just to rile her. She swallowed a lump in her throat.

A wagon stood by, unattended, full of barrels of apples—hundreds of them.

Would anyone notice if a few went missing? They were all so focused on the Robins . . . And Ellie's stomach was twisting inside out with hunger. She knew Twig was starving too.

Biting the inside of her cheek, Ellie edged nearer the wagon, jittery with nerves and shame. Just two apples—was this the price of her honor? Would she one day look back at this moment as the turning point of her life, when she threw it all away to pursue a career in crime?

Twig finally caught on to her and rolled his eyes at the anguish on her face. Ellie, bracing, was finally close enough to reach out—

". . . I'm telling you, he was Phoenix clan!"

Ellie froze, her fingers locked around an apple.

"What did he say?" she hissed to Twig.

"I heard it too! D'you think he means Nox?"

"Well, do you know of any other Phoenix clanners fluttering around?" Ellie released the apple and stepped closer to the crowd as the Robin clanner bent to grip the burlap sack at his feet.

"The Phoenix clan is a myth!" called out a woman. "Wings of fire and all that? C'mon, now. They're just a silly old story."

"They're not," insisted the Robin. "My son and I would be dead if that were so. The gargol struck out of clear skies and was on us both when the Phoenix appeared."

"Show us your proof, then!" shouted someone else.

"I will," said the Robin, and he whipped away the burlap.

The crowd gasped.

Ellie swayed on her feet.

There on the cart, in full view, rested a chunk of stone that she recognized at once, from its carved horns to its snarling snout.

At the Robin's feet rested the severed head of a gargol.

It was missing some pieces—a snapped tooth, a chunk of jowl, and its eye sockets were, Ellie noted with disappointment, empty of their skystones. But it was beyond all doubt a gargol's head. She'd seen enough of the monsters to know.

"A trick," scoffed the woman who'd spoken earlier. "That could have been carved by any Swallow clan stonemason. Flying islands, magic rocks that heal wingrot—now you want us to believe *this* too? Pah."

"No," said a portly Finch clanner standing behind her. "I've seen a gargol. Had one nearly snatch me before I made it into my house last year. And *that's* a gargol. Or his noggin, anyhow." He recoiled slightly, as if the head might still try to bite.

"The Phoenix did this," said the Robin. "He hit it with a wave of fire and it just . . . shattered. The rest of the pieces are back at my farm—too heavy to cart it all about."

Ellie and Twig exchanged a startled look. "Did you hear—"

"Yes," said Twig, flushing. "*Nox* did that."

She pressed her fingertips to her lips, then turned and shouted, "Where did he go?"

Heads swiveled to look at her. The Robin clanner shrugged. "Flew off like . . . well, like his wings were on fire. Which they were, of course."

"What direction?" asked Ellie.

"North, or maybe west?" He spread his hands. "Was hard to note, through the flames and smoke he left behind."

Ellie crushed her fist into her palm, trying to keep her excitement off her face. "What was he like? Did he seem . . . okay?"

Giving her a frown, the Robin clanner lifted a shoulder. "He seemed skittish. He was young. What does it matter? He was a *Phoenix*, and he killed a gargol with hardly an effort! That's what matters."

"He must have come from the islands in the sky!" shouted the

Finch clanner, jabbing a finger upward. "He's come to save us from the gargols!"

The crowd murmured and shifted, trying to get a closer look at the stone head. Ellie pulled back, dragging Twig with her.

"You really think Nox did that?" Twig asked, wide-eyed.

"What? Blew apart a gargol?" She grinned. "Of course. This is it, don't you see? This is proof that Nox is the key to reclaiming Tirelas! That Finch clanner said it himself—he's here to save us. Twig, that old woman was right about me. I can't change anything. But *Nox* . . . Nox can."

"I wonder if he'll see it that way," said Twig doubtfully.

Ellie shrugged. "We'll just have to make him understand that the world needs *him*. We know which way he went now. If we head north-west, maybe we can catch up to him."

"You . . . aren't going after him alone?" He dropped his chin.

"Twig, I'm not leaving you."

"You'll never catch him dragging me along."

He was right, and that was what hurt. Because she knew in the end, she'd have to set off on her own if there was any chance of finding Nox.

"It's okay," Twig insisted. "That farrier offered me work. I can stay here until you come back."

"The Goldwings . . ."

"If they show up, I'll just hide. Remember that canyon we passed a few days ago? I'll run and hide if I have to. There's a hidden cave behind that waterfall we saw."

"How do you know that?"

"A lizard told me."

She threw her hands in the air. "Of course a lizard told you."

"Ellie, I'll be fine. I'm not a helpless little kid, even though you guys sometimes treat me like one."

"We don't . . ." Her voice faded away as she realized he was right. Twig really wasn't much younger than she was; his small build just made him appear so.

"All right," she conceded at last. "But you must swear to stay on guard. I don't want to have to save your neck again."

"You mean like the last time?" he deadpanned. "The grand rescue where you got yourself thrown in prison *with* me?"

"Hey! At least we tried. If it hadn't been for . . ." Her voice trailed away, not wanting to finish that sentence.

But the words were written on Twig's face.

If it hadn't been for Gussie.

He sighed. "Wings up, Ellie. Find Nox and bring him back."

"I hope I can," she said softly. "I hope he'll listen to me."

"If there's anyone in this world Nox will listen to, it's you," he replied. "Anyway, if he doesn't, we both know you'll just drag him back by his toes."

Ellie laughed, but her heart only sank.

She wasn't sure Twig was right.

She wasn't sure *anyone* could reach Nox now.

CHAPTER EIGHT
· NOX ·

Nox dreamed he was back in Thelantis, standing on the gallows with Twig and Ellie. Only this time, the crowd wasn't silent. Instead, they were angry—at *him*.

"Freak!" they yelled. "Monster!"

They threw rocks, but not ordinary rocks—skystones. Glittering blue gems with sharp edges that cut and bruised. Skystones were supposed to be weightless, but these weren't. They struck his face and arms, no matter how he tried to avoid them.

"Burn him!" the crowd howled. "Burn him!"

Feeling a blossom of heat behind him, he turned, expecting to see King Garion.

But it was Ellie, holding a torch.

She smiled grimly and pressed the flames to his Crow wings, setting them ablaze. But then the fire leaped from his feathers and grabbed hold of her with a thousand searing hands. Ellie screamed, her eyes flooding with tears.

"Please, Nox!" she sobbed. "Please, stop!"

He reached out for her, only to see his hands were on fire too. Flames encased him like a second skin. He watched helplessly as cracks splintered over Ellie, and then she shattered like glass.

Where she had been standing, a creature appeared—a shadow

wreathed in flames, its eyes golden. Fangs bared, it leaped on Nox, jaws closing on his throat.

With a gasp, Nox awoke to the crackle of flames.

He hastily rolled away from the fire, his skin slick with sweat, and watched in horror as the barn he'd sheltered in burned around him. He'd stumbled into the building late last night, exhausted from flying, to fall asleep on the floor.

There was no point trying to stop the blaze. It was already out of control. He stumbled toward the door, coughing on the smoke.

It opened before he could reach it, and he skidded to a halt, wide-eyed and panting.

The man standing there had to be the barn's owner—a Finch clanner still in his nightgown. He gaped at Nox.

"Lad!" he shouted. "You're on fire!"

"I'm sorry, really. I—I didn't mean to—"

"Get out of there!" the man shouted, still clearly not realizing Nox was the source of the flames. "I'll get water! Roll on the ground or something, quick!"

The man ran toward the farmhouse across the yard and began frantically pumping water into a bucket. He seemed more worried about saving Nox—a stranger he'd caught sleeping in his barn—than saving his farm.

Shame burned in Nox's belly, hotter than any fire.

"I'm sorry," he whispered. "I'm so sorry."

Before the farmer could return, Nox launched into the air, rising through the plume of smoke that poured from the burning barn. With a crash, the roof caved in, and a glittering cloud of sparks shot into the air around him. He lost sight of the farmer through the smoke and flew higher, his eyes burning.

It wasn't quite dawn yet. The eastern sky was smudgy with pink. He turned his back to it and flew toward the darker, western horizon, where a few stars still glimmered. His stomach twisted with hunger and regret. At least, he thought sourly, the farmer would never know Nox had also stolen several ears of corn for supper the night before.

The bitter wind tussled with Nox's wings, choppy and unpredictable. He flew higher, trying to find gentler skies. Looking back, he saw his wings were still blazing too bright, his dark mood expressed through the tongues of flame streaming from his feathers like red ribbons. He was leaving a trail of smokeless fire behind him, bright as a beacon.

He flew faster, desperate to put the destruction behind him. But it seemed no matter how fast or far he flew, he couldn't stop destroying things.

Two days ago, he'd landed at a pond to rest and wash, not seeing the little Starling boy fishing on the bank. The kid had screamed and run as if Nox had been a gargol.

Four days ago, sick with hunger, he'd tried to steal a few bites of corn that had been left out for a herd of pigs. Instead, his wings had frightened the animals so badly they'd stampeded through their enclosure and nearly run straight into a river, where they would have all drowned. Nox had only barely stopped them by setting a fire along the bank, turning them back.

It had been one disaster after another, and now he added the burned barn to the list.

At least he'd done one thing right, leaving Ellie and Twig. He could only imagine how much harm he'd have done to them by now. His wings seemed to be getting more out of control with every passing day.

After several hours of flying, Nox was exhausted. He searched long and hard before he found a spot that seemed safe enough to land—a rocky river with a bank of smooth black pebbles. They crunched underfoot when he alighted. The place was as remote as any he'd ever seen, in a inhospitable region of rocky ground scored with gulches and little rivulets running out of the western mountains. Sandy soil mixed with black earth, and large deposits of flaky dark shale jutted out of the ground like the hulls of broken ships. It looked like no one had flown these skies in years, maybe never. Tough grasses and shrubs grew, but few trees.

The water was cold and quick. He splashed his face, then cupped his hand to drink.

But as he brought the water to his lips, he saw his own face reflected in the water . . . and beside it, the vague glimmer of watching eyes.

Startled, he dropped the water and spun around, but saw nobody.

"Hello?" He stayed very still. "Ellie, is that you?"

No reply.

"Great," he muttered, scooping another handful of water. "Why not lose my mind along with everything else?"

He drank until he felt sick, but it did nothing to banish the hunger pinching his belly.

Shivering from the frigid water, Nox wrapped his wings around himself, until he realized his feathers were singeing holes in his clothes. So he settled for curling up on the cold, damp pebbles. The pebbles hissed where he laid his wings, releasing steam.

He'd trade both his wings for a hot leg of lamb with plum sauce. Fantasizing about it, practically feeling the sauce running down his chin, Nox drifted between sleeping and waking, until a clatter of stone roused him as sharply as a dash of cold water.

Nox jumped up, looking all around, but saw nothing. Just a rockslide, perhaps? Or some small animal?

Still, he felt like he was being watched. His feathers bristled, and finally he took off again, flying through his exhaustion and sore muscles, following the river until it vanished underground. Then, seeing signs of civilization—a road, a shed, a plume of chimney smoke on the horizon—he winged higher again, into the upper, chilly layer of sky where the wind steadied but the temperature plummeted.

Twice he felt a shadow behind him and whirled in a rush of flames and feathers, only to see empty sky. But the hairs on his neck remained on end, the center of his back tingling as if feeling eyes on him. He saw no clouds, but that was no guarantee he wasn't being tracked by gargols. He couldn't understand why they hadn't attacked yet, if they *were* watching him.

The wind carried him farther and farther north, and the world below began to feel familiar. He realized at last that this was Sparrow clan territory, Ellie's home, and that the brown fields quilting the earth had been bursting with sunflowers the last time he'd flown these skies. He pressed onward in a hurry, until the farms faded away and the land turned wild, tangled with woods and rivers.

When he landed at last, dizzy with exhaustion, it was dark. The woods around him creaked and shivered in the wind. The trees here were mostly pine and other evergreens, their fallen needles a plush, bristling carpet on the ground. With the exception of the wind moving among the branches, the place was quiet. Disturbingly quiet. Thin flakes of snow landed on his wings and turned to steam.

Nox stood very still, peering into the gloom, his every sense on high alert. Was he being paranoid, or did that cracking branch sound too loud to be a squirrel or badger? Why wouldn't his heart stop thumping?

"Hello?" he called out. His voice felt muted by the snow and cold, like he was shouting into a pillow. "Who's there?"

Keeping his gaze fixed on the shadows, Nox slowly bent and picked up a branch with dead pine needles clinging to it still. He brushed the tip of one wing over it, and the needles caught fire with a crackle. Holding it out for a torch, he probed the dimness.

He hadn't actually *seen* anything, he reminded himself. Most likely he was just exhausted and wrung out from flying for hours, which would make anyone jumpy.

Gradually, his nerves quieted, and he let out a long breath.

"Ellie'd be laughing her head off if she saw me now," he muttered.

Then he turned around and came face-to-face with a pair of glowing blue eyes.

"Whoa!" Nox shouted, stumbling back. He raised his makeshift torch and gasped, expecting a gargol—but found a statue.

It was a girl, carved entirely of marble. Her wings were incredibly lifelike, even the barbs on her feathers rendered in fine detail. She stood with her hands clasped delicately in front of her, dressed in a simple, knee-length robe of stone. Weird.

She was beautiful, her hair and face carved in such detail it would put any Thelantian stonemason to shame. The marble was as smooth as glass, polished to such a shine that he saw himself reflected on her cheek. But her eyes . . . they were undoubtedly skystones, carved with irises and pupils of darker blue, lit dimly from within like little lamps.

How had he not noticed her when he'd landed?

Fascinated, Nox leaned closer to take a better look. He reached out to tap the statue's nose . . .

And then the statue *blinked*. "Hello, Phoenix."

Nox shouted and spread his wings, about to launch into the air—but quick as a viper, the girl swung her fist, knocking him in the temple with the force of a stone shot from a sling.

Soundlessly, he crumpled into an unconscious heap.

CHAPTER NINE
· ELLIE ·

*T*wo weeks.

Two weeks of searching and Ellie was growing desperate.

It was like Nox had vanished into the sky. What had changed? Had he turned in another direction? Been captured? Or worse—found by gargols? There was no telling, and Ellie was frantic. She contemplated turning back, regretting that she'd left Twig behind. Then she considered that Nox might be just around the corner, and if she gave up now, what if she missed him?

All she could do was hope some sign would appear, to point to which way she should go.

After a long night spent sleeping in her cloak, Ellie descended into a low, wooded vale, leaving the open prairie behind her. Around her towered the biggest trees she'd ever seen, cedars and firs that rose taller than any castle's towers. There was more than enough room to fly between them. She hardly even needed to zigzag. The air was cooler here, almost wintry. As she flew, she began hearing strange sounds ahead—knocking and clattering, and the occasional crash.

All at once, she burst out into a clearing bustling with activity. She'd stumbled into a logging camp, and all around her flitted burly, black-and-white-winged people hauling axes and awls and wedges. Nearly all of them had hair red enough to shame tomatoes. They sang robustly as they worked, felling trees with practiced skill.

"Axe and awl, swing and pound,
Hew the titan, lay 'im down!
Chop and hop, clear the ground,
Oaks a'tremble at the sound!"

A chorus of whoops filled the air as a tall tree began to groan and lean, while the loggers hacked at its trunk far below. Ellie watched in awe, until someone swooped in and grabbed her, and sent them both tumbling through the air.

"Hey!" she shouted, struggling to free herself and steady her wings.

"Watch out!" Her attacker, as it turned out, was actually her savior—she'd been right in the path of a falling pine, so focused on the loggers she hadn't noticed the tree plummeting toward her.

The pine hit the ground with a shuddering crash, sending up a cloud of dust and leaves. Ellie hovered, breathless at how close she'd come to getting crushed.

"Didn't you hear the warning call?" asked the boy who'd knocked her aside. He had the same black-and-white-striped wings and flaming red hair as the rest of his clan. He rolled his eyes at Ellie. "This is an active logging site, dummy. No place for strangers who don't have the sense to steer clear of a falling tree."

"Sorry. Thanks for saving me." She smiled shakily. "I'm Ellie, Sparrow clan."

"Harren, Woodpecker clan," said the boy, pressing a hand to his chest. "What are you doing here?"

"Looking for . . . a friend. He might have come this way. Dark hair, grumpy face . . ." She hesitated, then decided not to add *fire wings*.

Harren shrugged. She could tell he was trying hard not to look at her burns. They were healing—she could tell that by the infuriating itchiness—but the pain was still enough to make her dizzy at times.

"Dunno about your friend, myself," Harren said, "but if he's been through, someone in town will have seen him."

"Town?"

With a sigh, the boy waved. "C'mon. Day's nearly over anyhow, and I'm headed there myself."

Ellie followed the Woodpecker boy through the trees, admiring his skill in navigating the tight forest. His wings tilted and adjusted deftly, weaving through the trunks. Flecks of sunlight danced over his feathers like rippling water.

"There," said Harren a few minutes later. His voice swelled with pride. "Delven, clan seat of the Woodpeckers."

The town smelled of smoke and freshly hewn wood—cedar, oak, and pine. The houses were made of logs, with corbels, columns, and other architectural features skillfully carved in the shapes of animals and intricate patterns. The roofs were tiled in cedar as red as Harren's hair. Through the center of the town ran a river, its waters moving fast and choppy, turning several great wheels that powered lumber mills.

"Lots of strangers come through here," he said. "We're at a cross-roads, y'see—they say everyone passes through Delven at least once in their life. Anyway, best to start at the Lantern, over there— everyone goes there for drinks at the end of the day. Best place to ask around."

"Thanks."

"No problem. Watch the skies."

"Watch the skies."

She swooped toward the two-story building he'd indicated. The trees around Delven were full of Woodpeckers, many of them carving designs into the trunks, so that the pines and oaks had been transformed into towering works of art. There wasn't a bit of wood she could see that wasn't shaped into a bear, wolf, fish, or other elaborate figure. Twisting braided patterns wound up the trees like stitched seams.

Landing outside the Lantern, its name evident by the carved wooden lantern hanging over the door, she shook out her wings and then folded them, weary from the day's long travel. The river churned behind the tavern, frothing with whitecaps. The smell of freshly ground flour and baking bread greeted Ellie's nose, and she inhaled it hungrily. Her belly growled, reminding her she hadn't eaten since yesterday.

Above, the sky grumbled with coming thunder. Ellie smelled rain in the air.

She had a few coins left, earned several days prior when she'd stopped to help a stranded farmer reattach a wheel to his cart. Jangling them in her palm, she went inside and found a table in the corner; most of the others were occupied by loggers, who clustered in noisy groups around tables carved as intricately as everything else in Delven. Even here, people had pocketknives in hand and idly whittled at whatever wooden surface was within reach. The table she sat at featured an elaborate scene of stags racing through a glen. She ran her fingers over it, marveling at the detail.

"Thanks," she said to the Woodpecker girl who set down a mug of warm cider and a slice of bread with butter.

"You're not from around here," said the girl, glancing at Ellie's wings.

"Sparrow clan." Ellie flexed her feathers slightly.

"Ah! My mother swears by your wing oil. She loves the lavender-scented one."

Ellie smiled, feeling the familiar twinge of sadness when she thought about home.

"Hey," she said when the girl started to turn away. "Have you heard any weird rumors lately? About . . . I don't know, strange things showing up?"

"You mean like the Phoenix?"

Ellie's heart jumped. "He was here?"

The girl shook her head. "No way. But you're not the only person who's been talking about him."

"I'm not?"

"There's been rumors floating through here for days. Folks say they've seen a boy glowing in the night, wings aflame, and that where he lands, he leaves behind scorched grass . . ."

"Avie!" called a woman across the room—the girl's mother, Ellie guessed. She had the same auburn curls.

The girl, Avie, pressed her lips together. "Coming, Mama."

Ellie sighed and took a bit of the bread, which tasted even better than it smelled. Looking around the room, at the Woodpeckers gathered in groups of friends and family, laughing and chatting, she was suddenly reminded so strongly of her own clan that it brought a sting of tears to her eyes.

One of the groups, a trio of old men with braided red beards, looked a bit tipsy from their tankards. They began to sing, softly at first but quickly growing rowdy.

"Of old, they say, in lands away
Between the earth and sky
There soars a king o' feathers and flame
And all who see him sing his name.
A Phoenix born in golden light,
A Phoenix to burn away the night!

O watch the skies in darkest times,
To see him burning bright!
O watch the skies in darkest times,
My love, O watch the skies."

Clutching her cider, Ellie watched them raptly. They were launching into a second verse when the door of the tavern banged open.

Everyone in the room fell silent as five Goldwings strode in, just as a peal of thunder rattled the forest.

Ellie sucked in a breath and lowered her face, a cold sweat breaking out on her forehead. She tightened her wings, hoping they wouldn't notice the brown of her feathers, so out of place in this town of black-and-white wings.

But it wasn't her they looked for—it was the old men.

"What were you singing?" demanded the lead Goldwing, an olive-skinned man with a dark sweep of glossy black hair. Ellie knew by the tassels on his white armor that he was their captain. The others spread out, casting suspicious looks around the room.

"Back for more of Tilda's ale an' loafs?" called out one of the old men, raising a tankard the knight's way. "Thought you lot were aiming for the north."

"Well, of course the storm changed their plans," said the tavern owner, Tilda. She and her daughter rushed to press drinks into the Goldwings' hands, but the knights refused them.

"When we questioned you this morning," said the captain in a low voice, still focused on the trio of old men, "you said you'd never heard the word *Phoenix* before."

"That's right," hiccuped the elder. "Never have."

"I heard you singing it through the window."

"Sure you did, Woodpecker clan's got a song for every day of the year, y'know. As they say, our songs are the best! Well, no, actually they say Warbler clan's are the best. But there's something to be said for quantity over quality, eh? Ha! Anyway, they're just songs, man."

"Just songs? Songs about the very creature we interrogated you about?"

"Pshaw . . . little song never hurt anyone."

The Goldwing strode across the room and knocked the tankard from the man's hand, sending it flying into the wall with a clatter.

Everyone froze. Ellie clenched her hands into fists under the table.

The Goldwing took the old man by his collar and curled his lip. "How about you sing for *me*, then, you wrinkled old featherbag? Got any more illegal songs in that shriveled brain of yours?"

"Sir, please," Tilda said. "Why don't you and your companions sit and let us serve—"

"*Quiet*, woman!" The knight struck her across the face, and she fell with a shout.

Before Ellie half knew what she was doing, she'd jumped to her feet and opened her wings, her chair scraping over the floor.

"Stop!" she shouted.

Immediately a rush of hot regret warmed her cheeks, as each of the knights turned to stare at her.

"What's this?" said the captain, releasing the old man. "A little lost Sparrow, eh? You're far from home."

Ellie swallowed. Hard. She quickly folded her wings.

The last time she'd been the focus of a Goldwing's attention, he'd been putting a noose around her neck.

"I . . . I'm traveling with my father. He's an oil peddler."

The knight narrowed his eyes, taking a step toward her. With her back already to the wall, there was nowhere to go. They were between her and the nearest door.

"Wait a minute . . ." said the knight. "I know you."

"Huh?" Ellie's voice shot up an octave. "Me? I, uh, don't think so. I'm just a Sparrow—"

"Just a Sparrow," he repeated. "That's what everyone was saying after the Race of Ascension. 'Just a Sparrow,' but she beat out high clanners twice her wingspan. *Just a Sparrow* . . . but one of the most wanted outlaws in the Clandoms."

Ellie shook her head, her blood running cold. "No, you're mistaken."

"Am I? Am I mistaken in thinking your name's Meadows . . . what was it? Ella? Ellie?"

She bolted.

The door was blocked, but a window was set to her right, shut against the storm. She scrabbled with the latch, but before she could get it open, the Goldwings were on her.

They grabbed her arms and wings, the captain's fingers squeezing her alula joint so hard she cried out, fearing he'd break her wing. She didn't dare struggle, knowing the wrong movement would snap the bone. It was a dirty trick, one the old Ellie would never have expected from an honorable knight.

But if she'd learned one thing in the last few months, it was that there was little truly honorable about the Goldwings.

"Let go!" she snarled. "Let go of me, you—"

"Silence, girl!" snapped the captain. "I was there, you know, the day you were supposed to be executed! The day you started the riots!"

"I didn't start anything!"

"My brother had his wing clipped in that skirmish! He's grounded for the next *year* because of you!"

He wrenched her wing. Ellie screamed.

"The *king* will be very eager to see you," he said into her ear. "He knows you're involved with this Phoenix business. He knows you're the one spreading lies across his kingdom, to stir up treason!"

She couldn't reply; the pain in her wing was taking her breath away.

"Tie her up," the captain ordered. "As soon as the weather clears, we'll take this traitor back to the capital and finish what—"

Bang! The tavern door burst open, letting in a gust of storm wind.

"Hey!" shouted a voice. "Goldwing scum!"

The knights turned as one, to stare across the room at a stranger who stood framed in the doorway, his face and wings hidden under a dark cloak.

"Who are you?" grunted the captain.

"Catch me and find out!" With that, the stranger raced out again, and there shone a sudden blaze of fire in the street outside.

"The Phoenix!" cried Avie.

Ellie's heart tumbled. Nox? Could it be?

"To me!" ordered the captain, beckoning to his knights. "Dilan, guard the prisoner! The rest of you—after that boy!"

The knights stampeded out of the tavern and into the rain, which plinked off their white armor like music. Ellie wasted no time. While the remaining knight was distracted, she grabbed a bowl of hot soup still sitting on the table and flung it in his face.

He yowled and clawed at his eyes, then for her—but she was too quick. Ellie made for the window, throwing it open and rolling through before he could catch her. She landed on a muddy bank, with a short drop below to the river. The storm thrashed all around, thunder rolling through the forest.

"Quick! Into the water!" hissed a voice above her.

Flinching, Ellie looked up and spotted the cloaked stranger on the eaves over her head.

"Nox?" she cried.

"*Hurry!* They're coming!" The stranger dove at her, wings spreading. She had just enough time to see that his wings were *not* fiery gold when he grabbed her and propelled them both into the river.

Ellie barely had a chance to suck in a breath before her head went under. But she saw the stranger's plan at once. In the sky, they'd be spotted easily, even in the storm. Underwater, they had a chance.

She lost track of the stranger in the dark churn of the river and focused on swimming as hard as she could, letting the current sweep her along. Sharp rocks jutted from the river's bed, and with no way to avoid them, she collided painfully. Soon, the river quickened, bowling her over, and she had no choice but to let it drag her along.

When she could hold her breath no longer, she pushed toward the surface, gulping down air as lightning cracked above. The town was already shrinking in the distance, and she spotted a few dark shapes winging over the rooftops. The Goldwings were still searching. They hadn't figured out she'd fled by water and not air, but she knew it wouldn't take them long to catch on.

Swallowing another deep breath, she plunged under again, letting the current carry her, only surfacing when she absolutely had to breathe.

What seemed an eternity later, when her limbs began to wobble like seaweed, she made for the shore. Gasping and sputtering, weak with exhaustion, she dragged herself onto a sandy bank and flopped onto her back, her bedraggled wings spread wide. The rain had lightened, pattering over her face, and she had no strength to even shield her eyes.

"You all right?" asked a voice.

With a start, she sat up and looked around.

The stranger was crouched behind her, dripping wet. He'd lost his cloak in the river, it seemed. Now his face was in full view, as were his long, tapered high clan wings.

Ellie gaped.

"Prince *Corion*?"

CHAPTER TEN
· NOX ·

Something hard and cold jabbed Nox's cheek, over and over. His head felt like it had been split open by an axe. Pain thrummed through him in waves. Distantly, he heard a pathetic, whimpering whine, as if from a hurt dog. A moment later, he realized it had come from his own lips.

Jab.

What had happened? He remembered snow, and pine trees, and . . .

Jab jab jab.

A girl with blue eyes.

A girl made of *marble*.

Nox's eyes snapped open.

Groaning, he blinked blearily, his vision slowly clearing. He was in a strange place, with a strange face hovering over him. He stared for a long moment, until the spots were gone from his eyes and he was sure he wasn't dreaming.

"*You,*" he rasped. "You're real."

The marble girl, one stone finger still extended as if she might prod him again, retreated when he spoke. She knelt a wing's length away, watching him through her skystone eyes.

Nox raised a hand to his aching head, only to have his wrist catch. He looked down in dismay at the rusty, ancient-looking shackle on his arm. The chain attached to it snaked across the ground, the end looped around the iron bars of a balcony.

With a start, he turned and looked behind him, his stomach dropping.

The balcony on which he was trapped was part of what looked like an ancient stone manor, surrounded by rolling hills and patches of gnarled evergreen forests. A misty river flowed by, its water bright turquoise; from his vantage, he could follow its winding course across the pale green landscape, to where it reached a sudden cliff and tumbled away into cloudy gray sky. At a small pool below him, dozens of glowing moonmoths fluttered and danced, their light reflecting on the water. Twig would love that, he thought vaguely. The kid had gone starry-eyed over those moths the first time they'd seen them.

Moonmoths. Realization crashed into him.

There was only one place moonmoths gathered, after they broke free of their chrysalises and winged into the sky.

"Tirelas," he whispered. "You . . . carried me up here?"

He glanced back at the girl. She was watching him closely, her head cocked to the side. He wondered if she could understand what he was saying.

"What *are* you?" he asked, fighting to keep his voice even and friendly, when, in fact, his guts were churning with terror. He had a dozen ideas why the girl had carried him up here, and none of them ended with him leaving alive. Not wanting to provoke her into doing something rash—like, say, tossing him to her gargol friends—he forced a queasy smile.

The girl's lips parted, and she seemed to be struggling to speak. Her eyebrows bunched together with effort.

"I—I am Icara." Her voice was gravelly, like she hadn't used it in a long time. "Icara is me."

She touched her cold fingers to her lips, as if startled she could speak at all.

"Icara. Nice name. Really nice." He looked around again, swallowing. There were no gargols nearby that he could see, but there were a thousand places one could be lurking. "You, uh, all alone up here, Icara?"

"I have *friends*," she said defensively.

Right. Probably a hundred of them, all with fangs as long as his arm. His smile weakened as a wave of panic rushed over him. "Sure, sure. That's great. What about parents? Anybody else . . . like *you*?" In other words, was she the only walking statue here, or had he dropped into a whole city of them?

"My father," she said slowly.

"Great! Does he, uh, know I'm here?"

"If he did, you would be dead by now." She had an odd accent he'd never heard, her words clipped, each one snapping off her lips like a spark thrown from a fire.

"Oh," he said faintly. "Well . . . let's not tell him I'm here, huh?"

She considered him a moment. Then she said, "You're warm like the sun."

His wings tightened, the flames crackling over his feathers. "Yeah, you better keep your distance. My wings and gargols don't really get along. That is, if you . . . *are* a gargol?"

She moved closer anyway, reaching out but not quite touching his feathers. Their orange flow reflected on the smooth curves of her cheeks. "It's been so long since I felt warm."

Suddenly, she grabbed the tip of his wing, and in response, the flames in his feathers curled over her fingers like biting snakes. She only stared, bemused.

"Whoa," said Nox, eyes round.

"I am not so delicate as a gargol," she said seriously.

Nox swallowed, wondering what sort of creature could consider a gargol to be *delicate*.

Her curious fingers found his face again, prodding his cheek and chin. Then she grabbed his hand and turned it over, exploring his palm and the veins in his wrist.

"How alive you are," she said. "How soft and weak, like a mushroom."

"Uh . . ." Deeply uncomfortable but too terrified to resist, he remained still and studied her face as closely as she was studying him. She was more lifelike, more detailed, than any statue he'd ever seen, down to her eyelashes and the dark flecks in her stone cheeks that might have been freckles. Her hair was gathered in two stone disks over each ear, then hung in heavy braids that slid over her shoulders with faint rasps. Unlike the gargols, she had wings carved with feathers as fine as his own. She looked about the same age as he was.

"I didn't know gargols could look like you," said Nox.

"Like I said. I am no gargol."

She let go of his hand and turned her attention to his hair, and he yelped when she pulled out a strand of it. Pinching it between her fingers, she studied it as if it were the most fascinating object in the world.

"But I'm not like you either. I will live forever, and soon you will be dead." She said it so casually, she might have been telling the time of day.

He winced. "You'll live forever? Really? Are you being literal or . . . figger . . . furger . . . oh, what's the word? Gussie would know. Hey, stop! That hurts!"

She'd yanked on his ear as if it might open to reveal a hidden compartment.

"Are you going to let me go or what?" he asked.

"You're mine now. *Phoenix*." She rose and went through the doorway, into the room he hadn't paid much attention to till now.

Seeing his chain was long enough, he scrambled up and tugged at it, but there was no way to pull it loose. It looked like she'd bent the chains together herself, with her incredible strength. There were fingerprint-shaped indents in the metal. He held his wing against the links, thinking he might melt them off, but the metal didn't even get warm.

Giving up, he dropped the links and instead followed Icara inside. There was enough chain to go halfway in.

There was no telling what the room had once been. There were no furnishings of any kind. Shelves were carved into the stone walls, and these were filled with trinkets and baubles: ancient, tarnished jewelry, arrowheads and spear tips, a rusted dagger, coins of varying metals and sizes, and other artifacts he couldn't name, they were so misshapen or worn with age.

"Here," she said. "Water."

She thrust a tarnished goblet at him, its base studded with rubies, any one of which would have set him up for a life of ease in Thelantis. The water inside was sparkling and clear.

"You living sorts need water," she said. "Drink it. It's distilled from clouds, the Tirelan way. Better than any *groundwater* you earth crawlers could find."

"Hey," he said, offended. "We have wings too, you know."

"For now," she returned obliquely.

He watched her over the rim of the cup as he pretended to sip. Who knew what kind of poison she could have slipped in here? Then again, if she wanted to harm him, she'd had plenty of opportunity. His head still pounded from the impact of her fist. He doubted there was a soldier in all the Clandoms who would throw a punch to rival the slender girl in front of him. Her fingers only *looked* delicate; he knew now she was marble through and through, with the weight and strength of solid stone.

"I said, *drink*." She tipped the cup, forcing water into his mouth.

Spluttering, he choked it down obediently, though half ran over his chin and down his shirt.

"What do you *want* from me?" he coughed.

"You're a Phoenix."

"So?"

"*So*." Her head tipped, her eyes boring into him. "Your kind are supposed to be dead."

"Just give it a little more time. I'm apparently the last of us."

That brought a smile to her lips, albeit a small one. "As I am the last of mine."

"Uh . . . And what kind *are* you, exactly?"

"I am Tirelan." She raised a palm toward the vista outside, as if that should be obvious.

Right. Tirelans. The ancestors of all the clans on the ground, according to Ellie, and Gussie, and a legend he'd heard in the southern jungles. But no part of that legend had hinted that those ancestors might have been *gargols*. However the girl protested, he couldn't help seeing her as one.

"It's just you and your father? Sounds lonely."

She glanced back at him, and he was startled by the sudden sadness in her eyes. For a moment, she almost looked entirely normal, like any other girl.

Just as quickly, her eyes hardened again, blue as the sky and sharp as cut diamond. She took out a silver comb from her pocket and began scraping it absently over her hair, though the bristles were useless, of course. Her hair was solid marble. He shivered at the sound it made—silver scraping stone.

"I thought you were a trick at first," she said, combing away, "when

I saw you blazing along through the sky. For days I followed you, to be sure you were real."

Days? Nox shivered.

"Look, if it's a Phoenix you're after, I'm hardly a real one. In fact, up until a week ago . . . two weeks? I guess I lost track. Anyway, what I'm saying is, I'm really just a Crow. I don't know anything about Phoenixes, so whatever you want, I'm not your guy."

He tried not to think about what she might do if he did convince her. For all he knew, she might chuck him off the edge of the island with his wings bound and let nature do the rest.

"Perhaps you are a Phoenix." She shrugged, waving the comb. "Perhaps you are not. We will find out soon."

He recoiled slightly. "What does that mean?"

She walked to the balcony and held a hand in the wind, her eyes narrowing thoughtfully. "The winds will change soon, and then we will go."

"Go? Go where?" Nox eyed the chain, followed by a particularly large dagger on one of the shelves. He wondered if marble girls ever needed to sleep, and if so, could he reach the dagger? Would it make a dent in the metal of the chain? The links looked ancient . . . perhaps it wouldn't take more than one good blow.

"If you try it," she said mildly, "a hundred gargols will swarm you the moment you leave this island."

Nox started. "Try it? I wasn't going to try anything."

"My father set them as my guards, as if there were anything to guard me *from* up here." She sounded as surly as any kid lamenting a strict parent. "I haven't seen so much as a spider in over a century."

The room tilted around Nox. "Sorry, did you just say *century*?"

She lifted a shoulder. "Maybe two."

"How old are you?"

She looked confused by the question, but if she had an answer, he never heard it. At that moment, a familiar screech pierced the air.

"Gargol," he moaned. The flames on his wings burned brighter, making the room glow orange.

She scowled. "Get down. If they see you, I won't be able to stop them. Their instinct to kill earth crawlers is too strong."

Nox stayed low as a shadow flickered outside. The gargol flew back and forth, then seemed to wander off.

"Okay, *what* is going on here?" he asked, his voice high with desperation. "Who are you, *what* are you, and why am I here? What do you want me for? And will you let me go if I give it to you?"

"What I want," she said slowly, "is to live again." She reached out and planted her marble palm against his chest, then smiled wolfishly. "And I need a Phoenix's heart to do it."

CHAPTER ELEVEN
· ELLIE ·

"What are you *doing* out here?" Ellie asked, her mind still spinning.

She'd barely had the chance to say two words since she'd recognized the Eagle prince, before he bounded away again in search of cover. With the Goldwings still hunting them, staying on the open riverbank had not been an option.

So now they were holed up in a grove of poplar trees, soaked to the bone, shivering, and—in Ellie's case—still desperately hungry.

But she ignored the pain in her stomach and pinned Corion with a bewildered look. The last time she'd seen him, he'd been helping her, Nox, and Twig escape their own execution in Thelantis.

"Did you like my distraction?" Corion asked. "Knocked over a torch on the way out, but I got them, didn't I?"

Impatient, she nodded. "Yes, very clever. Thanks for drawing their attention and all that. Now answer my question!"

"Right." The prince's eyes lowered. He looked suddenly very tired. "Well, things have been a mess since you left Thelantis."

"You mean since your father tried to *execute* me and my friends."

"Yeah . . ." He grimaced. "Sorry about that, again. He's . . . going through some stuff."

Going through some stuff?

"Anyway," said Corion hastily, "where are your friends? And what happened to you? That looks painful."

She pinched her lips together, her hand going to her burns. The ones on her neck and face had started healing, but under the bandages on her arm, the skin was still raw and fiery. She would have scars there, she suspected.

Corion sighed. "Okay, fine. You don't trust me. That's fair. But I swear I'm not with the Goldwings. This isn't some trick. I really do want to help."

"Tell that to your father."

"I tried." Corion's gaze sank. "Believe me, I tried. He's not been himself lately."

"Did the king . . . ?" She winced. "Did he find out you saved us? Is that why you left?"

"No, nothing like that. He has no idea I helped you escape."

"Then what happened?"

"After your . . . near execution, the riots didn't stop for days," he explained. "My father had to bring in soldiers from all over the Clandoms just to get the city under control. Now people aren't allowed to leave their houses, and anyone who resists is imprisoned, their wings clipped. He sent me and my sister to Vestra for our own safety . . . though I'm not sure it wasn't more to do with the fact he didn't want us seeing how bad it was."

"Vestra," Ellie murmured. The seat of the Falcon clan—Gussie's home. She almost asked about the inventor who'd once been her friend, but found the knife of Gussie's betrayal was still lodged too deep in her heart.

Corion nodded. "We'd been there only a few days when I got a letter from Zain."

Ellie brightened at the mention of her oldest friend. Zain too had helped her and her friends escape Thelantis that day, proving he was still loyal to her despite his Goldwing uniform. "How is he?"

"That's why I'm out here," Corion confessed. "He told me his regiment was being sent on a very important mission, but he wasn't sure what it was. He sounded worried. Said Sir Aglassine was supposed to lead the mission, but she refused and got thrown in the dungeons for it."

Ellie shivered. The king had given an order Sir Aglassine wouldn't carry out? Something even worse than hanging three innocent kids and turning the Goldwings on his own people?

"I left Vestra at once," said Corion. "I have to catch up to Zain before . . . whatever happens, happens. If it's as bad as I think, maybe I can help. Maybe they'll listen to me."

He looked so wretched that Ellie knew he was telling the truth. She'd glimpsed how close Corion and Zain had become. Their bond was even deeper than she knew, if the crown prince was willing to risk everything to save the Hawk boy.

"What were you doing in Delven?" she asked. "I didn't see Zain there."

He shook his head. "Just passing through. Zain said they were headed home, so I'm going to—"

"Home?" breathed Ellie. "You mean *Linden*? The Sparrow clan seat?"

"Yes, that was it. Oh, it's your home too, isn't it?"

"Why is a Goldwing regiment going to Linden?" She shot to her feet, her hands tightening into fists.

"Like I said, I don't know. But I don't think it's for anything good."

The king knew Ellie was from Linden. He also obviously still blamed her for the riots and his loosening grip on the Clandoms. Ever since the day she'd won the Race of Ascension, she'd been a thorn in his side.

Ellie swallowed, feeling sick. Was this some kind of revenge, targeting her clan because he couldn't get to her?

"I got the shock of my life, seeing *you* in that tavern," said Corion. "But it has to mean something, doesn't it, that we bumped into each other?"

"What do you mean?"

"You have to come with me," he said. "To Linden. To figure out what my father's plotting. Look . . . he's not as bad as you think. Really. I know he *seems* like a power-hungry despot at times. But it's very stressful, you know, ruling the Clandoms and all . . ."

Ellie gave him a flat look until he finally lowered his gaze. The storm above was dissipating, thin clouds pulling apart in the wind until there was nothing left but grayish-blue sky.

"I'm already on a mission," she said. "I'm looking for Nox."

"The Phoenix?" Corion's eyes widened. "Is it true, then? I've been hearing stories about a kid with fiery wings. Thought it was just some wild rumor."

"It's true," she said. "It happened after Thelantis. Nox . . . changed."

She pulled out the Phoenix feather she'd been carrying in her pocket and twirled it so that it sent out tendrils of flame.

Corion let out a low whistle. "My father's going to molt when he hears that. He probably already *has* heard it. Your friend Nox gets to him like no one I've ever known."

"He must know Nox is the rightful prince of Tirelas," said Ellie. "Of course he's out to get him, if he thinks he'll challenge his throne." She watched Corion carefully to see his reaction. The throne was, after all, to be Corion's one day.

But the prince only nodded gravely. "I think that's exactly what he's worried about. And everything he's doing now is because he thinks the people will rebel to follow this Phoenix. It's . . . sort of an Eagle clan legend, I guess. We've always known about the Phoenixes, how they created the gargols to rule the clans and crush their enemies."

"Huh?" Ellie blinked. "That's not how it goes."

"Really? Are you sure? The Phoenixes were evil sorcerers who wanted to control everyone. It wasn't till the Eagles led a rebellion that the clans could be free."

Ellie shook her head. "That can't be right. If it were, why would *you* want to help Nox?"

He looked away, his face pale. "Because of Allyan."

"Who?"

"Nobody knows what I'm about to tell you," he whispered. "In fact, sharing this secret is punishable by death. Allyan was my sister . . . my youngest sister. She died when she was three years old. Of wingrot."

"Oh. I'm sorry."

"You'd think my father would want to do anything to find the cure, but he isn't interested. He says the skystones are fake, that the islands in the sky won't save us. But what if that's only because he fears returning to the sky means giving up his throne? Tirelas isn't like the Clandoms. The islands are too spread out to be ruled the way he does here."

"So that's it," whispered Ellie. "If he lets the people return to the sky, he loses them. He loses his crown. *That's* why he hates Nox so much."

"I don't care about crowns and thrones," says Corion. "Not when the price of keeping them is letting our people lose their wings, or even their lives."

Ellie studied him for a long moment. He couldn't possibly be more different from his father, despite the fact they had the same hooked nose.

"You're a good prince, Corion. If only the other Eagles were more like you."

He ducked his head, frowning. "Don't say that. I'm not better because I'm not like them. I'm still part of the problem. My father doesn't fight to keep control of the clans just for himself, but so he can one day shove it all on *me*, and so I can pass it to my heirs. That's what he told me, you know, before he sent me off to Vestra. He said, 'Everything I do, I do for the future of the Eagle clan.' So it *is* my fault, at least in a way."

The prince looked sick with self-loathing. Ellie didn't know what to say. So she only put a hand on his shoulder and gave him a sad smile.

He returned it, his wings lifting a little. "Will you go with me to Linden? You know the place, the people there. Don't you want to help them?"

Ellie chewed her lip.

She *did* want to help him, for Zain's sake and her clan's. But doing so would mean giving up on her search for Nox.

What if he never returned? What if he never became the leader the Clandoms needed to break free of Garion and return to their true home?

She remembered the last words she'd said to him before he'd died.

I still believe in you.

Ellie pressed her face into her hands and let out a long breath. She knew what she had to do, but it still hurt.

"Yes. I'll go with you."

If Nox was going to become a true Phoenix, he'd have to find his way alone. She'd done everything she could for him, more than she'd imagined she could.

Now . . . the rest was up to him.

CHAPTER TWELVE
· NOX ·

"Can I ask a question?" Nox didn't wait for Icara to answer. "When you say 'I need a Phoenix's heart,' you don't mean that, well, literally. Right? You're not going to yank my heart out and eat it with gravy, are you?"

Her face was expressionless as she replied, "I hate gravy."

"Strangely, that doesn't reassure me," he sighed.

They flew through an ephemeral world above the world, one made entirely of clouds, complete with sweeping valleys, deeply shadowed vales and gulches, mounding hills and towering mountains. Some clouds seemed frozen in place, while others flowed like slow, misty rivers or pooled like lakes. Still others, small and airy, drifted on the backs of quick-moving winds.

Nox felt as small as a speck of dust, following Icara through those strange skies. She navigated the world of clouds with bored familiarity, seemingly unimpressed by the way a banner of velvet mist soaked up the rose-gold light of dawn. The way a dark vale suddenly opened to a meadow of sun, where bundles of pure, fleecy white piled in disheveled heaps. The way the deepest, darkest clouds were brightly outlined, like silver stitching on the hem of a rich navy cloak, only to turn blindingly bright when they rounded to their sun-facing sides.

When he'd flown in clouds before, it had been in a state of panic and terror, dodging lightning bolts and hearing gargol screeches from every side.

He'd never imagined flying above the clouds could be *beautiful*.

Not that he wasn't still on his guard. Icara had assured him their path would be clear, but it wasn't like he trusted her. She *had* knocked him over the head, carried him off to who knew what corner of the sky, and then chained him up like a dog.

"Are we almost there?" Nox asked. Wherever *there* was; Icara was not forthcoming with details. He'd spent the whole night shivering on the cold floor of her little collection room, trading sleep for dread, expecting a gargol to drag him out at any minute. He'd even wondered if that might be preferable to whatever the marble girl had in store for him.

"I told you to stop asking that."

Nox waited a few more minutes, then asked, "So are we almost there?"

She shot him a severe look, and he grinned back a bit manically; he couldn't help annoying her. It was his nature, especially when he felt trapped. Porcupines had quills, skunks had spray, and Nox had snark.

"How do you even know where you're going?" he asked. "The landmarks up here change every five minutes."

She didn't reply.

"Are you *sure* there aren't any gargols around? Because I saw a shadow just now that I'm pretty sure had claws."

Still she didn't speak. Maybe she really was more statue than girl.

Nox tried again.

"When you said '*I want to live again*'"—he pitched his tone to a dramatic key—"what exactly did that mean? You were alive once? Like me?"

At that, Icara's wings flinched, interrupting her flight rhythm just slightly.

"So you *were* like me once." Nox stared at her. "What happened to you?"

She was silent for so long that he was sure she wouldn't answer. He had begun thinking up his next question when she suddenly spoke.

"Sometimes," she said, so softly he barely heard it over the rush of their wings, "when somebody sets out to save something, they destroy it instead."

That rattled Nox. Now *he* flew in silence for a while, before answering just as quietly, "Isn't that some truth."

Icara glanced at him, then looked forward again. "We're here."

They swooped right, then left, through a cluster of swirling gray cloud. Then Nox gasped.

Before him floated an archipelago of mountainous islands. Held together by massive chains, they drifted in unison in a pool of still sky, surrounded by a sea of clouds. On each island, misty ruins lay beneath curtains of dead vines and moss. Spires towered upward, most broken or missing large chunks, but impressive nonetheless. He had never seen buildings even half that tall on the ground. Nothing in Thelantis could compare—this place made the city of the Eagles look like a backcountry village. Hundreds of feet in the air, delicate walkways connected towers, with railings as intricately carved as lace. Fog flowed around domes and towers and great walls, giving the place a ghostly feel. It was plain the city was abandoned. Dark, crumbling windows and archways stared hollowly, making Nox think of the marble tombs in Thelantis's upper districts. This place had the same imposing emptiness.

There was life here, though, if only in the plants and land around the buildings. Forested hills and rocky mountains rose over the city, the highest of them white with snow. Below the peaks, evergreen trees ruffled in the wind, and on the lower slopes, autumnal trees shone with leaves of gold, scarlet, and deep purple. Here and there, ancient steps of white alabaster wound up the hills to ruined palaces that sat atop them like crowns. Waterfalls poured from the mountains' heights and wound through the ruins before tumbling into the sky. They fell hundreds of feet, then turned to airy mist carried away by the wind. Swarms of moonmoths shimmered in the air, sipping from their spray.

"This is Cyrith," said Icara. "The old capital of Tirelas and the clan seat of the Phoenixes. The shining city in the sky. At least, it *used* to shine."

"And the gargols?"

"Busy elsewhere, with my father." She flapped a hand dismissively. "They won't be back for a while. You're safe with me."

He was not at all sure of that, but he had little choice now. If he wanted to be safe, he should have stayed on the ground.

But if this was really the city of the Phoenixes, maybe, just maybe, there was something here that could teach him how to control his wings. Or better yet—to change them back to the way they'd been. If he could figure that out, maybe he could still get his old life back. He could return to the Clandoms, to Ellie and Twig.

Icara landed at last on a marble plaza in front of a large agora, its interior open to the outside and the roof supported by rows of columns. He tried to imagine people going up and down the shallow steps, their wings blazing like his own. Looking around, he felt a tingle of recognition.

"I've been here before," he murmured. It had been the day his mother died. "Only it was full of gargols then."

Icara shook her head. "You shouldn't have come. You riled them."

"Yeah, I know that now," he sighed. "So this is where the high clans lived?"

"High clans?"

"Yeah, you know. The Hawks, Eagles. The . . . Phoenixes."

Icara shook her head. "There were no *high* clans in Tirelas, or *low* clans either. Only the clans. Equal. The same."

Nox blinked. He had trouble imagining such a thing.

"The Phoenixes did live here," Icara added. "And others, people from all the different clans. This was where everyone wanted to be. There was a saying: Everything happens in Cyrith." Her tone was wistful.

He watched her, noting the way she looked around, as if remembering the place the way it had been. Remembering the unanswered question still lingering in his mind, he asked, "Icara, were you . . . were you *here* when this place was full of people?"

She pointed across the steps. "That's where we used to meet, me and Lua and Fleck. They were Owl clanners. We liked to sit on the rooftop and watch the Phoenix warriors fly in at night. Their wings lit the sky like lanterns."

Her finger traced the sky, as if following the Phoenixes' flight path in her memory.

Nox stood like a statue, eyes wide.

Icara wasn't old.

She was *ancient*.

"You've been up here for over a thousand years?" Nox asked, his voice hoarse with shock.

"My father says time means nothing to us now," she replied, but he heard doubt in her voice. Then she seemed to shake it off as she darted up the steps and into the vast agora, weaving in between the columns while Nox hastened to keep pace. For being made of marble, her feet were light as a dancer's.

"This was the best place in Cyrith," she said dreamily. "The Forum. It's where the best practitioners of all Legacies came to display their talents. My father worked here, with the other Swallow clan stonemasons."

"Legacies?" Nox echoed.

"Specialties. Gifts. The abilities clans carried in their blood."

Nox's mind whirred like the cogs in one of Gussie's inventions. "My friend Twig can hear the emotions of animals and people. He always said it was a Legacy of clan—"

"Mockingbird," Icara finished, nodding. "A powerful Legacy, theirs. They understand any language, and the strongest of them can even read the unspoken whispers of the heart. Or they could, anyway, before they fled to the ground."

Nox nodded, much becoming clearer in his mind. "I've heard people say that every clan has a legacy. I always thought that meant, you know, Sparrows farm and Crows steal. It's like a clan tradition. But that's not what it means at all, is it?"

"Legacies are much more than that."

"They're magic, aren't they? Twig's ability is a kind of magic. And the skystones . . . they make those Legacies stronger."

"I suppose." She danced away, starting to seem bored by the conversation.

"What about Sparrow clan?" he called. "What's their Legacy?"

Icara slowed, looking thoughtful.

"Seeds," she said at last.

"Seeds?"

"Any seed planted by a Sparrow was said to be blessed. It would grow no matter its conditions, and its fruit would be richer and more plentiful. Their harvests were always the best."

He wondered if Ellie would appreciate knowing that *farming* was her clan's lost magical talent.

"We're not only losing our wings on the ground, are we?" he said. "We're losing our clan magic."

"Because you've been without skystone too long." She paused, peeking at him from around a column. "No more Cormorants singing the fish out of the sea, no more Petrels foretelling the weather, no more Weavers spinning cloth that never tears. My father said it was bound to happen . . . your Legacies fading from your blood, your wings crumbling from your backs."

The way she said it, almost tauntingly, sent a chill down Nox's spine.

"My father knows much about skystone," she added. "More than anyone else. That's why we're still up here, and *you* are all down there."

"Did you say you're Swallow clan?"

"Yes."

He glanced at her wings, now recognizing their tapered shape. "Stonemasons," he murmured, his heart beginning to pound. "Swallow clan are stonemasons. They carve the most incredible statues . . ."

His eyes flickered back to Icara's marble face.

"I'm bored," Icara said suddenly. "Come on. The Phoenix palace is this way!"

He scrambled to take off as she soared away, swallowing the questions still bubbling in his throat.

They flew over two more islands, both of them covered in dense ruins, before reaching the centermost island. Its underside cliffs were tangled over mountains of skystone like roots around rocks. Five massive chains, each link wide enough for Nox to comfortably fly through, tethered the island to the rest; it held its smaller neighbors in place like the hub of a wheel, the center of the archipelago drifting in slow formation.

The blue light from the skystones glowed on Icara's marble skin. She led Nox across the great gulf between the islands, following one of the chains. It anchored deep into the island's underside, and they lifted on a thermal to soar above the heart of the city.

"There," she said, pointing needlessly, because the palace was obvious.

It was shaped like a crown with many towers rising in a ring around a wide, circular hall. Its roof was a high latticed dome that looked fragile as glass from a distance. But as they flew nearer, Nox saw why it had withstood the test of a thousand years: The dome was veined with skystone, which made it nearly weightless.

They flew through one of the holes in the latticed roof and landed in a vast chamber. Trees and shrubs tangled in untamed chaos, but he guessed that once it was a well-groomed garden that had divided the room into sections. They stood in the center, where six thrones were set in a circle, facing one another.

Nox walked around them, feeling suddenly daunted.

"The palace my friends and I visited, sunken beneath the ground . . . I thought that was the Phoenix throne."

She waved a dismissive hand. "That was just one of their schools. They liked to send their fledglings away for their learning, to keep them out of trouble here in Cyrith."

In that case, what he'd taken for a throne room had perhaps been some sort of ancient headmaster's chamber. He shivered, imagining being summoned to a place like that just to be reprimanded for cutting class.

"Why are there *six* thrones?" he asked.

"Three kings to judge in peace and war," said Icara in a singsong voice. "Three queens to guard the skies we soar."

"There were six of them!" Nox scoffed. "And I thought having *one* king was bad."

"One *is* bad," she replied. "At least, the Phoenixes thought so. Their way, nobody ever got too powerful. If one of the kings or queens went bad, the others were strong enough to remove them."

"What if all six of them went bad?"

"I don't know. They're gone now anyway, so what does it matter?"

"What happened to them? They must've been pretty sorry kings and queens to have let the gargols run everyone off the islands."

"Oh, they tried to stop them." She laid a hand on one of the thrones. "It was a terrible battle. Many, many people died, all across Tirelas. But the Phoenixes were always few in number. My father's gargols were *legion*."

Nox's heart stopped. Started again.

"Your *father's* gargols? As in . . . he commands them?"

"As in, he *created* them and commands them." Icara suddenly grabbed hold of his arm, her grip like iron. "Come on. It's this way."

"What is? He did *what*? Your father—Icara, wait! Where are you taking me?"

She dragged him across the room, toward a raised, round platform of stone. A great ashmark—or, as Nox now knew, the Phoenix clan crest—was engraved on the floor.

Still struggling against her grip, Nox cried out, "Icara, what do you *want* from me?"

He was expecting the worst—a knife to his throat, like some kind of sacrificed animal. His wings spread, their flames burning hotter.

She placed her hand on the wall, still holding him in place over the ashmark.

"I want to know if you're truly a Phoenix," she said. "Fortunately, they have a test for that. Unfortunately, if you fail this test . . . you die."

She pressed a stone on the wall, and with a groan, the floor beneath Nox split open. He dropped, too slow to open his wings before Icara had shut the trapdoor above him.

Nox plummeted into nothingness, his scream swallowed by the dark.

CHAPTER THIRTEEN
· ELLIE ·

The sunflower fields lay brown and barren, the turned soil encrusted with a rime of frost. A tingle danced over Ellie's scalp as she flew. Her heart was a lump in her throat.

Home.

After nearly half a year away, she was finally returning home.

At least, she hoped she could still call Linden that. The whole flight here, she'd envisioned every possible scenario that might await her, and it was hard to imagine her clan greeting her with anything other than contempt. After all, she'd turned her back on them, fled like a thief, and then embarrassed her clan chief and Mother Rosemarie, the Sparrow who'd raised her, in front of King Garion himself. Her people were probably ashamed to be associated with her.

But that wouldn't stop her from doing whatever it took to protect them. She didn't know what Garion had planned for Linden, but she doubted he was throwing them a parade.

When the town finally appeared on the horizon ahead, Ellie banked lower and landed with a flutter. Corion dropped beside her a moment later.

"We're here," she murmured.

He nodded grimly. "Not much cover, is there?"

"Not this time of year."

"So what's the plan?"

Gently scratching the healing burns on her arm, she gave him a thoughtful look. They'd been journeying together for six days now, but it still felt weird to be traveling with the crown prince. Despite the fact his father wanted her head, Ellie hadn't found a reason not to trust Corion. He seemed genuine in his concern for Zain and his desire to help. And he wasn't uppity or demanding, the way she imagined most high clanners would be. He'd helped make camp each night, finding firewood and fetching water with a skin he carried on his belt, all without a word of complaint. Just as if he'd been doing that kind of thing all his life. He was thoughtful and polite, and clearly determined to reach Zain as fast as possible.

"We sneak in," she said. "And hope we're not too late."

They had no way of knowing whether the Goldwings had already been to Linden or not. If they had, then there was a good chance Ellie and Corion's rescue mission would be in vain. She tried not to think about that.

"After you," said the prince, sweeping a hand. "This is your territory, Sparrow."

"Right." She inhaled deeply, breathing in the familiar scent of the soil, still tinged with the woody fragrance of the sunflowers. They had been in full bloom when she'd last been here. Seeds were still scattered across the ground, and she gathered a sundried handful as they walked, munching on them while she thought.

Their best approach would be from the west, in the tall grasses that grew on the dormant fields. At least they wouldn't have to worry about running into people. This time of year, nearly everyone in Linden would be busy indoors, with the Sparrows gathered in their barns and shops, pressing the seeds they'd harvested into oil.

The nearer they got to town, the stronger the smell of the fragrances grew. This had always been one of Ellie's favorite seasons, when she'd spent hours at the oil presses, or with a mortar and pestle, grinding herbs, dried flowers, and seeds to make the scents that would be mixed into the sunflower oil. She could smell them all now, gentle on the wind. It smelled like a honey day, when the Sparrows scraped the beehives to make the ever-popular honey-scented oil that would be shipped all over the Clandoms.

But despite the smell, Ellie soon realized something was different today.

There was no smoke rising from the perfumery, the big barn where most of the scents were mixed. And no Sparrow fledglings were perched on the eaves, munching on stolen bits of sweet beeswax.

"Something's wrong," she whispered to Corion.

He gave her a worried look.

"This way," she said, angling toward another building—the bottle barn, which should have been busy as well, with Sparrows transferring the freshly scented oils to the bottles they'd be sold in. But it was also quiet, the windows dark.

"That's our way into town," she whispered. "Someone there should know where the Sparrows are."

"Can't we just fly?" Corion frowned. They were still in the town's outskirts. Linden itself was off in the distance, a muddle of thatched rooftops blending into the dry landscape.

"This way is better. You'll see."

They ducked through a side door and into the dark interior of the bottle barn, where a wave of familiar smells and sights swept over Ellie, leaving her stomach in a twist. There was her old station in the corner, where she'd spent so many hours screwing the corks into the filled bottles with the other Lost Sparrows.

No one was there now. The whole place was deserted.

A pit opened in her chest.

Something was *very* wrong.

She hoped desperately they weren't too late.

"Here," she said, lifting a cellar door to reveal a staircase. "This tunnel runs all the way into town. It's where we store the oil before it's shipped, for temperature control. If there *are* Goldwings in Linden, they won't see us coming."

She went down first, taking a lantern from its hook on the wall and lighting it with the Phoenix feather. All it took was a twirl of the quill, and the barbs sparked with fire.

The tunnel smelled of packed dirt, sunflower oil, and cedar. Barrels of the oil were stored neatly against one wall and, farther down, rows and rows of shelves held the glistening bottles waiting to be shipped. Ellie's reflection flickered over them as she passed.

"Nearly there," she whispered.

The tunnel ended in another staircase and cellar door; this one opened in the back storeroom of the oil shop in Linden. More shelves of oil rose all around, stacked in tall shelves. The air smelled of dust and oil and beeswax. She cracked the door cautiously, saw no one, and clambered out, blowing out the lamp. On quiet feet, she approached the curtained doorway to the front of the shop with dread.

Pulling the cloth aside, she peered out through the dark, sweet-smelling shop and the paned window at its front.

"There they are," she whispered.

"The Goldwings?" asked Corion, spying over her head.

Ellie nodded. "And the Sparrows, the mayor, everyone."

It reminded her of the day she'd left Linden—the whole town gathered in the square. Only that day, they'd been joyful and noisy, celebrating the Trials and the victors who were going on to the Race of Ascension. There had been music, feasting, dancing . . .

Not today.

Even from the back of the shop, Ellie could feel the heaviness in the air. No one was laughing. No one was dancing. She saw the familiar faces of her own clan, as well as those from other clans who had made Linden their home. They were all wide-eyed and silent, wings folded tautly.

"I have to get closer," she whispered. "C'mon."

They crept through the shop to the window. Ellie sat with her back against the wall, her head turned to peer through the corner of the glass.

"I see Zain," murmured Corion, from the other corner.

She nodded. She'd seen him too, standing with the other Goldwings in the center of the square. He looked queasy, but he kept his chin high, his armor polished to a perfect shine.

Her heart skipped a beat as she counted them. And counted. *And counted.*

Fifty.

Fifty knights stood in Linden.

Corion caught her eye, his mouth a grim line.

Why so many? It was like an invasion force. She'd never in her life seen more than three Goldwings in Linden at once.

No wonder the people looked so tense. Whatever was going on, this was no ordinary visit from the king's knights. And they were led by a familiar face.

"The Stoneslayer," Ellie groaned.

The general, who'd earned his nickname by once slaying a gargol, had a particular hatred for Ellie, after she, Nox, Gussie, and Twig had stolen a skystone from his fortress back in the summer. He'd been out for their heads ever since.

The Stoneslayer stood with his Eagle wings spread wide in a show of intimidation, his fierce face with its sharp nose and dark sideburns commanding the attention of every person in the square.

Ellie crawled to the door, to press her ear to the crack so she could listen in.

"... dark times indeed, when the king of the Clandoms cannot trust his own people. You've no doubt heard the dangerous rumors of islands floating in the sky—honestly! As if such a thing were possible! Or worse, of this charlatan flitting about, calling himself the Phoenix, burning down the countryside in his quest to terrorize honest, king-fearing folk."

Ellie watched the people react, some nodding, eager to show their loyalty. Her breath caught in her throat when she spotted Mother Rosemarie and the Lost Sparrows, her old housemates. All stood still, obedient and demure, while Mother Rosemarie watched the Stoneslayer with narrow eyes.

"It is unfortunate, then," said the general, "that the king has learned of the treason which foments among his people—yes, even here in the farthest reaches of his kingdom."

Kingdom? Since when were the Clandoms a *kingdom?* Ellie brushed the question aside as unimportant, though, focusing more on the new knot of dread forming in her belly. She had a bad, bad feeling about where the Stoneslayer was going with all this.

"It's come to our attention that this outlaw, this villain, the so-called Phoenix trickster, has at his right hand a coconspirator of none other than Sparrow origin—the traitor Ellidee Meadows."

Ellie clapped a hand over her mouth, smothering a gasp. Across the room, Corion shot her a worried look.

The reaction outside was little different. Every non-Sparrow in the square turned to stare at her clan. In turn, the Sparrows all shrank together, eyes widening and wings tensing with uncertainty. They looked to their chief, Donhal, whose face had gone bright red.

"Sir!" sputtered the chief. "Ellie Meadows has not been seen in Linden in months! I'm sure no one among us has the least idea what she—"

"Enough!" snapped the Stoneslayer. "We have our orders from the king himself. In his wisdom and his desire to protect his people, he has determined that no amount of treachery will be tolerated! Whatever treason was born in this Meadows girl, it is contagious and must be stamped out. Which is why today, by His Majesty Garion's decree, *every* Sparrow in the Clandoms will be punished for treason."

A cry rose from the townsfolk, Sparrows and others alike. The Goldwings bristled, crossbows appearing. A few bolts fired into the ground quickly quelled the noise.

Ellie reeled, nauseated, the shop spinning around her as she fought for breath.

Skies above—this was happening because of *her*!

Davina, the mayor of Linden and an Oriole clanner, stepped forward, raising a calming hand toward Donhal and the other Sparrows. She serenely nodded to the Stoneslayer, the picture of respect and deference. But Ellie could see the tremble in the bright orange feathers that crowned her wings.

"Surely the king cannot intend to *shatter* the Sparrow clan," she said. "Such a sentence requires a formal vote of the high court judges, and there is a process of appeals that must be—"

"Enough!" The Stoneslayer flapped a wing, silencing her. "We are beyond such judgments now, Mayor. After all, the shattering of the Crow clan did not stop the thief who riled the gargols against us all, did it? No. We have entered a new era, one in which judgments of paper and ink are no longer enough to keep the Clandoms safe. The king has ordered a different sentence upon the Sparrows."

"What—what sentence?" gasped Davina.

"The punishment will be carried out immediately!" shouted the

Stoneslayer, ignoring her. He waved a hand to his knights, several of whom stepped forward with a large crate between them. They set it down and opened it to reveal neatly packed pairs of large, toothed saws.

Ellie stared, her blood running backward.

She'd seen a saw like that before—in the hands of the doctor in Khadreen, the one who'd "treated" Twig for his wingrot. Those saws had one purpose and one purpose only.

The king had sent his knights to Linden not to protect the Sparrows . . . but to cut off their wings.

CHAPTER FOURTEEN
· ELLIE ·

Corion had to lunge across the oil shop to grab hold of Ellie, to stop her from bursting through the front door.

"Let go!" she hissed. "I can't let them do this!"

"If you hand yourself over, what's to stop them from doing it anyway?" asked Corion. He was nearly twice her size and had no trouble pulling her away from the door. Pinning her down by her shoulders, he gave her a hearty shake. "Listen to me, Ellie! There's nothing you can do."

"They're going to cut off their *wings*," she snarled. "Your father ordered it!"

His face flashed with pain. "Yes. I know. But we can only help them if we stop and use our *heads*."

"Then think fast!" She pushed him away, her eyes burning with tears of rage. "Because they're not waiting around!"

Already the knights were pushing the Sparrows into a line. Wails and pleas rose from her clan, but she saw no one fight back. They were too afraid of the crossbows trained on them and the fearsome glares of the Goldwings. Conditioned to obey the white uniforms, they would never rise up, not even to save themselves.

Only Ellie could stop them.

But *how*?

"Wait!" a voice rang out. "This isn't right! No one told me we'd be chopping off people's wings!"

Ellie and Corion gasped as Zain pushed through the knights to confront the Stoneslayer.

The captain stared at the Hawk boy with a wolfish smile, as if he'd been expecting him to say something. Ellie got the horrible feeling Zain had been assigned to this mission on purpose, as a test of loyalty to see whether he'd side with his neighbors—or the king's orders.

Well, it looked like he'd failed the test, and the Stoneslayer was delighted.

"Mutiny, Zain of the Hawks?" he barked. "Very well. You can lead the line."

Shouts of protest rose from another faction—Zain's family, Ellie realized, were clustered on the far side of the square. Tall, broad, and Hawk to the bone, they pressed forward with all the aggressiveness the Sparrows lacked. *They* weren't used to being shoved around by high clans. They *were* a high clan. But the knights outnumbered them five to one, and when half the Goldwings turned their crossbows on them, the Hawks were forced to freeze in place.

"Apologize to your captain, Zain!" called out Zain's father. "You took an oath before your king."

"Don't shame us this way!" his mother added.

Ellie realized then, with sinking horror, that it wasn't the Stoneslayer they were angry with at all.

It was *Zain*.

They were siding with the Goldwings over their own son.

If anyone knew what it was like to feel the betrayal of one's own people, it was Ellie.

"We have to save him!" Ellie said to Corion.

This time, the prince didn't argue. He'd gone pale, and nodded dazedly. She'd been right in her suspicions—he cared deeply for Zain.

"Any ideas?" he asked.

"You're asking *me*?"

"Well, when it comes to starting riots and saving people, that's sort of *your* specialty, isn't it? Why do you think I asked you to help me on this mission?"

"I don't know. Maybe because I was the only option you had?"

He shook his head. "You don't get it, do you? You're a warrior, Ellie Meadows. As good as any of the Goldwing recruits—you *won* the Race of Ascension!"

Ellie felt a flush of warmth at his words. Still, despite Corion's confidence in her, she was just one Sparrow—and there were fifty fully fledged Goldwings out there.

Goldwings who were currently tying Zain's hands in front of him, preparing to hack off his wings.

"Right," Ellie whispered. She tapped her fingers together. "I need to think. Need a plan. Something to distract them long enough that you can grab Zain and get him out of there."

Corion nodded, his eyes watching her desperately. "Hurry, Ellie."

"I'm trying!" She squeezed her eyes shut, her mind racing. If only Nox were here—his big, fiery wings would be the perfect distraction.

Ellie gasped, her eyes popping open.

"What?" said Corion, frantic. "Don't tell me you've run out of ideas!"

"No," she sighed. "I have the perfect idea."

It was the thought of carrying it out that made her feel sick.

But there was no time for regret. The Goldwings were forcing Zain to his knees in the center of the square. The Stoneslayer himself picked up the bone saw and approached him with a look of barely contained satisfaction.

"Wait here," Ellie said. "As soon as you hear the signal, grab Zain and *fly*. Head for the Forest of Bluebriar—that's the only place you'll be able to hide around here. I'll catch up with you later."

"But what are you—"

She didn't have time to explain. The Stoneslayer gave the order for the pair of Goldwings holding Zain to extend his wings, giving him a better angle at their bases.

Ellie had mere seconds to save him.

She limped through the shop and dropped through the hatch to the storage tunnel, landing awkwardly on one foot. As she stumbled down the tunnel, cursing her bad leg for slowing her down, she dragged her hand and wing along the shelves, knocking dozens of oil jars to the floor, where they shattered and spilled. Each one represented hours of hard labor by her clan—some of it her own work—but Ellie couldn't worry about that now.

At the other end of the tunnel, she bent and held out the Phoenix feather, touching its tip to the long trail of slippery oil she'd left behind. With a slight twirl, it flamed, caught the oil, and fire roared up.

She didn't have a Phoenix, but over the last few months, Ellie had gotten pretty good at starting fires all on her own.

The harsh warnings of the elder Sparrows thundered in her head, her mind replaying all the stern voices that had drilled into her brain the dangers of open flames around the sunflower oil.

This was exactly what they'd been afraid of.

The tunnel now raged, an inferno of flame. Stumbling back from the heat, Ellie whirled and grabbed a barrel of freshly pressed oil, tipping it over and letting it cascade down the steps. The fire chased it hungrily, leaping out of the tunnel and into the warehouse.

Time for Ellie to get out of there.

Fast.

She took to the air, coughing as smoke spread through the room.

The burns on her arm seemed to scream with new pain in response to the fire. A high ventilation window in the roof was just wide enough for her to squeeze through, as below, flames engulfed the presses, perfumes, and barrels and barrels of sunflower oil.

Ellie hovered in the sky over the barn, horrified by her own handiwork. That oil was her people's entire year's income, their only source of food for the winter, clothes for their children, shelter against storms . . . And she'd destroyed it all in less than a minute.

The warehouse fire filled her vision, but then a sudden groan and crack drew her attention to the ground between it and the town. The tunnel was collapsing. Ellie clapped her hands to her face, eyes wide. The heat was eating away the wooden beams that supported the tunnel, and where the ground caved in, jets of flame shot up, leading toward Linden in a fiery trail.

But had her distraction worked?

Was Zain all right?

She flicked her wings and sped toward the town, flying low, just as a wave of people rose from the square. So the smoke hadn't gone unnoticed. Goldwings, Sparrows, and other clanners rose into the sky, shouting. In the town, someone began ringing the alarm bell outside the mayor's house—two sharp, repeating clangs that meant *fire*.

Averting her face—burns or no burns, any one of the Sparrows would recognize her immediately—Ellie landed behind the tailor's shop and edged around the corner, peering into the square.

She was just in time to see Corion—his face hooded—flying directly at the Stoneslayer. He bowled the knight over before the Stoneslayer even realized what was happening. Grabbing the saw, Corion turned and swung it like a sword at the Goldwings still gripping Zain's arms. As he did, his hood fell back.

"The prince!" gasped the general.

In the chaos, it seemed only a handful of the knights were paying attention to the scene, but that one moment was all it took: Corion had been exposed. The Goldwings hung back uncertainly.

"Grab him, idiots!" shouted the Stoneslayer. "Prince or no prince, we serve the *king*, remember? This is treason!"

"Zain, let's go!" Corion yanked Zain by his wing, startling the boy into motion. They both took to the air.

Ellie was about to take off after them when a Goldwing planted himself in her path.

"Stop, Sparrow!" he ordered, lowering a spear at her chest.

She froze, eyes wide.

Then out of nowhere, a stone came flying. It pinged harmlessly off the knight's armor, but he turned to see who'd thrown it.

It was the opening Ellie needed.

She launched into the air and tore off after Corion and Zain.

CHAPTER FIFTEEN
· NOX ·

Nox hit solid ground and crumpled, wings sprawling, legs shaking.

But alive.

So far.

If you fail this test, you die, echoed Icara's words.

Nox sat in shock for a moment, then rushed up to the ceiling, wings fluttering frantically as he tried to pry open the trapdoor, but it was no use. His panic caused a surge in flames to roll from his feathers, filling the air with heat and illuminating the room into which he'd fallen.

He sank down again.

There were no windows, no hidden seams or levers. The place was dismally solid, each wall bare rock with no features or instructions to offer guidance on what he should do next. It reminded him of the cells below the palace in Thelantis.

The ghost of his old mentor, the Talon, was probably having a belly laugh right now—this was just the sort of thing he'd always warned Nox about. *Traps only catch fools*, he used to say.

The only option out was a doorway, which gaped as if waiting to swallow him up. It clearly led downward—underground, not to the open sky he wanted. It felt unsettlingly like a throat waiting to swallow him.

"A test," he muttered. "What fun."

He pulled in a deep breath of stale air, then walked through the doorway. At least he didn't need a torch.

He could sense the weight of the stone all around him, solid and thick as a tomb. Here and there, veins of skystone ran along the walls, glowing blue in the darkness but fading when he came close, the light of his wings overpowering the faint gleam.

"I thought this was a test!" he called out. "Feels more like a long walk. What— Oh."

He stopped abruptly as the tunnel ended in a blank wall. Or rather, it took a sudden sharp turn—straight *down*. He'd nearly walked right off the edge and into the pit below.

Nox groaned. *"Are you serious?"*

With a sigh, his stomach starting to knot, he knelt and peered down the vertical chute. It extended into utter darkness, but was wider than his wingspan.

Clearly, the only way forward was *down*.

Nox dropped into the pit, spreading his wings and descending as slowly as possible. There was no telling where the bottom was, and he didn't care to hit it at a speed that would break his ankles. As he descended, he heard a sound over the rush of wind from his feathers—a *drip drip* of liquid running down the walls around him.

"Water?" he wondered. That would be welcome. He was getting thirsty.

But when he angled too close to one of the walls, his wingtip brushed the dark runnels of liquid and it caught flame.

Not water.

Oil.

Nox yelped as fire raced down the chute's walls, chasing the rivulets of oil trickling down the stone. The passage below became a churning inferno.

Despite being fireproof, every instinct in Nox's body rebelled. He reversed course, flying upward—only to see the fire had spread that way too. He was closed off in both directions. The heat was unbearable; he might have been immune to the flames themselves, but soon he was drenched in sweat.

For a moment, he hovered in place, his mind locked by fear. Should he go up and hope Icara would let him out?

No. He wouldn't beg at the door like a beaten dog. He didn't have much of himself left after he'd come back to life on that beach, but he still had his pride. He would press on and hope to find another exit.

Tucking his wings and rolling forward, Nox made a reckless dive. He plummeted through the fiery chute, teeth gritted, sweat stinging his eyes.

He was committed now.

The ground appeared all at once, so suddenly he nearly slammed headfirst into it. But at the last possible second, he flared his wings and slowed, sending a rush of flames curling all around. His stomach dropped as he realized how close he'd come to smashing his skull.

He found himself hovering in a massive underground tunnel; it seemed too perfectly round, the floor too smooth, to be natural. Landing gently on the stone, he looked up and saw the flames in the chute slowly extinguishing, the oil trickling down the walls having burned away.

Folding his wings, Nox stared into the passage, wondering what waited in the darkness ahead. It was large enough to drive several wagons through, side by side, and the ceiling was high enough to comfortably fit a two-story building. Veins of skystone traced the walls, ground, and ceiling, polished smooth but revealing no hidden message or sign.

The only things of note were the thin stone screens that lined either side of the tunnel, carved with intricate but random patterns. They were about shoulder height, and served no purpose that he could see, except to make the passage slightly narrower.

Suspicious that there might be traps laid out ahead of him, Nox spread his wings wide, letting the flames light the tunnel.

Then he gasped as a shadow sprang up on the wall.

He mistook it at first for his own shadow, but the angle of the light was wrong. And an odd side effect of being a living torch was that Nox usually had no shadow at all.

No, this was definitely cast by the carvings set in front of the wall. They weren't just random patterns—they'd been shaped to cast the shadow puppet, with Nox as the lamp. He'd seen something similar once in Thelantis, when a theater troupe had used cut paper and a candle to project a shadow play on the walls of the city. Nox remembered that day fondly, not because he particularly enjoyed theater, but because he'd picked a record number of pockets among the audience.

The shadow figure beside him now was not a Phoenix. Nox measured his wings against the shadow's and found his own to be larger and more tapered. No, judging by the wings, the shadow was definitely a Crow. Nox would know that shape anywhere. It had been *his* shadow for thirteen years, following him faithfully until the day he'd died.

He folded his wings, and the shadow dimmed and shrank into a meaningless blotch. When he opened them again, the light of his feathers brightening, it once more rose into a distinguishable shape.

Staring, Nox took a few steps forward, watching as his movement made the shadow transform again, causing it to shift and move. The figure came to life, walking, raising his hands, as lifelike as if he were an actor moving on a stage. As long as Nox kept walking, the shadow walked with him.

Gradually, more shadows cropped up. The Crow was joined by

others like him, a whole village full of people. They rose on either wall, tall and short, male and female, young and old. The first Crow moved among them as if they were family, carousing with friends and ruffling the hair of the little fledglings.

Then, as Nox kept walking, other shadows formed—much larger, with wings like tattered sails, and long as snakes, these were creatures like Nox had never seen before. They moved with liquid fluidity that meant they couldn't be gargols. Some had as many as thirty legs, their heads long and pointed. These creatures dove on the Crows, killing many. Nox recoiled as the shadows burst and faded, elders and fledglings alike falling victim to the vicious creatures.

Drakkan.

The name of the creatures tolled in Nox's head like a distant bell, deep and reverberating. He was certain he'd never heard it before. But it felt as if it had been hiding in the back of his mind all his life, only to flicker to the surface now.

A chill ran over his skin.

Finally, the first Crow took flight, separating from the others and winging away by himself. Nox chased him, his heart pounding.

"Where are you going?" he shouted. "They're dying back there—your clan! They need you!"

The Crow fled on, and Nox felt a rush of sudden, shameful heat in his cheeks.

He heard Ellie in his memory.

We need you! You can't run from this!

Feeling sick, Nox nearly turned back, but there was nowhere to go back *to.* He had to keep moving forward, had to make it through this strange test, or he'd never see the light of day again.

So he and the Crow went on, until new shadows sprouted—a conical mountain spewing smoke.

"Volcano," Nox murmured. He'd heard of them and seen paintings in the geology books Gussie used to identify the gems his crew stole. Mountains of fire and lava, smoke and ash.

The Crow flew around it, his shadow a tiny speck now beside the massive volcano. Then, as if this had been his plan all along, the Crow dove into its pit.

Nox gasped. "Idiot! What are you—"

The Crow emerged again a heartbeat later, clutching something in his hand. He held it high in triumph . . . then swallowed the thing. Nox started. What in the skies was going on?

He caught his breath as the Crow fell to the ground in obvious agony. He twisted and writhed, and as Nox watched, he felt a chill run down the back of his neck, his every vertebrae icing over. What had the fool swallowed? No wonder he was in agony—the thing had to have been boiling hot, coming out of a volcano's mouth.

Then, slowly, the Crow's wings disintegrated into ash, and new wings grew in their place—larger, swirling wings with feathers that shifted like flames.

"Ah," said Nox dryly. "So that's it. This is the story of the first Phoenix."

Whatever the Crow had plucked out of that volcano, it must have been what sparked the transformation—the same transformation Nox had gone through on the beach. He grimaced, supposing he should be glad Ellie hadn't chucked him into a volcano, at least. He wouldn't have put it past her, if she thought it would save him.

Nox continued, the story unfurling alongside him. The Crow-turned-Phoenix returned to his village and, in a truly impressive display of shadow puppetry, battled and drove off the vicious drakkan with their many legs. The creatures slithered away into the dark, and the Crows celebrated by following their hero to the volcano.

One by one, they dove inside to swallow whatever it was the first had eaten. They all transformed just as he had.

Just as Nox had.

"Phoenix clan," muttered Nox, eyeing his ancestors warily.

They were all around him—the shadows of his forebears, the fire-winged kings and queens of Tirelas. They walked when he walked, flew when he flew, inescapable. He even took to the air, spreading his wings and flying down the twisting tunnel, but they flew alongside him, over him, swooping all around as if energized by his attempt to flee. It seemed the farther he went, the more of them sprang to life, leaping up out of the rock to haunt him.

"Where are you taking me?" he murmured. "What do you *want* from me?"

Despite himself, Nox found his heart beating faster as he was herded. Anticipation swelled in his chest, until he felt like he would burst. More and more shadows joined the procession, and it seemed they too felt the expectant tension building in the tunnel air. They swooped and circled and dove, hurrying him along. He could almost hear them whispering in his ears.

Was this what it felt like, to be part of a clan?

The question took him by surprise.

As a Crow, he'd never known his people. They were dispersed to the four winds, their clanhood shattered by the Eagles generations ago. With no chief, no seat, no common creed to bind them together, they had sunk into the cracks of the world like scattered grain, sep-arated by more than just distance. By law, no more than five could gather in the same place. And so even in their own country, they were exiled from their own kind.

But flying down that stone passage, surrounded by the shadows of the Phoenixes, Nox felt something he never had before—a connection he hadn't even had with his fellow thieves. Perhaps it came close to the feeling he got with Ellie, Twig, and even Gussie before she'd betrayed them, but it was also different in a way he couldn't explain. Not a deeper or stronger connection, exactly, just . . . different. And no less important. All he could think was that it reminded him of his parents, in the happy *before*: before his father's execution, his mother's imprisonment, his life as a thief.

Still, they were only shadows, and the feeling was faint at best, a vague hint at what he had been denied in his life. It left him empty and wanting.

Finally, the tunnel ended in a round chamber. He landed with a fiery flutter, and the shadows vanished; the carved screens ended at the chamber's entrance. Suddenly alone—the Phoenixes may have only been shadows, but they'd still *felt* alive—he became aware of how cold this place was, and how cut off from the sky. He shivered.

THUMP.

Behind him, a stone door dropped from above, sealing off the exit with no sign of a handle or trigger to open it again. The way forward was obvious: Another door waited at the opposite end of the room.

He walked toward it, his eyes dropping to the floor, where words had been carved deep into the stone. Like a pathway, they led him forward.

> *Wings of light, heart of flame,*
> *Face your shadow, speak its name.*
> *The truth will shine in golden eyes,*
> *From ash alone may a Phoenix rise.*

Whatever that meant.

Nox stopped in front of the door. It was huge and round, and a massive carving covered its entire surface.

"The ashmark," he muttered. It was the largest one he'd ever seen. He put his hand to it, then dropped it and stepped back to look for any handles, levers, or other ways to open it.

There were none.

"Huh. Now what?"

He looked over his shoulder at the door he'd come through, his heartbeat rising. Perhaps this wouldn't be as easy as he'd thought.

"All right," he said aloud. "I get it. This is the test, isn't it? And that's some kind of riddle." He scuffed a shoe over the words carved in the floor. "Solve the riddle, and I'll know how to get out, right?"

Blazing skies.

He hated riddles. He hated anything that was designed to make others look stupid. And besides, he'd never been good at solving them.

What he wouldn't give now for Gussie's brain, or Twig's ability to sense what others couldn't, or even Ellie's hardheaded determination. He paced around, amusing himself by imagining Ellie forcing open the door with a solid headbutt.

But the smile dropped from his face the moment he heard the heavy grind of stone on stone.

Whirling around, Nox gave a strangled yelp. The large slab blocking the door had begun to move, grinding over the floor, pushing toward him. It sealed against the walls and ceiling, leaving no gaps through which he could escape. He put it together in a single, horrifying instant.

If you fail this test, mocked Icara's voice, *you die.*

If he didn't solve that riddle within minutes and open the great door, he would be crushed to death.

CHAPTER SIXTEEN
· NOX ·

His skin clammy with sweat, Nox stared at the massive stone door. The sound of grinding rock bearing down on him was terrifically distracting. When he needed to be thinking of answers to the floor riddle, all he *could* think was how much it would hurt to be slowly crushed to death.

"*Face your shadow . . .*" he muttered. "*Speak its name.* But what in the skies does it mean? And what am I supposed to *do*?"

He tore at the door's seams with his fingernails, to no avail. He pounded on it and called for Icara. He pressed every stone, trying to trigger some hidden mechanism. Nothing worked. Icara, if she heard him—which he doubted—ignored him entirely. He was on his own, with nothing but his useless brain to save him.

He paced in a frantic circle, his wings half-open, and chewed on the cuff of his sleeve.

Wings of light, heart of flame.

Flame.

Flames were the only tool he had to work with. Surely that meant something.

He thought of the gargol he'd slain in the wheat fields, and how it had shattered like glass when he'd sent a rolling wave of fire over it.

Catching his breath, Nox faced the door and spread his wings.

How had he done that again? He couldn't remember. It had happened in an instant.

"Okay, door," he growled. "Take *that!*"

He gave a mighty forward flap, and sent a few flames curling and flickering into the air, but not nearly the inferno he'd produced against the gargol.

Useless!

Face your shadow, speak its name, read the riddle on the floor.

What shadow? What name?

Looking over his shoulder, he saw the stone was halfway across the room. His time was half up.

Cursing, Nox tried again, his pulse racing faster. Still his reluctant flames sputtered and died in the air. He'd spent so much time trying to suppress the fire that now, when he truly needed it, it failed him.

Nox stepped closer to the door and pressed his feathers to it, but it didn't burn or crack the way the gargol had.

> *The truth will shine in golden eyes.*
> *From ash alone may a Phoenix rise.*

Well, Ellie had seen to that last bit.

You're alive, she had said to him on the beach. *I'd save you again and again and again if I had to. Because you're alive and that means we have hope.*

"Hope," he whispered, his eyes starting to burn with tears. "Still have hope, right?"

But he wasn't feeling hopeful. He was feeling more lost than he'd ever been, trapped in that stone room with death grinding down on him with dreadful inevitability. Lost, afraid, and very, very alone.

Pressing the heels of his hands to his eyes, Nox dropped onto his knees. He racked his brain, but no more words of wisdom fell out. No epiphanies, no memories with answers hidden inside them. He had nothing.

"I'm not one of you," he cried out.

The voices of his Phoenix ancestors did not answer.

"You hear me?" He lifted his face, wet with tears. "Maybe I have your wings, your blood, but I'm no Phoenix! I'm just a stupid kid, just a Crow thief with no family, no home! I never asked for this and I *don't want it*. So there! I fail your dumb test, can you just let me *go*?"

His voice rose to a shout, and the last three words echoed around the chamber before they were swallowed by the unrelenting grumble of the stone behind him.

Let me go, let me go . . .

He felt a stirring in the back of his mind—the creature again, snarling. It raised its fiery hackles, and he could feel its hunger reaching for him, a fire in search of fuel. Whenever it appeared, destruction followed.

"No, no, no," Nox moaned, pushing against it. Sweat poured down his neck as he fought to control it, to keep it from consuming him. He thought of cold things—of snow and ice, of stone and chilly ocean water—until the creature fell asleep again.

Only then did he breathe, his chest aching.

More than ever, he was a prisoner. His wings were his chains, binding him to this doom. Curse Ellie for forcing this fate on him! Curse his ancestors, for designing this impossible test! And curse Nox himself, for being too stupid to find his way out of it. Too stupid or too weak or too . . . too *Crow*.

"All my life I've never been enough," he raged, rising to his feet and pacing, speaking to whatever ghosts of the Phoenixes still lingered here. "I wasn't strong enough to save my father, or fast enough to save my mother. I couldn't save Twig's wings, or save my friends from Gussie's betrayal. I can't save *anyone* but somehow I'm supposed to save them all? Blazin' skies, you couldn't have picked a *worse* descendant!"

Still his only answer was the grind, grind, grind of stone on stone.

With a wild yell, he knotted a hand into a fist and punched the door. He pulled his knuckles away bruised and bloodied. Then he sank to the ground, drained of ideas and strength.

Let this place crush him, then.

There was nothing he could do to stop it.

Grimacing, he curled up and let his wings go slack on the floor, but nothing could stop the shudders that wrenched his body. His teeth chattered so hard he tasted blood.

He felt rather than saw the stone as it bore down. It was as if it were compressing the air, squeezing him even before it reached him.

Nox shut his eyes, his head spinning.

So when the door began to open, at first he thought it was just his dizziness.

But then he swallowed a cool draft of fresh air, and he fell forward as the door gave way, collapsing on the other side.

"What—what in the skies . . . ?"

Gasping, Nox crawled the rest of the way through, yanking his wings out just before the great stone ground over the floor where he'd been sitting.

He'd been mere *seconds* away from being crushed to pulp.

Had he solved the riddle by accident?

Choking with relief, his skin cold and trembling, he looked up to see Icara standing over him, her hand on the lever that had, presumably, caused the door to open.

Ah. So he hadn't solved it after all.

"Did you find it?" she asked. She bent to grip his shirt. "Did you *find it?*"

"Find what?" he choked out.

"A Phoenix heart, fool! Do you know *nothing* of your own clan? A firestone! Was there a firestone in there? I've been trying to break into that place for centuries, but could never get past the stupid flames. *Did you find a firestone?*"

"I—I don't even know what that is! There was nothing in there but shadows!"

For a moment, he was sure she'd bash his skull in, she looked so furious. But then, as if called by some voice he couldn't hear, she suddenly let go and stepped back, her shoulders hunching. "I guess you're no Phoenix after all. You may have their blood, but not their heart."

Unable to speak for the adrenaline and terror still pulsing through him, Nox only gaped at her. He wasn't sure his wings would ever work again, they were shaking so badly.

The chamber had emptied him into a small alcove set in the island's lower cliffs, little more than a crude cave. If he fell from the edge, it would be a long, long drop to the ground. Beyond the precipice rose a wall of heavy gray cloud, obscuring any view of the sky beyond or the world below.

After a while, Nox managed to rouse himself to his feet. As his terror faded, it was replaced by a feeling almost as strong: *anger.*

"So what if I'm not a Phoenix?" he shouted. "Why should you care? Why should anyone care? Why can't you all just *leave me alone*?"

Wondering why he was suddenly so full of rage, Nox spun to the half-open door and the solid wall of stone now behind it. At least the blasted thing was silent now. He looked around but saw nothing that might hint at what the answer to the riddle had been.

The wind howled at him. Icara had turned away, her arms folded and her expression bitter.

"What am I missing?" Nox shouted at the doors, spreading his hands wide. "What about me isn't enough for you?"

Of course there was no answer.

And Nox wondered why he suddenly cared.

CHAPTER SEVENTEEN
· ELLIE ·

"I can't help you if you won't stop squirming," Corion said calmly.

Zain screwed up his face. "But it *hurts*!"

"It's a splinter, Zain, not an arrow in your gut. Sit still!"

"They were going to cut off my *wings*." The horror rasped in the Hawk boy's voice.

"I know." Corion's own voice was shaking. "I know, but they didn't."

They'd managed to escape Linden and disappear into the Forest of Bluebriar, but only barely. It had taken hours to lose the Goldwings chasing them.

Now they were sheltered in an old oak, high above the ground. Above them, the bare branches of the trees clacked like bones, stirred by a frigid wind. They'd have to build a fire tonight or risk freezing, but Ellie wanted to be sure they hadn't been followed before daring to light one. For now, she paced back and forth along the branch, her chest buzzing as if filled with wasps. Her hands were in fists at her sides, clenching and unclenching.

Zain yelped as the prince finally pulled the splinter from his thumb and held it up like a trophy.

"There! Better?"

Grumbling, Zain sat up. "You shouldn't have done that."

Corion's lips quirked. "What, saved your life from this deadly and terrifying sliver of wood?"

"No, you shouldn't have gone to Linden."

"You practically asked me to in your letter."

"I thought you'd, I don't know, talk to your father about it or something. Not fly out like a blazin' fool—" Zain blanched, as if suddenly remembering who he was talking to.

"It was Ellie who saved you, really," Corion said. He looked up at her. "You were brilliant back there."

Unable to bottle her fury any longer, Ellie turned and kicked the trunk.

"That *monster!*" she snarled. "That evil, slimy coward! He wants to come for *my* clan? Cut off their wings, call them traitors? I'll tear off his feathers one by one! I'll drag him into the sky and sling him to the gargols, let them rip him apart! *Argh!*"

She kicked the tree with her other foot.

Zain and Corion stared at her, eyes wide.

Breathing hard, Ellie dropped down, sitting with her back against the trunk and her legs dangling off the branch. Her chin lowered to her chest, and she struggled to get control of the rage thrashing inside her.

If only she didn't feel so *helpless*.

Hot tears burned her cheeks.

What if the Sparrows were being de-winged this minute, while she hid out in the forest like a scared rabbit? There was no reason to believe the Stoneslayer wouldn't finish the job he'd been sent to do, even after the destruction she'd caused back in Linden.

She had to go back and . . .

That was where her brain stopped. And do *what*, exactly? How could she possibly hope to rescue her entire clan from the Goldwings? She had no more distractions up her sleeves, no more ideas.

What could *she* do, alone, against the full might of King Garion?

You are nothing. The old woman's words echoed in her brain like a curse. *You can do nothing.*

Her helplessness made her rage burn all the hotter. She curled up, head on knees, hands still in fists.

"I don't understand," said Zain softly. "I knew the king was going off his head, but ordering an entire clan to have their wings chopped off?"

"It was brave of you to say what you did back there," said Corion.

"The prince is right," Ellie added, giving her old friend a considering look. "You were the only one who was willing to say anything."

"Well, if you must know," Zain mumbled, "I only did it because . . . I thought, *What would Ellie do?*"

Ellie blinked. "Really?"

"Yes. And look where it got me," he moaned. "Did you see my father's face? My mother's? They think I'm a traitor."

"Aren't you?" said Ellie viciously. "I am. And you know what? I'm proud of it. You should be too. The king is a monster. Anyone who's *not* against him is just as bad as he is!"

"He's not really . . ." Corion looked down at the splinter still pinched between his thumb and forefinger, his eyebrows bunching together. "I did try talking to my father, you know. After he burned down Knock Street, I asked him why he would go to such lengths over one penniless Crow."

"He knew what Nox was, didn't he?" asked Ellie.

With a glance up at her, Corion nodded. "I think he suspected. He took me into a locked part of the palace I'd never seen before. It was like some kind of museum, with a bunch of old relics and . . . a pair of severed wings hanging on the wall."

Ellie's gut twisted. "What kind of wings?"

"Golden, shining wings. They looked forged out of metal. Not real. They looked like . . . well, you have one."

From her pocket, Ellie drew the feather Nox had dropped on the beach. It shone like tempered gold and was warm enough to ease the chill from her cold fingers.

"Yes," said Corion. "Just like that."

"Phoenix wings," Ellie breathed.

"He said he'd cut them off a Phoenix woman when he was much younger, and that he'd nearly lost his life doing so. She was a sorcerer, able to control fire. He said she tried to kill him, and that if he hadn't got her first, she would have wiped the Eagles out to take our throne."

"Tanra Corvain," she whispered.

His eyebrows lifted. "Yes, that was the name."

"Nox's grandmother." Ellie shut her eyes. "She disappeared years ago."

"Oh . . ." Corion's eyes widened. "You—you don't understand. I know it sounds bad, but he's not evil. My grandfather was the one who told him to always beware the Crow clan, because they carried the blood of Phoenix sorcerers. They would kill us given half the chance. He's doing what he was told he must."

"*You* were raised that way," Ellie pointed out. "And you don't go around chopping off people's wings or burning down neighbor-hoods. The reason your father hates Nox is because he knows Nox could become a symbol the people would rally to—and then he'd have a real fight on his hands if he wants to keep his throne. He's a coward and a murderer!"

Corion winced. "Look, I know why you hate him. I'm not say-ing you're wrong to hate him either. I just don't think fighting is the answer. I want everyone to come together and try to understand one another better. I want *peace*."

Ellie stared at him. "You don't want peace. You want to avoid the truth. You want to avoid facing the fact that your father is a monster who has to be stopped. What we saw today in Linden? That was not the kind of thing you just forgive and forget. We can't have peace as long as he's on the throne."

He lowered his gaze. "But if we could only—"

"The *only* thing you need to do," she said, "is pick a side. Are you with him, or are you with us?"

Corion wouldn't meet her eyes, but his jaw hardened as he stared into the cold forest.

"So . . . what now?" asked Zain hastily, clearly trying to change the subject. "I'm sort of new to this whole fugitive thing. Do we just . . . hide out somewhere?"

Ellie hesitated. Not long ago, she'd have said no way, she'd never hide out like a coward while people were suffering. She'd have said they ought to fight back with everything they had.

But now . . . she wasn't so sure anymore.

She'd tried everything she could think of, and it hadn't been enough. Everyone thought she was the girl who never gave up, who always had a plan, who kept trying and trying for as long as it took.

But what happened when *all* her plans failed? When her every attempt seemed to only make things worse? People had died because of her. She'd driven Nox away. Her clan were branded as traitors, who might even now be wingless or worse on her account.

Who was she, to have ever thought she could make a difference?

"I have to go to Robinsgate," she said tiredly.

"The Robin clan seat?" Corion frowned. "Why?"

"I left Twig there, and I promised to go back for him." That, at least, she should be capable of pulling off.

The boys exchanged looks. Then Corion said, "All right, when do we leave?"

Ellie tilted her head. *"We?"*

"You're the girl with all the plans," Corion said. "Who else would we follow?"

A few weeks ago, she would have blushed with pride at hearing those words from the Eagle prince. Now she cringed.

"I don't have a plan," she said. "I don't know what comes next. I don't know what to do. Even if I did, I . . . I don't think I'd be the person to do it." Turning her face away, she added, "You shouldn't follow me. I'm not what you want me to be."

I'm not what you want me to be.

Nox's voice.

Nox's words.

"Well, we can't sit around here," Corion pointed out.

"And where he goes, I go." Zain crossed his arms. "I'm still a knight, and it's my job to protect you, Your Highness."

Corion's smile was brief and shy, spots of pink in his cheeks.

Ellie sighed and slumped down on the branch. Fine. Let them follow her if they wanted. They'd realize soon enough she wasn't leading them anywhere, and then they'd leave.

Just like Nox.

CHAPTER EIGHTEEN
· NOX ·

The apple was small, withered, and likely wormy—but it was the most delicious thing Nox had ever tasted.

He devoured the entire fruit in three bites, core, stem, possible worm, and all, then began hunting for more. The ancient orchard Icara had brought him to was overgrown with weeds and vines, and the original trees were long since gone, but a few of their descendants had managed to sprout among the undergrowth, offering their shriveled, meager fruits to Nox's eager hands.

"Mmf," he moaned, chewing another. "Sky apples just taste *better*, you know what I mean? Oh. Maybe you don't. How long has it been since you . . . ? *Can* you even . . . ?"

His voice trailed away as he caught sight of Icara's icy expression.

She had barely spoken to him since the Phoenix test that morning.

He'd hoped that, given his failure in the test, she might free him. No such luck. He wasn't sure what more Icara could want from him now, but when he'd timidly asked if he could leave, she'd given him a glare that had nearly turned him to ash. He'd moped around a bit longer, while Icara stared at the clouds in deep thought, before finally telling her he was sure to starve to death in minutes if he wasn't allowed to eat.

Begrudgingly, she'd led him to one of the smaller, outer islands in the Cyrithine archipelago, where they'd found the orchard.

Pocketing the last few apples he'd found, Nox hopped onto the wall to watch the marble girl, scattering a few moonmoths that had been perched there. Icara was systematically tearing small trees out of the ground and snapping them in half, then hurling the pieces angrily. They spun off the edge of the island and fell. He could only hope they were drifting over a wasteland and not some poor town.

"Can't you just let me go?" he asked. "Clearly, I can't help you with your problem."

She froze, her hands around a slim sapling. "What's so great about the ground, that you're dying to get back to it? Got someone waiting for you?"

He dropped his gaze. "Not exactly."

"Then you're lucky." She coldly snapped the sapling and tossed the pieces down. She stalked toward him, pressing her face so close to his he was forced to lean back. Her skystone eyes swirled with icy anger. "Forget them. Forget them all and stay in the sky with me. They're done for anyway."

"D-done for?" Nox stammered. "What do you mean?"

She shook her head, stepping back. "It doesn't matter. It's too late anyway."

"Too late for what? Icara—"

"Maybe you could have stopped it, if you were a true Phoenix. But clearly you're not. You couldn't even break through one measly door on your own. You don't have a chance against my father."

"Your father? What's he got to do with . . . ? Icara, is he planning something?"

She shrugged.

"*Icara!*" Nox's voice rose with alarm. "What's he going to do?"

"If you'd found me what I wanted, maybe I'd have told you. Maybe you'd have time to warn them. But you failed."

"If he's planning some kind of attack, you *have* to tell me!"

She sat on the stone wall, drawing her knees up and wrapping her arms around them, a statue of petulance. "I don't and I won't."

"Will people die?"

She glanced up, a savage little smile on her lips. "Lots."

His heart drummed faster. He wished he could shake the answers out of her, but she'd probably snap him easier than those trees. "What can I do to make you tell me?"

"Only one thing, and you already failed at it."

"You—you want a firestone, is that it? What *is* a firestone anyway?"

Her eyes were fixed on the ground, and for a long moment, she didn't speak. Then she took one of the pendants off her necklace and held it up. It looked like an ancient earring, with an amber stone set into a silver teardrop.

"My grandfather and the other Swallows used to fly down to the ground to mine stones they could carve. Marble and many other types of stone aren't found in Tirelas, not naturally, so they had to haul it up from below. One day, in the mountains, my grandfather found this."

She laid the earring in Nox's palm.

Nox looked closer. "It's *glowing*. Like a skystone."

But skystones were blue, and this stone was brown, the light within it soft orange.

Icara replied, "It's an earthstone. My father thinks they're the source of the ground, soil, rocks. Just like how skystones are the source of the sky and clouds and weather. He calls them *origin stones*, and says there might be many kinds of origin stones— seastones, nightstones, starstones."

"Firestones?"

She nodded. "Nobody ever saw them, but there were rumors the

Phoenix clan had one, maybe many. It was said these were the source of their clan Legacy, which was always so much more powerful than all the other clans'. The ability to withstand fire, to transform their wings, to create and control flames . . . There are some pretty wild Legacies out there, but this was far beyond what anyone else could do. My father said the only explanation was that they had found another type of origin stone, the firestones, to amplify their power."

Nox handed the earring back. "And you want one."

She nodded. "I need it . . . to change myself."

"Into a Phoenix?" He grimaced.

"No. To change myself *back*." She knotted her hand into a fist around the earring. "My mother and I were sick, dying probably. My father wanted to save us, so he used an earthstone's magic to turn us to marble. He changed himself too, making us all immortal, but no longer quite . . . alive. These he gave me so I could still fly." She touched her skystone eyes. "He was the best stonemason in our clan, but with the power of the earthstones, he became the sorcerer Demetrace."

"The gargols," breathed Nox. "You said he created them."

Icara nodded.

The gargols had been *made*. And their creator was still alive, somewhere up in these skies. Nox glanced around uneasily, as if the stone sorcerer might jump out from behind a gnarled apple tree. "But a firestone can turn you back to normal?"

"Maybe. *He* says so, anyway. Centuries ago, I begged my father to undo the magic. I didn't want to be made of stone. I didn't want to live forever, not if it meant being alone up here. What kind of life is that?" She looked out across the ruins of Cyrith, her skystone eyes glinting as if filled with tears that could never fall. From her pocket she pulled her comb, and she ran her marble thumb over the bristles.

"It's no life at all," she finished. "I have the whole sky to myself, but I'm still a statue, stuck in place. Never changing, never growing up . . . Even if it meant being sick again, I'd rather have a real life while I could." She sighed. "But my father got angry. He told me the only magic that could undo his would have to come from a raw firestone— the magic of life, warmth, and rebirth. I thought it was impossible. I've searched all of Tirelas, every ruin, every island, but never found a sign of a firestone. The last place one could be was inside the Phoenix test, but nothing helped me get past the fire tunnel."

"I wouldn't have guessed fire could hurt *you*."

She drummed her fingers on her marble arm; it sounded like pebbles pinging off rock. "I'm not indestructible, remember. The first time I tried to get through the tunnel, I got this."

When she raised her arm, he saw a fine, hairline crack running from her wrist to elbow.

"If I'd continued, I might have shattered from the heat," she sighed. "And when I tried to get in through the back door, it stayed locked. I think it's rigged not to open from the outside unless someone's already gone through the fire, to keep non-Phoenixes from ever breaking in. You're lucky it did unlatch at last. I guess even the Phoenixes wanted to be sure they could get their kids out if they failed the test. I must have tried a hundred times to get in there, and nothing worked."

"But then you saw me." Nox gave a weak smile.

"Then I saw *you*. A real Phoenix. You're not even supposed to exist. My father did his best . . ."

"To wipe out the Phoenix clan?" Nox said acidly. "Yeah, people have a habit of trying that."

"It was my fault," she said softly. "After my father turned us to stone, the other clans got angry. They said he had too much power, and that what he'd done to my mother and me wasn't right. Nobody should be immortal, they said. Not even the Phoenix kings and queens had that kind of power. And he was going to teach the other Swallows how to use earthstones, to make themselves immortal too. But the other clans petitioned the Phoenixes, who outlawed earthstones and ordered my mother and me to . . . to be destroyed."

Nox's mouth opened with horror. "*Destroyed?* But you'd done nothing wrong!"

"We existed." She shrugged, looking down at her comb. "That was enough. They managed to capture my mother, and they . . . Well, we're immortal, but not invulnerable. They crushed her into a thousand pieces and then they came for me. And my father just . . . snapped. He created the gargols and sent them to battle the Phoenixes. They were a small clan, always had been. Their fire wasn't enough to save them. But the gargols didn't stop there. My father . . . I think between transforming himself and seeing my mother die, he lost what it meant to be alive. To feel. To love. The gargols went after the other clans, and he did nothing to stop them. They drove everyone away, killed anyone who resisted, and they've guarded Tirelas ever since."

So there it was—the truth behind the gargols, and why they haunted the skies, killing anyone who flew too high, all because of one man's anger. Well, not *just* because of that. The Phoenixes had played a part in it too.

Nox stared at the clouds roiling beyond Cyrith's borders. "They took your mother from him, so he took the sky from them."

She nodded. "Anyway, you were my last chance at being normal again. And now I have none." She lifted the comb and pressed it gently to her lips. "You know, sometimes, I can still feel her brushing my hair. This is all I have left that was hers."

Nox looked away, feeling a violent tug in his chest as he thought of his own mother. "You really think a firestone could undo your father's magic?"

"He seemed to believe it."

"What about the gargols? Could firestones destroy them?"

She looked at him thoughtfully, as if the idea hadn't crossed her mind before. But after a moment, she nodded. "I guess they could."

Nox's heart began to race. He already knew his own fire was strong enough to destroy a gargol, but he also knew he alone could never take on a whole sky of the creatures.

But if he could find something to give the Skyborn to help *them* fight the gargols . . . He pictured himself placing that kind of power in Ellie Meadows's hands. Would it ease the guilt he still felt about burning her, then running away like a coward?

Besides, if the Skyborn had the power to fight the gargols, then they wouldn't need a Phoenix. He could be rid of *destiny* once and for all. The clans would have the strength to save themselves.

"If I get you a firestone," he said slowly, "you'll tell me what your father's planning?"

Her eyes narrowed. "What do you mean? What secret are you hiding?"

With a sigh, Nox closed his eyes. His mind filled with dancing shadows. "There weren't any firestones in the tunnel. But . . . there was a story."

"A story?"

"About the first Phoenix." He looked at her, but he could still feel the shadows flickering in his memory. "About how he *became* a Phoenix."

Icara's eyes widened.

"Tell me," she said.

Nox bit his lip. He didn't like where this was leading, not one bit. He almost wished he'd said nothing at all.

"*Tell me.*"

But if there really was some terrible attack brewing against the Skyborn . . . he might be the only one in the world able to stop it from happening in time.

"Fine. If you can find me a volcano," Nox said, wondering if he'd soon regret his own words, "I think I can find you your firestone."

CHAPTER NINETEEN
· ELLIE ·

"Twig? Where are you?"

Ellie flitted between precipices, navigating the narrow canyon with care. High walls of striped rock towered on either side of her, crossed by horizontal bands of gray, red, and brown. Dry winds howled through the space, as if searching for escape from the canyon's deep confines. She avoided these; they were strong enough to send her tumbling if she wasn't careful. Far below, a yellow narrow river churned over huge rocks, its dull roar reverberating off the cliffs. Ellie's every sense was on high alert; there were hundreds of places to hide in this maze of rock, and Goldwings might wait in any one of them.

The knights had been crawling all over Robinsgate, just a few miles to the southwest. Ellie, Zain, and Corion hadn't even gotten close to the town; they'd passed a family on their way out, who warned them to turn back.

It seemed that word had spread of the Robin clanners Nox had saved. The knights had come and confiscated the gargol head the man had been displaying. Then they arrested the entire Robin family, dragging them off to fates unknown. That news had sickened Ellie, and the feeling hadn't faded. The Goldwings were not gentle with anyone who spoke of Phoenixes or Tirelas. It seemed not an hour went by that she didn't remember the old men singing in Delven, or the shattered farm with the dusty, hollow-eyed children, their parents' graves still fresh.

Ellie hoped Twig had gotten out in time. He'd promised if there was trouble in Robinsgate, he'd run to this canyon and hide. But what if Goldwings had followed him?

She landed on a high ledge to rest her wings and think. Zain and Prince Corion dropped beside her. They had been her constant shadows since Linden, though she couldn't say she minded. It was better than flying alone, and besides, having Zain as a friend again was a comforting surprise . . . even if he only had eyes for the golden-haired prince.

"Spread out and look for a waterfall," she told them. "He said there would be a waterfall. And Zain . . ." She pointed to his cloak and epaulettes. "If he sees you looking like that, he'll never come out."

"Oh, right." Zain reluctantly took off his Goldwing uniform, leaving himself dressed in a white linen shirt and tight-fitting gray trousers. He patted the cloak, as if it were a beloved pet he were sending away. Corion patted his shoulder consolingly.

"This place is probably crawling with outlaws," said Zain, looking around. "Perfect spot for a thieves' den."

"Good thing I brought along a strapping young Goldwing to protect me," Ellie said.

"Yeah, a strapping young Goldwing with no sword, no bow, not even a sharp, pointy stick," moaned Zain. "If we do meet any robbers, all I can really do is jump at them and yell *Boo*."

"I'm sure they'd find you terrifying," Corion reassured him.

They took off again, flying just close enough together to hear one another's voices as they searched the canyon. If there *were* outlaws or Goldwings nearby, they'd probably hear them coming a mile off, the way their voices echoed. But it would take days to search the entire place if they stuck together, and Ellie wasn't willing to leave Twig alone any longer than she had to.

Nearly an hour later, Ellie finally found the waterfall. Calling to the others, she swooped toward it.

They got soaked flying through the cascade and landed in the dark mouth of the cave, shivering and shaking water from their wings. Ellie saw no sign of Twig, her heart dropping, but the cave appeared to be more of a tunnel delving into the dark. Perhaps he was deeper within.

But after another half hour of fruitless wandering, Corion sighed. "There's no one here," he said.

The tunnel had branched into a maze, and Ellie was starting to worry they wouldn't be able to find their way out again, despite the arrows she was drawing on the walls with her charcoal stick. She lit the way with Nox's dropped feather, holding the quill like a torch. The feather was starting to lose its glow, she noted. The light it gave off was dimmer and dimmer by the day. She tried not to read too much into that. Wherever he was, Nox was okay. He *had* to be okay.

"Just give me one more hour," she said. "I have to be sure . . . *Wait.* Did you hear something?"

"My stomach rumbling," complained Zain. "It's been hours since—"

"No—*that!*" Ellie lifted a finger as, behind them, a small, furry creature came scurrying on sharp little claws. It was carrying a large white mushroom nearly as big as itself.

Ellie gasped. *"Lirri?"*

The creature froze just long enough to glance at her, clearly displaying the white horns on her head.

"Lirri!" Ellie cried.

"What's a Lirri?" asked Zain. "And is it rabid? It looks rabid."

With a hiss, the animal turned and sprinted away.

"C'mon!" Ellie picked up her pace. "Follow her!"

"Follow a *rat*?"

"Just trust me!" Ellie began sprinting, desperate not to lose the little animal. Lirri glanced back at her, squeaked in alarm, and scurried faster, still hampered by the mushroom she was dragging along.

"I get that you're hungry," Zain called, "but eating *rats*, Ellie?"

"I don't want to eat her! I want her to lead me to—" She skidded to a halt, sucking in a breath.

Behind her, Zain and Corion both yelped as they tried to stop, crashing into Ellie's outspread wings.

"What the—" Corion pushed her feathers aside and stared. "Who's that?"

Ellie's vision had gone red. She clenched her teeth together. *"You!"*

A girl stood in the tunnel in front of her, her hands raised defensively. She had a large knapsack looped over her shoulder, and such a variety of satchels, pouches, pockets, and packets strapped to her clothing that she looked like a peddler. Her long, tapered wings were striped in the pattern of the Falcon clan.

"Hello, Ellie," said Gussie. She offered a weak smile. "Surprise?"

Ellie rushed her, making a fist.

The girl blocked her punch. "Stop! I don't want to fight!"

"I bet not." Ellie remained in a fighting stance, her pulse pounding in her ears. "You just want to sneak around and stab me in the back. *Again*. That's your style, isn't it? This is a trap! I should have known!"

A tear glistened in Gussie's eye, but Ellie didn't trust it for a second.

"I'm sorry," Gussie said.

"Sorry? *Sorry?*" Rage made Ellie's mind spin. *"Sorry* doesn't even begin to fix what you did! Are you here to finish the job? Looking for Twig so you can turn him over to the Goldwings again?"

"What? No! Lirri found *me*, if you must know. She acted like she wanted me to follow her and I figured Twig must be in trouble. I've been following her for days, thinking—"

"Trouble!" roared Ellie. "You hand us over to our deaths and *now* you worry about us being in trouble?"

She threw another punch, and Gussie had to drop her knapsack to defend herself. They sparred down the tunnel, Ellie driving Gussie farther and farther back. The Falcon blocked her fists but didn't return blows of her own. Zain and Corion hung back, wide-eyed, as if afraid to intervene.

"You left us for dead!" Ellie shouted. "Nox *did* die!"

"What!" gasped Gussie. She tripped and fell backward, landing hard. Ellie pounced, straddling the Falcon girl and grabbing her by her collar. The swell of tears in the girl's eyes stopped her.

"Nox is dead?" whispered Gussie.

"He didn't *stay* dead," snarled Ellie. "No thanks to you!"

"Stop!" cried a voice. "Stop fighting!"

Ellie looked up as a small figure came barreling toward them.

"Twig!" she and Gussie shouted in unison.

Then Twig tackled Ellie, driving her off Gussie and slamming her into the wall.

"*Stop fighting!*" he cried, pinning Ellie with as much force as he could muster.

Panting, Ellie glared at the Falcon girl, who stared back miserably, not even bothering to pick herself up off the ground.

Instead of pushing him off, Ellie wrapped her arms around Twig. "You're okay! When I saw Gussie, I thought you'd been captured again."

"Well, I'm not. And if anyone should be mad at Gussie, it's me. She betrayed me first, remember."

"Then go on," said Ellie. "Tell her how you feel! She deserves to hear it!"

He gave her a strange look and stepped back. "All right. I will."

Gussie swallowed but didn't make a move to defend herself as Twig stood over her. Instead, she shut her eyes and nodded, as if ready to accept whatever punishment he decided to dole out.

"Gussie," he said, "I forgive you."

"What?" Ellie gasped.

Gussie's eyes shot open. *"What?"*

Twig offered her a hand. "I forgive you. I know why you did it, and I know you're sorry."

"But—but—" spluttered Ellie.

Gussie took Twig's hand and let him help her up, still looking uncertain.

"Twig . . ." she whispered. "They had my little sister. They threatened to—"

"I know," Twig said. "I know all of it."

His eyes went vacant, his body still, and Ellie knew he was using his ability to read emotions, his focus on Gussie.

"You really are sorry," he murmured. "You've been beating yourself up over it for weeks."

"I hate myself for what I did!" Gussie burst out. "King Garion told me he'd personally torture my sister if I didn't turn you all in. I couldn't let him . . . I didn't know what else to do! I'm so sorry, Twig. Ellie. I know you hate me. You *should* hate me."

Ellie stared in disbelief. Stoic Gussie, Gussie who prided herself on putting reason above emotion, who had never shed a tear that Ellie had seen . . . was *sobbing*.

"I took my sister home to Vestra the day you were supposed to be executed. I couldn't bear to be in the city when it happened. When

I heard you'd all escaped, I was so relieved I fainted. Fainted! Like some kind of Peacock clan actress!" She gave a bitter laugh. "When Lirri came crawling through my window three days ago, I thought I was seeing things. Then when she pulled my sleeve, trying to get me to follow her, I dropped everything. I didn't even leave a note for my family. I just *flew*, because I thought . . . if there was any chance to fix my mistake . . ."

Twig gave Ellie a beseeching look.

But Ellie shook her head. She couldn't forgive Gussie yet, she just couldn't. Even knowing the girl had been forced to choose between them and her sister . . . She touched her throat, remembering the feel of the noose. Gussie might as well have dropped it there with her own hands.

"How do we know the king doesn't have your sister still?" she asked coldly. "How do we know this isn't another trap, that the minute we step outside there won't be fifty Goldwings waiting to stuff us with arrows?"

"Because of me," said Twig. He stepped closer to Gussie, protective. "Because I'm looking into her right now, and she's telling the truth. And because even more importantly, *Lirri* trusts her. Or she'd never have brought Gussie here."

Ellie still couldn't relax. The strength of her anger frightened her; she hadn't realized how much of it she'd been carrying until the moment she'd seen Gussie's face.

But one by one, she pried her fingers out of a fist.

Twig looked between them until he seemed convinced Ellie wouldn't start throwing fists again. Then he knelt and grinned, holding out a hand.

"Lirri! I knew you'd find me!"

The pronged marten scurried up his arm and ran laps around his shoulders while he laughed. Then she burrowed into his hair and fell fast asleep, her tiny chin resting on his forehead.

"I hate to interrupt this, um, exciting little reunion," said Corion, "but any chance we could get out of these tunnels already? This place gives my *feathers* goose bumps."

Gussie blinked. Then blinked again.

"Is that . . . the *crown prince*?"

"And where's Nox?" asked Twig.

"Oh, yeah," Gussie said. "What's this about Nox dying but not dying? And what happened to your face?"

Ellie sighed, her fingers brushing the tender, pink skin still healing on her face and neck. "Right. I'd better fill you both in."

CHAPTER TWENTY
· NOX ·

The journey took so many days that Nox lost count. He and Icara flew from island to island, rarely touching the ground. Nox was getting used to the upper skies, where the wind flowed like great rivers. Closer to the ground, it raced in quick streams, tumbling and unpredictable, but the higher they soared, the steadier the sky. Icara knew the winds well and showed Nox how to read the air he couldn't see, just by feeling the temperature around him and studying the way the clouds in the distance moved.

He thought constantly about what her father might be plotting with his horde of gargols. Scenes played out in his head—towns slaughtered, fields burned, fledglings snatched screaming from their parents' arms. But no matter how he pressed her, Icara would not say a word about it, except to assure him there was still time . . . if they hurried.

He began to wonder if there really was some dark plan in the works, or if Icara was just stringing him along to get what she wanted.

But what if there was?

What if she wasn't bluffing at all, and something terrible was coming, and the only chance the clans might have of saving themselves was for Nox to find a magic rock in the heart of a volcano?

He had never more missed his simple days as a thief.

Nox foraged on the islands they landed on. While most of the foliage had succumbed to the cold, the ruins of ancient villages often hid wild carrots, onions, and other root vegetables still nestled in the soil. Whenever he ate, he wondered about the people who'd planted the gardens long, long ago.

"It won't be much farther now," said Icara at last. "We'll reach it this afternoon."

They stood on the edge of a deserted floating island, too small to have been settled and holding only grass, a few twisting trees, and a small pond at its center, where rainwater drained and collected. Amazingly, there had been a few brown fish circling in its waters. Nox speared one and roasted it by holding it over his own wings.

"Great," he murmured. "Can't wait."

Icara gave him an amused look. "Nervous?"

"Me? Never."

Laughing, Icara stepped off the edge, dropping into the open sky before opening her wings. Nox hurriedly finished off the fish, licked his fingers, then followed her.

Far below, the ocean glimmered like a sheet of gray silk. They'd flown beyond the eastern coast of the Clandoms days ago, and Nox had seen nothing but open sea ever since. But he trusted Icara's sense of direction by now. She hadn't been wrong so far. She knew when an island would be waiting just over the horizon for Nox to rest on, knew when the weather would turn nasty and they should fly above it, when a patrol of gargols would pass and they should take shelter. After the first few days of traveling, he'd felt more and more at ease, glad to let Icara take the lead.

But today, his nerves started buzzing again. In the distance, a string of islands appeared. Not floating islands but true, ocean-bound ones, like dark ink splotches against the sea.

"They're called the Embers!" said Icara, shouting over the wind's roar. "Each one's a volcano, but the last time I was here, only one of them was on fire. We'll aim for that one."

He nodded, his stomach turning over. The islands drew inevitably nearer, and an hour later, they swooped over the first of them. Laid out in a line, the Embers were all small, mountainous, and lush with jungle growth except for the northernmost. This last was nothing but black volcanic rock, shaped like cloth in folds and wrinkles. At its center rose a conical peak with a deep depression at its top. Even before they reached its shores, Nox smelled the fumes, saw the plume of ash and smoke billowing upward.

The blood drained from his face.

Why, oh why, had he ever suggested this?

Why hadn't he just kept his mouth shut?

They circled the island once before landing on the highest point of the volcano, a bank of ash and soot.

Below, the ground dropped away in a steep cliff, down, down, down to a pit of molten lava.

He'd expected something like a lake filled with liquid fire, based on the illustration he'd seen in Gussie's geology book. But what he saw below was far worse. The lava bubbled high as hills, boiling and livid, bursting in places to fling globs of fiery red high into the air.

Nox swallowed. Hard.

"Good thing you're immune to fire," said Icara.

He shot her a wild-eyed look. "Aren't *you* immune? Why can't you go down there? You're supposed to be the immortal one."

She shook her head, turning over her arm to show the crack running from her wrist to elbow. "Remember? Even marble shatters if it gets hot enough."

Nox stared down for a long moment, watching the lava bubble

and burst. His hands were slick with cold sweat. Sure, he couldn't get singed by a candle or even a house fire . . . but it wasn't like he'd tested how far his fireproof-ness went. He had no idea what his skin could withstand; if marble had a breaking point, surely he did too. And did lava even count as *fire*? Maybe he had no immunity to it at all.

He had a bad, bad feeling about the whole thing.

Nox shook his head. "You know, on second thought, maybe we could work out some other deal? I could steal you a giant ruby, for example. Or a princess's crown! What about puppies? Do you like puppies?"

"I want a firestone," she said icily.

His stomach turned over. "I can't do this, Icara."

The hairs on his neck rose as her marble hand closed on his wrist, squeezing so tightly his fingers began to turn blue.

"There's not much time left," she said in a voice that wrapped around his throat like a garrote. "Two weeks, in fact. Only two more weeks until my father attacks the ground. I haven't seen him this angry since my mother's death. Your people will never escape what he has planned."

Nox shut his eyes, his throat in a knot. "I guess if my ancestors could do it . . ."

She released him at once, but the red imprint of her fingers still circled his wrist. "Good boy."

Gritting his teeth, Nox watched the lava boil and spray. He took a deep breath, then dove.

The heat rising from the fiery pit created a massive thermal. When Nox first swooped into the volcano, it merely lifted him high into the sky. He fought against it, wings stretched wide to hover.

This was no good. He'd never reach the interior flying normally.

Every attempt only swept him high into the air again. His wings were sails caught by that hot, vertical wind.

There was only one option.

Nox shut his eyes, drew a deep, deep breath, and then tucked his wings and dropped headfirst into the volcano.

This time, the thermal didn't lift him into the sky. Instead he pierced it like an arrow, falling faster and faster toward the boiling lava. Hot wind screamed past his ears; sweat poured from his skin. He wanted to shut his eyes, but if he did, he might not see the surface of the lava in time and plunge right into it.

Hotter and hotter, the air burned his lungs. Noxious fumes made his head swirl and his vision distort. The fire might not kill him, but the smoke and fumes very well could.

As Nox neared the lava, flames broke out on his clothes. He patted them frantically, and then, at last, spread his wings.

Banking hard, Nox landed on a jut of rock just above the surface of the lava. He yelped and ducked as a bubble burst below, sending up a hot spray.

Coughing, Nox looked around through watering eyes. What would a firestone look like? Would it be visible at all, or buried under stone, impossible to reach?

He flitted around the lava, flying from rock to rock, but found nothing that might be a magical stone. What if they were underneath the lava itself?

Sickened with dread, Nox lay on his stomach and stretched a hand downward, fingers trembling. Twice he snatched his hand back, breathing hard, unable to force himself to go through with it.

The third time, he touched just one finger to the surface—and screamed as pain shot through his hand.

He yanked it back and cradled it against his chest, tears streaming down his face. He stared in horror at his fingertip, which bore an angry, bright red burn.

The first in his life.

So he *did* have limits, and he'd found them at the bottom of a raging volcano.

Head now spinning with pain in addition to the toxic air, his clothes breaking out in flames that had to be smothered under his palm, Nox stumbled up and backed away from the lava. He bumped into the sheer inner wall of the volcano's pit.

Plumes of smoke and hot air shimmered around him. He coughed harder, doubling over, sweat weeping from every pore. His lips cracked in the heat, and his skin was turning red. The heat was breaking him down, seeping through his fireproof armor, scalding him from the lungs out. It was getting hard to breathe.

He pressed a hand against the stone to steady himself, only to gasp and snatch it back when he found the surface scalding hot—and then saw it: an ashmark carved into the rock, above a small depression. There was another above it, and three more to his left. The more Nox looked, the more he saw—ashmarks over empty pockets in the rock, as if something had been removed.

There *had* been firestones here, but they were gone now. All of them harvested by his ancestors.

"Nox!"

He looked up to see Icara hovering halfway up the volcano's opening, fighting to keep from being swept away on the thermal. She seemed unwilling—or unable—to descend any farther.

"Anything?" she asked.

"No," he croaked. "They're . . . the Phoenixes took . . ." He dissolved into a fit of coughing, his lungs clotted with smoke.

"Keep looking!" Icara shouted.

"I—" He choked again.

"Keep looking!"

Nox could only shake his head. He dropped to his knees, gasping for air that didn't come. He was suffocating from the inside. Somewhere in the back of his mind, the creature of fire and darkness howled and scratched its claws as if wounded.

"Nox! You said there would be firestones!"

He looked up at her, but she was only a gray blur through the haze of smoke and tears on his eyes. "I . . . I'm . . . sorry."

Nox pitched into darkness, his head slamming the rock.

CHAPTER TWENTY-ONE
· ELLIE ·

"Let me get this straight," said Gussie. "Nox died, literally *died*, and you resurrected him . . . by setting his body on fire."

They were following Ellie's trail of charcoal arrows out of the tunnels, walking in single file. Ellie, still bristling whenever the Falcon girl spoke, nodded tightly. "That's right."

"And he came back to life—after being *dead*—with a new set of wings."

"Fire wings," said Twig.

Without a word, Ellie handed the Phoenix feather to Twig, who passed it to Gussie.

"Careful," he warned. "It's hotter than it looks."

Its soft orange glow lit the walls around them. When Gussie twirled it, a curl of flame leaped from the barbs.

"He's really a Phoenix," whispered Gussie, mesmerized by the feather. "I heard rumors, but . . . I didn't know what to believe, honestly. And you have no idea where he flew to?"

"I had to stop searching when I met Prince Corion."

She told Gussie and Twig about Linden and the Sparrow clan, feeling her rage start to boil all over again. Horror was plain on their faces as they listened.

"Will he take the wings of every clan?" Gussie asked Corion.

The prince grimaced. "I . . . don't know. I would have said *no way* a few days ago, but . . . maybe I don't know my father as well as I thought."

"People without wings are easier to control," Ellie pointed out, repeating something Nox had once said to her.

"But would he really go that far?" asked Zain.

"Would the clans let him?" asked Gussie. "I can't imagine everyone sitting back and just *letting* it happen."

They walked in silence, contemplating both ideas. Ellie didn't doubt for a moment that the king was capable of such a move. The only question was, how far would he take it? Would he cut off the high clanners' wings too, or just the low clans' like the Sparrows? At the end of it all, would he be the only one left who could fly at all? *Would* the other clans rise up if he tried it, or would they surrender meekly like the Sparrows had?

She shuddered.

"So what's your plan?" Gussie asked her.

"Why do I always have to be the one with the plan?" she snapped. "Why is it up to *me* at all? What do you expect me to do, face Garion's entire army by myself?"

"Uh . . ." Gussie's eyes darted to Twig, who looked just as startled by Ellie's outburst.

Sighing, Ellie lifted a hand. "Let's just get out of these tunnels, okay?"

Finally, they rounded a corner and stepped into a beam of sunlight shining through the tunnel's exit. The waterfall shimmered beyond, a rainbow dancing in the spray. Ellie put up a hand to block the light, wincing as her eyes adjusted.

But then she felt a prickling along her scalp. Just as Twig started to run ahead for the open air, she grabbed him and pulled him back.

"Wait!" she hissed.

A shadow fell over the tunnel's exit.

"Gargol," Ellie warned. She waved at the others to go back, then chanced a peek out the side of the exit, around the waterfall's edge.

Two gargols circled in the sky above, as if waiting for them to set foot in the open.

Ellie retreated quickly and reported to the others.

"Great," moaned Corion. "We're trapped until they get bored and leave."

"At least they're too big to fit in the tunnel," said Ellie, but her stomach churned nervously.

"We could make a run for it," said Zain. "Sneak out, fly low and fast, try to get away before . . . What?"

He frowned at Ellie, who was frantically shaking her head. She glanced pointedly at Twig.

"Oh." Zain's eyes flickered to Twig's wingless shoulders. "Right."

Twig sighed. "I knew it'd come to this again. You won't get far with me along, just admit it, Ellie. If those gargols attacked while we were in the open, you'd have to choose—either fly and save yourself or stay with me and die."

"I'd never leave you like that."

"I know. Which is why you shouldn't have come back for me at all. I'm useless."

"Well—" started Gussie.

Ellie cut her off with a sharp look. As far as she was concerned, Gussie didn't get a say in any of it.

"Twig, you're *not* useless. You can communicate with animals and read people's minds. And even if you couldn't, you're a person. *No one* is useless. We'll make it work."

"Emotions," he corrected her. "I read emotions."

"Wait—he can *what*?" asked Corion.

"Long story," said Ellie. "Another time. Twig, don't start this again. I'm not leaving you behind and that's final."

Gussie tried again. "If you'd just listen—"

"You're *not* part of our group anymore," said Ellie. "That was your choice, remember? Stay out of it."

"But—"

"There's a third gargol now," warned Zain, who'd taken up watch at the exit. "Smaller. If it smells us, it could wriggle its way in."

"Get away from there before he *does*!" Ellie said. "We just need—"

"You *need* to listen to me!" said Gussie hotly. "For just one minute, Ellie, will you shut up?"

Ellie stared at her, her jaw hanging open. "What are you—"

"Shush!" Gussie pleaded. "Just *shush*. Can you do that?"

Ellie glared at her but nodded once.

Blowing out a breath, Gussie removed the knapsack from her shoulder. "What I'm trying to tell you is, ever since I heard you all escaped Thelantis, I've been busy. Working on a new invention. Something . . . to prove to you I'm still on your side, and that I want to fix things. I mean, I know I can't fix everything, but there is something I can do. I think. I haven't really tested it yet, but . . ."

"Tested *what*?" Ellie burst out impatiently.

"This." Gussie opened her knapsack and took out a folded tangle of metal, cloth, and string. "It's for Twig. And if it works . . . it might be the most important thing I'll ever invent."

She opened the contraption then, and Ellie gasped.

Wings.

Fine metal rods in place of bones, cloth instead of feathers, and delicately threaded strings to bind it all together, like sinew. But most striking of all were the fragments of skystone she'd somehow welded into the metal rods.

"For me?" whispered Twig, eyes wide.

"They're a prototype, really, but I think they're ready to test. I was going to do it myself, but then Lirri showed up and, like I said, I just took off then and there."

Reverently, Twig reached out to touch the framework of the metal wings. "I . . . could fly again?"

"I'm not saying they'll replace your old wings, and you'd have to remove them on the ground, and keep them well oiled. But with some fine-tuning . . . yes, I think you could fly again. The trick was fitting them with skystones. Without those, they'd be way too heavy to fly. But the skystones lighten them enough that they should feel almost the same as your old wings. Luckily I had a few left, though it meant taking apart my skystone compass."

Twig launched himself at Gussie, wrapping his arms around her neck in a massive hug. Gussie looked startled, then pleased, and gave Ellie a tentative smile.

Ellie only stared back, her expression grave. *Those better work*, she mouthed. Gussie nodded, her smile slipping.

If she'd come all this way only to give Twig false hope, Ellie would strangle her.

"Can I try them on?" asked Twig eagerly.

Gussie helped him with the complex task of strapping on the wings, fitting them over the stumps of his old ones. But before she could finish, Zain began shouting.

"It's onto us! Go go *go!*"

Ellie whirled just as the smallest of the three gargols burst through the waterfall and shoved its way into the tunnel, slithering like a lizard, its wings scraping the walls and sending sparks flying.

"RUN!" she yelled.

They burst into motion, pelting down the tunnel with no regard for direction. Zain led the way, taking whatever turns or bends he saw. Limping in the back of the group, Ellie could hear the gargol screeching and scraping behind them, getting closer.

Blast these tunnels! They were just narrow enough that she couldn't spread her wings to fly. And if she couldn't, there was no way Zain, Gussie, or Corion could, with their larger wingspans.

Their only hope was to *run*.

But the gargol was gaining fast. It scrabbled over the rock, screeching and pulling down chunks of the wall and ceiling with its claws. A cave-in might get them before the monster did. The others could outrace it, but Ellie limped along, cursing her bad leg. It buckled when she tried to turn a corner, and she fell onto her hands and knees.

"Go!" she said when the others turned to look back at her. "Just go!"

Instead, Twig skidded to a halt and stepped between her and the gargol.

"TWIG!" Ellie screamed.

She gaped in horror as the boy raised his hands, as if he could push the gargol back by sheer force of will.

"Stop!" he cried out. "You don't want to do this!"

The gargol screeched, stopping just within striking distance of Twig. But it didn't attack. Instead it glowered at him, waiting. The only light in the tunnel came from its glowing skystone eyes, the blue light barely enough to see Twig's face by. Ellie froze, afraid any movement might provoke the creature to snap off his head.

"You're confused and scared," said Twig. His hand strained in the air, as if he were pressing against an invisible force. "I can hear it. Deep down, you don't want to hurt us."

The gargol yowled like an injured cat. It had a head like a lion's, with a long, sinewy body and great clawed paws.

"Deep down," Twig said, "you want . . . you want to go home. Hear that? *Home.*"

Ellie stared in disbelief as the gargol seemed to consider Twig's words. Was he actually *communicating* with the creature? Everyone knew gargols couldn't be reasoned with. They were mindless killers.

Twig stepped closer to the gargol.

"Twig, get back. *Please.*"

"I can hear him, Ellie. Deep, deep down . . . he's frightened."

"*He's* frightened?"

Ignoring her, Twig reached out a hand, inching closer to the monster. Skies, was he going to try to *pet* it?

"You're not a monster," Twig said, still staring into the gargol's skystone eyes. "Someone *made* you like this. Someone twisted you up inside. Who?"

He stretched his hand closer. The creature slowly shut its horrible jaws and stared at Twig as if entranced.

For a moment, Ellie believed he'd done the impossible—tamed a gargol, at least long enough to save their lives.

Then the tunnel, already weakened by the gargol crashing through it, collapsed.

Huge slabs of rock slammed into the creature, crushing it to the ground. It thrashed and screeched, but for now, it was pinned in place.

"Twig!" Grabbing his arm, Ellie pulled him along.

They hurried onward, and this time, Lirri took the lead. The little marten bounded ahead, waiting at every fork to guide them the right way. Twig told them to trust her, and sure enough, Ellie shouted in alarm as she rounded a corner and found herself blinded by daylight, tumbling off a precipice and into the open canyon.

She spread her wings, catching herself, and lifted to hover in front of the exit. The others gathered on the edge, the tunnel exit yawning around them. Far below, the yellow river hissed and coiled like a rattlesnake. A few rocks knocked loose by Zain's feet tumbled free and fell toward the water.

"We have to fly," Ellie gasped out. "The other gargols will find this place in no time. Gussie, do those wings work?"

"I—I don't know!" Gussie was frantically trying to finish fitting the wings to Twig's back. "I told you I haven't tested them!"

Zain pointed behind them, into the tunnel. "It's free! I can hear it getting closer!"

The gargol hadn't stayed pinned for long. And Ellie couldn't imagine it would stop for Twig again, not after gretting brained by falling boulders. Its enraged screeches, echoing down the tunnel, seemed to prove it.

"Gussie!" Ellie shouted.

"There!" Gussie gasped out, pulling the last strap tight across Twig's chest. "It either works or it doesn't."

That wasn't the answer Ellie had been hoping for, but she grabbed Twig's hand. "Well? Do they feel all right?"

He moved the stumps of his old wings, and the metal ones moved with them. "M-maybe," he stammered.

"Your Highness, we have to go," Zain said.

"What about him?" Corion asked, watching Twig test his new wings.

"It's my job to keep *you* safe," Zain said. "Let's go!"

The pair of them launched into the air, but Corion hung back, waiting. "We can't leave them here!"

Ellie looked into the tunnel, where the gargol had just rounded the last corner, its claws gripping the walls and its teeth flashing as it shrieked.

"Twig, it's now or never!" she shouted.

"Don't overthink it," said Gussie. "Pretend they're your old wings."

"They're *not* my old wings!" Twig cried.

"You're strong, Twig," Gussie urged. "You can do this!"

He drew a deep breath, pushed Lirri's head deeper into his pocket, and then took a running leap off the precipice.

Twig dropped like a stone.

Ellie's heart seized. She went into a dive, even knowing it was useless, that she'd never catch him in time.

But then, all at once, his metal wings spread wide. The shards of skystone embedded in them flashed in the sun. Twig swooped awkwardly, wobbling a bit, but found his balance and pumped the wings a few times. He lifted up, eyes wide with joy.

"Look at me!" he cried. "Gussie, I could kiss you! WOO-HOO!"

He tried to turn a loop and nearly plummeted all over again when the wings buckled. But he turned himself upright again, grinning. The others fluttered around him, Gussie looking smug.

They'd leaped just in time. The gargol roared at the tunnel's exit, mindless with rage. Ellie's stomach flipped, until she realized the thing couldn't fly. The tunnel collapse had crushed one of its wings. It flapped the other uselessly and scored the cliff walls with its claws.

"Let's get out of here," Zain said uneasily. "Before its buddies hear that and catch up."

"Where are we going now?" Twig asked.

"We need someplace safe," said Ellie. "Where we can figure out what to do next."

As if they could do anything at all, but she didn't want to say that aloud.

"I know a place," Gussie said. "My family has a summerhouse not far from here, less than a day's flight. It's safe, I promise. And trust me . . . it's the last place anyone would look."

Trust her?

Despite Twig's new metal wings, Ellie was far from trusting Gussie. She likely never would again.

But Twig nodded eagerly, while Corion and Zain looked willing enough.

"There's food," Gussie said to Ellie. "*Lots* of it. And hot baths."

Twig's smile twisted into a grimace. He felt about baths the way most people felt about boiling lava.

"Sounds like a trap," Ellie said.

Then again, if there was ever a trap worth risking, it was one that included a meal, a tub of warm, clean water, and soap. She was starting to smell like one of the creatures tucked in Twig's pockets—and that was nothing compared with how *Twig* smelled.

"All right," she said reluctantly. "But only if Twig gets the first bath."

He shot her a horrified look. "*What?*"

"Fair enough," Gussie replied, wrinkling her nose. "I'll wrestle him into it myself, if I have to."

Twig moaned.

"Can we work this all out later?" Zain's voice squeaked as he turned a barrel roll overhead, his eyes scanning every direction. "We're flying from gargols, remember?"

Ellie didn't need the reminder; a screech echoed through the canyon. The other pair were still hunting for them.

They took off as if shot from a sling, five pairs of wings flashing in the sun.

CHAPTER TWENTY-TWO
· NOX ·

He had failed again.

Nox shuddered and curled around himself, but not even the cool rain splashing on his skin could drive away the memory of the volcano's heat. The drops that landed on his wings hissed, turning to steam.

His clothes were singed tatters. His shoes he'd thrown away completely, the soles gone. Soot was smeared over him from head to toe, and his burned finger still stung. He almost wished Icara had just left him in the pit.

Instead, she'd carried him out and laid him on the edge of the volcano's island, near the crashing waves that bubbled over the dark gray stone. Shortly after, rain began to fall, but even it smelled of ashes.

It was a fitting place for him, he thought, here on the edge of the world, in the ashes, soot, and smoke.

"Are you done sulking?" asked Icara.

He barely moved, only sliding his eyes to where she stood over him, her hands on her hips.

"Just leave me to die," he moaned.

"I don't know why *you're* the one pouting. I'm the one who really lost here. Now I'll never be normal again." She dropped to sit beside him, taking out her comb and running it absently over her hair. The rasping sound it made grated on Nox's nerves.

He sat up, leaving a few ragged scraps of his shirt on the ground.

"I let her get into my head again," he said. "I keep falling for that, over and over, thinking I might actually do something right . . . and every time it ends in more failure, more disappointment."

"Her?" asked Icara.

He drew up his knees beneath his chin. "Ellie Meadows."

"Ah. The girl who sparked your transformation."

"Yeah . . . at least, the girl who tried."

A wave splashed over the rocks below, leaving clumps of foam piled in the crevices. Nox licked rainwater from his lips; they were parched and cracked from the heat he'd endured.

"Face your shadow, speak its name," he muttered.

"What?"

"It was carved in the tunnel, back in the Phoenix palace. Some kind of riddle. But I couldn't solve it in time to escape. If you hadn't opened the doors, I'd have died in there." He looked at her. "You don't know what it means, do you?"

"No idea."

"It's been eating at me for days." He sighed and pushed back his wet hair, but it only flopped forward again.

She tilted her head. Rain ran down her smooth cheeks, making her marble skin shine. "I thought you didn't care. I thought you didn't even *want* to be a Phoenix."

"I don't. I didn't. I don't know." He groaned and pressed a hand over his face. Then he pulled it away and yelled, "Why is it whenever I try to do something good, it comes back and punches me in the nose?! Why is it that I fail over and over at everything I try? Is it because I'm stupid? Weak? Scared? What's *wrong* with me, that I can't stop messing up everything I touch?"

"Don't ask me," Icara returned stiffly. "I'm no oracle."

"You know who is? An old woman in a cave, up in the Aeries Mountains. You know what she said? She said—according to Ellie—that I'm supposed to be some kind of destined hero. A flame that'll stop the sky from falling. Who in the blazing skies looks at *me* and thinks, *Oh yeah, he can save the world*?"

"I get your point." Icara narrowed her skystone eyes. "No hero whines half as much as you do."

"Yes! Exactly!"

"She really said that? That the sky would fall?"

"Supposedly. Aren't prophecies always vague like that? I bet it didn't even have anything to do with me, it was just Ellie putting her own ideas—"

"Look," said Icara. "You have problems. I get it. But I don't particularly care." She stood up and brushed soot from her white robe. "Seems to me you just have to decide what you want."

"What I *want*," he replied firmly, "is to be left alone."

"Well, wish granted."

She leaped up and opened her wings. The rain made a soft drumming sound on her marble feathers.

"Wait!" Nox yelled, jumping to his feet. "You promised to tell me what your father's planning. Is it true? Is something terrible going to happen?"

"I said I'd tell you *if* you found a firestone."

"I dove into a blazin' volcano! What more do you want?"

"I want a firestone. And clearly you aren't going to get me one."

"Right, right, so you can be alive again. Well, sorry to break it to you, Icara, but living isn't just about what your skin's made of! There's not much point in being alive *here*"—he pressed his fingers angrily into the soft flesh of his forearm—"if you're dead in *here*!" He thumped his chest.

Icara gave him a withering look. Then she took off without another word.

He tried to follow her, but she flew as if fired from a crossbow, too fast even for his wings. Nox floundered in the air, trying to keep up, but in minutes Icara had vanished into the gray clouds, heedless of the rain.

He hovered uncertainly, looking back at the smoking volcano, then at the clouded sky that had swallowed Icara.

Surely she'd return eventually.

But as time stretched on and the sky remained empty, he realized she'd abandoned him here on the edge of the world.

She really was made of stone.

Nox sank down to land back on the island's black shore, his feathers dripping. Thunder rolled, a deep, groaning boom that warned the storm would soon worsen.

He was pretty sure he could find his way back to the Clandoms . . . if the sky islands they'd hop-skipped on their way here hadn't shifted much on the wind currents. Which was unlikely. If he flew south, he could follow the line of volcanic islands to the southern jungles, he thought, but his knowledge of the region was hazy and based only on vaguely remembered glimpses of maps here and there.

With a wild cry, Nox kicked at a stone with all his strength, sending it whizzing into the sea with a large splash. He pulled at his hair, breathing fast. He watched the sky in hopes Icara would return and laugh at his expression, tell him it had only been a joke.

But hours passed. The storm did worsen, thunder and lightning lashing the island, rain sheeting down, the drops as sharp as needles. His wings steamed, their heat matching his mood. Not bothering to find shelter from the elements, Nox paced, and Icara did not return.

Then again, why should he care?

After all, wasn't this exactly the sort of place he'd been looking for? Someplace his wings couldn't burn down anything or hurt anyone? Someplace he could be alone, untroubled and no trouble to others, with plenty of fish in the sea to eat? The other islands were all overgrown with jungle, bananas and coconuts enough to feed him for years. His clothes were falling apart, but when you were the only one on the deserted island, what need was there, really, for clothes at all? He could be a wild, naked hermit for the rest of his life. He barked a hoarse, bitter laugh at the image.

Finally, exhausted and shaking, he sank down and wrapped his arms around his knees, staring at nothing.

Should have listened to me, he could hear Ellie saying. She would shake her head and scrunch her lips to the side in disappointment at him, the way she had so many times before.

Nox's head tipped forward, his forehead resting on his bare knees.

Should have listened to Ellie.

He drew a breath, tasted the blend of salt and ash in the air.

Then his head snapped up.

"Should have listened to Ellie," he whispered. "I should have, shouldn't I? She told me what I had to do, and I ignored it. Like an idiot."

Because that was the most annoying thing about Ellie—she was always right. And sooner or later, no matter how much he resisted, Nox seemed to come around to admitting it.

Ellie had told him where to go, weeks ago, on that blasted beach where he'd woken from the dead and stepped into this nightmare.

And so, shaking out his wings, Nox rose and set his jaw.

He decided, at last, that he would listen.

CHAPTER TWENTY-THREE
· ELLIE ·

"Blazin' skies, Gussie," Twig said. "You're not rich. You're *rich*, rich."

Gussie looked a little embarrassed as she led them to what she'd called a house but Ellie was pretty sure most people would call a *castle*.

Gray stone walls three stories high loomed over them; at each corner of the rectangular building rose a tall turret with a pointed roof. The grounds were expansive, covered in snow-laden gardens with frozen fountains, paths of crushed stone, and statues of horses and Falcon clanners.

"You're sure it's empty?" Ellie asked skeptically.

"Nobody comes here in winter. There should be a few guards around to make sure nobody robs the place, but I happen to know they spend most of their time at an inn a few hours' flight east of here, drinking and cheating travelers at cards. I'll scout the place to be sure, though."

She opened a scullery door, picking the lock expertly, then disappeared inside.

Ellie waited with her wings half open, ready to take flight at the first sign of trouble. Zain and Corion leaned against the wall and dozed, while Twig experimented with his new wings, opening and closing them and looking wholly at ease. Ellie envied his ability to trust so completely, even though she wished he'd be a little more on guard.

Finally, Gussie returned and nodded. "All clear."

The inside of the house was even more luxurious than the outside, the walls covered in paintings and tapestries, the floor inlaid with pearl mosaics. Their footsteps echoed through room after room, where they passed furniture covered in canvas. Snow melted off their shoes and clothes, leaving a trail of water that soaked the fancy carpets. Gussie sheepishly described each room they walked through: the music room, the sitting room, the other sitting room, the room guests sat in before they went into one of the sitting rooms.

In the grand entry hall, they stopped in front of a massive painting of two stern Falcons and four children.

"Gussie," Twig said, cocking his head. "Is that *you*?"

He pointed to a fat-cheeked fledgling scowling on her mother's knee. Gussie sighed.

"Wait a minute," said Corion, peering at the plaque under the portrait. "You're from the *Berel* family?"

She winced. "Not that they like to admit it. They don't talk about me much outside the family. Comes from being the greatest disappointment of their lives, I suppose."

"Your uncle is Havanor Berel, the chief of the Falcon clan!" he exclaimed. "And one of my father's generals. I had dinner with him just a few weeks ago. He's terrifying."

"Yes, I heard you were in Vestra, Your Highness," she muttered. "And I heard you flew off in the middle of the night. My family was in a frenzy, trying to track you down. Your father blamed my uncle, you know, for letting you slip away."

"Sorry." The prince grimaced.

She shrugged. "Not my problem. The pantry is this way, if you're hungry."

Not long later, they had a feast spread out in the kitchen, and Gussie lit a fire that soon melted the cold from their wings. She helped Twig unfasten his mechanical wings and laid them out to dry. Taking a cloth from a drawer, he lovingly wiped each metal feather and polished the skystones until they shone.

Then they sprawled on the floor and dined on jars of preserved figs, honeyed chestnuts, spiced apple cider, pickled vegetables, and foods Ellie didn't even have names for. Zain and Corion made a game of daring each other to eat increasingly larger bites of a cheese that smelled like goat feet, and which was the only delicacy Ellie passed on.

"This is the best day of my entire short life," groaned Twig, sharing a jar of peach jam with Lirri. "Gussie, I can't believe you left all this to eat moldy garbage bread with me and Nox in Thelantis."

"I never thought I'd miss moldy garbage bread so much," Gussie said quietly.

"Not me!" Twig declared, opening another jar. He took a deep sniff of its contents and sighed happily.

Ellie ate until she couldn't move, then lay in front of the fire and stared up at another portrait of little fledgling Gussie, in which her scowl was even deeper.

"I'm surprised they left them up," Gussie said, following Ellie's gaze. "After they sent me on my farflight, they took down every portrait of me in our house in Vestra. I guess they forgot to sweep this place too."

"What about your sister?" Ellie asked, her eyes shifting to the baby sitting beside Gussie in the portrait.

"Evie?" Her voice was soft. "I talked to her, after . . . what happened in Thelantis. I think I scared her into staying home, for now. She saw how it broke me, giving you all up to Garion in exchange for her safety. It was the hardest thing I've ever done, Ellie. And I know it was wrong."

Ellie tensed, still unwilling to forgive her. As good as a full belly felt—and as much as she was anticipating the hot bath still to come—she resented every moment they spent in this too-large house. She didn't want to accept Gussie's help or her food. But it wasn't just Gussie's betrayal that made her feel out of place here. Seeing how the high clans lived, feeling outnumbered with just her and Twig the only low clanners in the room, she felt acutely the gulf between her own life and Gussie's and Zain's and Corion's. It was as if the size of the walls around her had been built purely to remind her how small she was in their world.

In the sky, she thought, *everyone will be equal.*

If they ever managed to return to Tirelas, maybe it would be a chance to build a fairer world, one where there were no high or low clans, just *clans*.

But thinking of Tirelas inevitably made her think of Nox, and thinking of Nox made a sinkhole open in her chest.

"Do you think Nox will come back?" Twig asked.

Ellie jumped, flashing him a look. "Did you just read my thoughts?"

"Why would I have to, when you're doing *that*?"

She looked down and realized she'd taken out Nox's feather and was absently twirling it between her fingers. "Oh. Sorry."

"Everyone in Vestra has been talking about him," said Gussie. "Not openly, of course. The Goldwings are arresting anyone who does."

"What are they saying?"

Gussie lifted a shoulder. "That he's come to wage war on King Garion, and that he's behind the gargol attacks. The usual mix of truth and lies, I guess, but it's strange, hearing everyone talk about Nox. *Our* Nox. He's gone from an anonymous thief to the most infamous name in the Clandoms." She gave a grim smile. "No wonder he flew off. If I were him, I'd never come back either."

"He'll come back," Ellie said.

"What if he doesn't?"

Ellie looked down at the feather. "The real question is, when he does, will people follow him to Tirelas?"

"My father thinks so," said Corion quietly, his face pale. He sat shoulder to shoulder with Zain, leaning on the Hawk boy with his knees drawn to his chest. "And he will do whatever it takes to stop that from happening. After what we saw in Linden, I know that much."

"If we don't return to the sky," Ellie said, "the lucky ones will lose their flight to wingrot. The unlucky ones will die of it."

Twig shuddered, setting down his jar of jam as if suddenly robbed of his appetite.

"So, what's the plan?" asked Gussie. "We just sit around waiting for Nox to show up?"

Ellie shrugged.

"Oh, c'mon, Sparrow. This isn't like you! You're always scheming up something."

"That was before you turned us over to the king," Ellie snapped. "That was before Nox died. Before he left. Before . . . I realized changing the world isn't as easy as spreading some rumors and flashing a few skystones around."

"Maybe it's not about changing the world for *all* people," replied Gussie. "Maybe it's about changing it for just a few. The right few. Me, Twig, Nox. We wouldn't be here, you know, if it weren't for you."

She was just trying to get onto Ellie's good side again. Besides, considering where *here* was, they'd probably have been a lot better off never having met Ellie in the first place.

"Well, this party got depressing," commented Zain.

Corion snorted. "Party?"

Zain frowned. "You're right. It's not a party. Parties have music and dancing." He jumped to his feet. "I can fix that!"

"Zain! Where are you—"

The Hawk boy leaped onto the large kitchen table, grabbing a copper pot that hung from a rack above it. He began drumming on it and marching up and down the tabletop.

Ellie groaned and covered her face. "Not one of your songs, *please!*"

"Zain can sing?" asked the prince, eyes wide.

"*No,*" she replied emphatically. "That's the problem."

"Oh, I can sing," Zain pronounced, beating away on his pot. "What's more, I can *rhyme.*"

He launched into a terrifically off-key tune that Ellie recognized as a Hawk clan flight song, but with words of Zain's own devising.

> *"Oh, we might all soon die horrible deaths*
> *We might die screaming painful breaths!*
> *Something something to rhyme with breaths*
> *I don't know where I was going with this next!*
> *Hey, skies ho, away Hawks go!*
>
> *Oh, we might all be doomed for a hangman's noose*
> *But there's hope 'cause this Phoenix kid is still on the*
> *loose*
> *I don't really know what he's supposed to do*
> *But Ellie thinks he's important, so, whoop-de-doo!*
> *Hey, skies ho, away Hawks, go!"*

The prince laughed so hard he fell over and banged his chin on the table. Blood began gushing from his lip, and immediately Zain dropped his pot with a clatter and rushed to Corion's side. Rolling her eyes, Gussie handed them a cloth.

"You chipped a tooth," Zain said, horrified. "Your Highness, I'm so sorry. This is all my fault."

The prince stared at him, then gravely put a hand on his cheek. "Sir Zain, I'd give a *whole* tooth just to hear you sing again."

Zain paused in his careful dabbing at the blood on Corion's chin. "You don't understand."

"Huh? What do you mean?"

To Ellie's shock, there were *tears* in Zain's eyes. She'd known the Hawk boy her entire life, but she realized suddenly that she couldn't recall a single time that she'd ever seen him cry.

"You don't *understand*," he said again, his voice so soft she could barely hear him. "This is all my fault, Your Highness. You're in this trouble because of me. If I hadn't opened my big mouth back in Linden, you wouldn't have had to save my neck. Now they probably all think you're a traitor. What if your father—"

Corion stopped him with a hand on Zain's lips. "The day I got your letter, I knew I had to make a choice. Him or you." He smiled, lowering his hand. "I made my choice, Zain. And I don't regret it for a minute."

Zain stared, the cloth in his hand still frozen on Corion's chin.

Ellie coughed then, and the boys startled, as if suddenly remembering there were other people in the room.

"Right," Gussie said loudly, averting her eyes. "How about those baths?"

Later that night, Ellie lay in a bed the size of a wagon, feeling impossibly small dressed in some Falcon clanner's nightgown. The only part of it all that felt right was the Sparrow clan sunflower oil she'd freshly applied to her feathers. She'd nearly wept when she found the jar in the bedroom wardrobe, still with the seal on it. When she'd opened it, it had smelled like home. Which had only made her think of the

Sparrow clan and the Goldwings with their bone saws. Then she *did* cry, sick with worry for her clan. Face pressed into a pillow embroidered with leaping hares, Ellie sobbed until her body ached.

Perhaps that was why she didn't hear the intruder until it was too late and his hand was on her shoulder.

Ellie froze, her eyes flying open. She reached for her knife, only to remember she'd lost it weeks ago, when she'd been captured by Goldwings in Thelantis.

"It's all right!" whispered the shadow standing over her. "I'm a friend, Ellie Meadows!"

Slowly, the hand lifted away, and Ellie didn't hesitate. She rolled out of the bed and grabbed the staff leaning on the wall. She'd found it while snooping through Gussie's house, in an armory tucked inexplicably between an art gallery and a sewing room.

"My friends are sleeping just down the hall!" she said, scrubbing away her tears. "If I scream, they'll come running with swords and spears!"

She hadn't been the only one to raid the armory.

"Friends?" The intruder sounded confused. "I thought you were a prisoner."

"What?" Ellie shook her head. "Who *are* you?"

She fumbled for the Phoenix feather, which she'd left wrapped in damp cloth by the bed. Holding it up, she frowned in further bewilderment.

The man standing there was no Goldwing, as she'd first feared. He was a Gull clanner, of all things, his long gray-and-white wings half spread. Middle-aged, with thinning hair and a short beard, he was dressed in warm winter clothes, ragged but well mended. With his hands raised and in plain view, it was clear he was unarmed. She was sure she'd never seen him before in her life.

"How do you know my name?" she demanded.

"So you *are* Ellie Meadows?"

"Answer my question!"

"Everyone knows your name," he replied. "You're the Sparrow who discovered the cure for wingrot. I saw you win the Race of Ascension months ago."

Ellie blinked. "Everyone knows my name?"

"I'm sorry. I didn't mean to startle you. When I saw you flying with three high clanners, and one in a Goldwing uniform, I thought you might be a prisoner. I sneaked in here to save you . . . and to ask for your help. Those high clanners are *really* friends of yours?"

Her head spinning, Ellie lowered the staff slightly. "My help? Who are you? What do you want?"

"My name is Brennec. I'm traveling with a group of people, half of them very ill with wingrot. Please, we need your help." His gray eyes seemed sincere as he lowered his hands, pleading. "We need you to lead us to Tirelas."

CHAPTER TWENTY-FOUR
· NOX ·

Nox landed with a whisper of wings, flames swirling away. He was so exhausted that his knees buckled the minute he touched the ground. He landed hard, hands flinging out to keep from planting his face in the mud. Not that he wasn't already filthy, covered in grime and sweat.

For days he'd flown, hard and fast, sometimes through the night, gargols or no gargols. He stopped only to eat, drink, and take short naps, before rising and pressing onward again. He was thinner than he'd ever been, but harder too, his back and shoulders muscled and aching from constant flying.

Yet somehow, following an inner sense of direction he'd never known he had, he'd made it.

Thraille.

The clan seat of the shattered Crows.

It couldn't have been a more inhospitable stretch of land, tucked away behind the ever-clouded Thornmoors, against the western mountains. But for his clan, once, this had been home.

Thraille was set in a muddy clearing surrounded by tall, bristly pine trees. All that was left of the place were stone foundations and a few rotted timbers where there had once been houses. A large circle of paving stones must have been the town square. He walked around slowly, his heart throbbing in his chest. His family had once lived here—not distant, vague Phoenix royalty, but normal Crows. They'd filled this square, flown these skies, and probably perched in those tall pines as fledglings on their first wobbly flights. They'd gathered here for celebrations, marriages, funerals.

And then the Eagles had come and burned it all to the ground, scattering the Crows like dandelion seeds on an uncaring wind.

According to the letter his grandmother had written to his grandfather, there was a secret buried in Thraille—the explanation of why the Eagle clan had shattered the Crows. A secret linked to the Corvain family line. She had set out to uncover that secret, but it was a mission from which she never returned.

Had she made it to Thraille?

Had she unearthed the secret before she vanished?

Nox hoped to find out.

He began searching the ruins, house by house. It was difficult to tell where they had stood; those without stone foundations had rotted away entirely, and all he had to go by were slight, rectangular depressions in the land where the houses had been.

His spine crawled as he searched. Everywhere he looked, he could picture the Crows who'd lived here. He wondered if any had died that day, when the Eagles attacked. Had they fought back? Or had they fled, as he so often did when trouble found him?

As time passed and his efforts turned up nothing, Nox's hope turned sour. What was he even looking for? If he found it, how could it make a difference?

He'd flown in a fervor for weeks, so certain that the answer would be here, simply because Ellie had said it would be. Well, Ellie couldn't *always* be right, could she? He'd clearly failed again. There was nothing—

Nox froze in front of an old house site on the edge of the town. It had a stone outline, and two stone pillars that might have once supported a porch roof.

And there, on the stone threshold where the door had once hung, was carved an ashmark.

It could have been nothing. After all, people had been putting ashmarks outside their homes for centuries.

But the *way* it was carved, set on the ground, not up high where it could supposedly ward off gargols . . .

He couldn't ignore the tingling on his scalp, or the slight tremor in his wingtips.

Nox ran his fingers over the stone walls that outlined the house. They rose as high as his waist, and along the inside he found many small notches carved into the stone, made to mark the growing wingspan of fledglings. Names were written by each set—*Rus Corvain, Saryn Corvain, Roth Corvain*—and dates, some of them five hundred years old, so worn he could barely make them out.

"This is where you lived," he murmured. "My family. The Corvains."

In the back of the house's layout, where he guessed the bedrooms might have been, he found one stone that didn't match the others. It was taller and wider, and the ashmark carved into it had been cut by a steady hand, to match the one on the threshold.

Hands shaking, Nox eased the stone out of the wall.

Behind it, as if waiting for him—an iron box.

He took it out and found the lid locked fast, but that was no trouble. Nox had picked nearly half the locks in Thelantis, and this one required only a probe with a stiff twig. It clicked open.

Pausing a moment to draw a deep breath, Nox opened the box.

The first thing he noticed was a red glow, soft as candlelight. There was a rolled piece of paper, bound with string.

But beside it, gleaming on a bed of faded cloth . . .

"A firestone," Nox breathed.

It was perfectly round, cut into sharp, smooth facets. The light within shifted slowly from red to orange, orange to yellow, like slow-moving fire. It didn't float as a skystone would, but when Nox picked it up, it sat warmly in his palm, emanating gentle heat.

"They *are* real," he whispered.

He closed his fingers around it, feeling the warmth, the weight. He wondered what kind of magic was bound up inside it, and felt a little afraid, but he didn't set it down.

"Blazin' skies of blue." Nox shook his head. "Ellie was right again."

He couldn't even be annoyed about it.

He opened the paper next, his heart going cold as he read the hasty script.

I leave this letter for my husband, or my son, or whatever foolish, brave Corvain might follow my flight to this place. This secret is too important to be lost, but I must be quick. The Eagles are tracking me. They know what I am, what all us Corvains are, or might become, anyway. It all makes sense now— the warnings we've passed down, parents to children, for generations. Never tell anyone about our immunity to fire. Bury us in water, a deep lake or the ocean is best—never burn our dead, as the other clans do. Now I understand: we are not Crows. At least, not fully. It happened to me by accident—a fire in an inn on my journey here. I was the only one to escape but my wings burned away, replaced by . . . something out of legend. It must be connected to this stone somehow, whatever it is. Why else would my ancestors have hidden it here? In any case, I cannot return to Khadreen, not with my wings as they are now. Perhaps I can run, and once I lose my pursuers I'll return for this stone. Or perhaps they will catch me. Either way, I leave this note and the odd stone in the hopes that my descendents find a way to rid ourselves of this curse . . . or perhaps to find the purpose for it. May you have better luck than I.

Beware fire. It can affect us after all, as it turns out.
Watch the skies.

Tanra Corvain

Releasing a long breath, Nox sat back.

So. His grandmother had transformed into a Phoenix too, in nearly as dramatic a fashion as Nox had. And then she'd found the firestone buried in Thraille, but had left it behind. Had the Eagles caught up to her in the end? They must have. She'd written that she would return for the stone if she escaped them, but it was still here.

Grief for the grandmother he'd never known pulled at his heart. Grief, and anger. The Eagles again. Always it was the Eagles who destroyed his family. He tried to imagine Tanra, a vague figure with fiery wings, crouched in this same spot. Alone and afraid, as he was. Hunted, as he was.

May you have better luck than I.

With a shudder, he rolled the paper carefully and replaced it in the box. But he kept the firestone. It nestled, warm and bright, in his palm.

Now what?

Could he even find Icara, to give the firestone to her? Maybe she would finally tell him what Demetrace was planning. Or should he keep it, try to figure out how it worked? He cursed Gussie for her betrayal; if she'd been part of his crew still, he'd give it straight to her. She could figure anything out.

Ellie? He had no idea where she was, or Twig either.

And what could one firestone do against an army of gargols, anyway? Even if it could be used as some kind of weapon, how far would it get anyone against an entire sky of monsters?

"Ellie would know what to do with you," he said to the stone. He couldn't take his eyes off the mesmerizing pulse of the light.

Find the purpose for it, his grandmother had written.

Thinking of the shadow puppets in the Phoenix test, he raised it tentatively to his lips. It was too big to swallow. So he licked it.

Then felt immediately idiotic. Nothing happened, except his tongue got a bit scalded.

"Stupid," he muttered. He dropped the stone into his pocket—the last remaining pocket he had on his tattered, singed clothing—and rose to his feet. He was too hungry to make important decisions right now, anyway. He'd eat, sleep, sleep some more, and then maybe—

WHOOMPF.

The sound boomed through Thraille and the trees beyond, making the very ground shake under the impact of something *big*.

Nox choked on his own breath, then whirled.

A gargol the size of a ship stood crouched in the center of the town ruins, watching him through skystones eyes, each one bigger than his head. It had the face of a bull, but with twenty horns instead of two, and wings large enough to flatten a village in one swipe.

And it hadn't come alone. Smaller gargols—each still five times Nox's size—crept around it and toward him, with faces like bats, like lizards, like wolves. Their teeth chattered. Their wings shivered with anticipation of a kill.

Nox swayed on his feet, rooted by horror. Where had they come from? Had they been tracking him this whole time? Had Icara told her father about him, or sent the gargols herself?

Shaking himself free of his petrified trance, Nox shot upward.

He didn't get far.

A gargol claw closed on his ankle. Another bit down on his arm, fangs sinking through his skin.

Nox could do nothing but scream as they dragged him down.

CHAPTER TWENTY-FIVE
· ELLIE ·

"Down here," said Brennec, waving at a snowy gulch filled with smooth gray stones. The rocks created a kind of warren, full of little pathways and hidden rooms, shaded from view above by thick, overhanging branches, all brittle with cold. By the light of a torch Gussie carried, Ellie saw rivulets of snowmelt dribbling down the stone walls to form small pools, their surfaces limned with ice. It had taken them well into the night to reach the spot, and the dropping temperature had left them all shivering. Ellie walked with an arm around Twig, trying to keep his skinny body warm, but his teeth were chattering all the same.

"I still think this is a bad idea," muttered Gussie. "This guy broke into my house, after all."

"*We* broke into it first," Ellie pointed out.

"Almost there," said Brennec, sounding apologetic.

It was a good hiding place. She'd have been totally lost if not for the Gull's guidance. After several minutes of following the twisting pathways, he finally stopped in a large opening, surrounded on all sides by wet rock and sheltered by several moss-laden logs laid across the rocks overhead. Once, a fox stuck its head out of a burrow to nuzzle Twig's hand before scurrying away into the dark.

"It's all right!" called the Gull. "It's me, Brennec. Come out, I've brought a surprise!"

Heads and wings began to pop out from behind the rubble of rock, one by one. They crept out cautiously, people of every age, size, and feather, even a few high clanners. Most were in groups of two or three, families and friends, Ellie guessed. In each group, inevitably, one was wingless or near it, their wingrot progressed to the point where they'd lost most of their feathers. A few lit candles and held them up to take a better look at their visitors. Their breaths rose in frosty clouds.

One, a boy with gnarled wings, ran to Brennec and wrapped his arms around him. Brennec smiled and patted his head.

"My nephew Brayden," he said to Ellie. Turning to the others, he said, "The sky smiles on us today, friends. I've brought to you Ellie of the Sparrows!"

The people exchanged looks, eyebrows lifting and mouths opening.

"*That* Ellie?" asked a Warbler clan woman holding up an older, wingless woman who might have been her mother.

"That Ellie," confirmed Brennec. "That Ellie who, according to the stories, discovered the cure for wingrot."

They looked at her then and waited, until she gave a hesitant nod of confirmation. She'd been flattered when Brennec had asked for her help, but in the cold night, with all those faces staring at her, she began to feel doubt.

"You know the way to the islands in the sky?" someone called out.

Elli nodded.

"Is it true they're full of skystones?"

"Big ones, small ones, more than we'd ever need."

"And gargols?" asked Brennec's nephew in a small voice.

"Those too," Ellie said gently.

"Will you take us there?" asked the Warbler. "We only need a handful of stones, right? We just need to grab them and get back before the gargols ever know we were there."

They all stared at her, expressions ranging from skepticism to hope, but each one tense with anticipation of her answer.

"I . . ." Ellie looked around at them. "It's not as simple as that."

"We know." Brennec held his nephew close, his own face grimly creased. "We've made three attempts already. Twice, we failed to find anything at all. The third time, we couldn't make it past the gargols. We . . . lost four people."

Ellie exhaled slowly, but the hard knot that had suddenly formed in her chest only tightened. "And you're still sure you want to try again?"

"Look at us. Do we have any other choice?"

Every one of them was clinging to someone else, desperately, out of fear and determination and hope. No, Ellie thought. They looked like people who'd dive down a gargol's throat if it meant saving the ones they loved.

Still she hesitated.

She thought of the gargol's head she'd seen in Robinsgate—proof of Nox's powers—and wished he were here instead. *He* was the one who should be leading people into the sky, not her. What could she do against gargols? The last time she'd faced one head-on, it had smashed her leg to pieces. She carried the pain of that meeting with her every day, a sharp and visceral reminder of the danger that waited above.

Gussie was shaking her head, her mouth twisting in a grimace. "I don't like this. Last time we went up there, we nearly died."

His eyes on Ellie, Twig murmured, "She'll go anyway."

"I haven't decided that yet," Ellie said.

Twig smiled, as if he knew something she didn't. Was he using his ability to read her emotions? "Ellie. You'll go."

She shut her eyes, knowing Twig was right. Knowing she'd made up her mind the minute she'd heard their request. Of course she'd go, because these people needed her . . . and because she was still trying to prove a bitter old woman wrong.

You are nothing.

You can do nothing.

"I'll go," she whispered.

"Then I guess I'm going too," sighed Gussie.

"And me," added Twig, flexing his new wings. "You all have been to the islands how many times now? And I haven't even seen them once!"

"I'll go too," said Corion, making Ellie jump. She'd almost forgotten he was here, his face hidden in a fur-lined hood he'd found in Gussie's manor. They'd decided it might be unwise to have him recognized by the people they were going to help, not when his father was hunting anyone who even mentioned skystones. According to the king's new laws, these people were practically condemned to death. As it was, they were eyeing him and Zain warily; there was no hiding the fact of their wings.

Zain's eyes popped. "You'll *what*?"

"They're my people," said the prince. "My responsibility."

"You're not king yet!"

"*Shhh!*" hissed Ellie, glancing nervously at the others.

"Your concern for me is sweet," said Corion gently, putting a hand on Zain's cheek. "But this is my duty."

Zain looked green. "If you're going, so am I."

Corion's mouth opened, then shut, and he sighed. "I guess I won't be able to talk you out of it."

"Not a chance."

Drawing a deep breath, Ellie turned back to Brennec. She met his eyes, then gave a small nod.

Breaking into a grin, he turned to the others and raised a fist. They didn't cheer exactly, but their expressions brightened and they gave Ellie grateful smiles.

She tried to return them, but only felt queasy.

This was wrong, all wrong. She had a bad feeling about the whole thing but didn't know what else to do. They'd go without her, they'd said. If they did, and they all got shredded by gargols, she'd certainly feel even worse.

"We'll have to wait until conditions are right," she said.

"What conditions?" asked Brennec.

She gave him a grave look. "It means we need a storm. A really *big* storm."

It came the next day, howling and freezing, scouring the earth with sleet. The trees hardened and glistened, limbs coated in ice. This was no pleasant snowy afternoon, with gentle flakes drifting idly to the ground. No, this was a storm with teeth, a storm that froze everything it touched.

This included the two dozen Skyborn preparing to hurl themselves into its depths. Ellie shivered, and not just from the cold.

"They must affect the weather," Gussie said absently, watching the storm from beneath the rocky overhang they huddled under. "The islands, I mean. They're always floating atop clouds. It would be interesting to study."

Ellie shook her head. Only Gussie would think about scholarly contemplation at a time like this.

"This is madness," said Zain. "Utter, complete lunacy."

Ellie had to agree. Normal storms were bad enough. But this was a different beast. Instead of lightning, this storm was laced with flying shards of ice as sharp as glass. Instead of thunder, it had the terrible, bone-deep cold. She wondered if they could fly in it at all, or if their feathers would freeze before they ever reached the island that may or may not be hidden inside the clouds.

Looking around at the people they'd leave behind on the ground, though, she knew there wasn't much choice. Most of them didn't have until spring. The wingrot would take their wings by then, if not their lives.

It was now or never.

Like Corion, they'd all taken warm clothes from Gussie's family home, though Twig had refused anything with fur. It wasn't stealing, Ellie figured, when they had Gussie's permission to take the stuff. She tightened the leather strings around her new boots, securing their thick woolen lining to her skin. Their warmth did little to ease the cold in her bones. Her blue cloak was lined with fleece, and delicate silver embroidery outlined the wing holes cut in the back. It was the fanciest thing she'd ever worn, but she told herself she'd chosen it for its warmth, not for how pretty it looked.

"Are we ready?" she asked Brennec at last.

He nodded. "Watch the skies, Ellie Meadows."

"Watch the skies."

Final hugs and teary farewells were exchanged, as those with wingrot prepared to wait out the storm on the ground. Ellie stood with Zain and Corion and gripped her staff.

Zain gave her a crooked, slightly manic grin. "Some things never change, huh?"

"What do you mean?" she asked.

"I mean, here I am, about to do something completely stupid, all because Ellie Meadows said it was a great idea." He cuffed her lightly with his wing. "This is just like the time you made me eat that poisonous bullberry just so you could try out the medicines you'd been mixing up for your healer's apprenticeship."

"Ha!" Ellie rolled her eyes. "As I remember it, *you* ate that because you thought it was a blackberry, and you were lucky I was around to save your ungrateful feathers."

"Oh yeah. Well, it *did* look like a blackberry."

"It was *orange*!"

He shrugged, still grinning. Ellie returned the smile, feeling just as anxious about the mission ahead, but glad that the strange paths of fate had somehow brought her and Zain back together. There had been a time, just weeks ago, when she'd thought their friendship was lost beyond all saving. He might be more featherbrained than a newborn fledgling at times, but she was glad he would fly beside her.

"Would you think me an idiot for saying I'm a little excited?" asked Corion. He grinned nervously, even though his teeth were chattering.

Ellie and Zain stared at him, then said in unison, *"Yes."*

"The sky islands!" He spread his hands. "Our ancestral home, if Ellie here's to be believed. Come now, that's got to have your curiosity roused, Zain."

"The only thing roused about me," Zain returned, "is panic."

"We'll make it," Ellie said, with far more confidence than she felt.

When they took off, it was in grim silence, not that words could have been easily exchanged over the howling wind. Ellie led the way with Twig and Gussie, followed closely by Brennec, Corion, and Zain. The others trailed after.

She clenched her teeth and flew with the bitter wind, letting it lift her up and out of the forest, over the frozen trees and into the sky. The world below was brittle with cold, the last of autumn's color fading under the onslaught of the storm. Even if there were no gargols to fear, flying in such weather was one of the most dangerous things Ellie had ever done. Ice pellets stung her cheeks, and soon she was blinking frost from her eyelashes. Even when she'd raced up Mount Garond in the Race of Ascension, she hadn't felt a cold like this. It dulled her senses and slowed her wings, made even her teeth ache.

But she pressed on, hoping gargols minded the cold as much as she did. Maybe they'd all stay tucked in their ruins above, shivering and harmless.

Only she never got the chance to find out, because when the attack came, it wasn't gargols at all.

It was Goldwings, an entire regiment of them bursting out of the forest with crossbows and spears, and the Stoneslayer leading them.

CHAPTER TWENTY-SIX
· ELLIE ·

"Ellie Meadows!" roared the Stoneslayer. "I should have known." She gaped, trying to understand what she was seeing.

Dozens of Goldwings were converging on their little band from all directions, each of them armed. Their white armor and cloaks blended into the pale, snowy sky, making them difficult to see. Brennec and his band grouped together, looking bewildered and terrified.

"Attempting to contact your gargol friends, are you?" said the Stoneslayer.

"Of course not!" Ellie yelled. "Don't be stupid! We're only—"

"Only following a known traitor!" He pointed his spear. "Your days of sowing dissension end now. We've been trailing you since Linden, girl, waiting for you to lead us to your cabal of coconspirators. Now that we've found them, you'll all suffer the king's judgment."

"Enough!" The command in Corion's voice drew everyone's attention. "As your prince, I order you to lower your weapons and withdraw!"

Gasps rose from Brennec's band. The prince had flung back his hood and now glared at the general with blazing eyes. He seemed every inch an Eagle in that moment, and every inch the crown prince, with his dark gold wings spread wide.

Eyes turned back to the Stoneslayer, who only sneered. "You're no prince of mine, *boy*. Or perhaps you didn't hear? You've been disowned."

Corion paled. "Wh-what?"

"That's right, brat. You rank less than a worm, as far as I'm concerned. Though the reward for your capture is considerable . . ." He raised in voice to his troops. "Take the *former* prince alive! The rest have earned their fates."

The sky erupted as the soldiers rushed to obey.

Bolts zinged through the air, followed by screams. The Goldwings had also brought nets, which they threw over their targets and then soared coldly away, letting the netted ones fall screaming and helpless.

"Gussie!" Ellie screamed. "Get Twig out of here!"

He protested, but Gussie swooped to him at once and pulled him down, toward the safety of the forest below. His metal wings were nowhere near nimble enough to save him from the bolts and spear thrusts.

Reeling from the suddenness of the attack and the ruthless brutality of the Goldwings, Ellie hurled herself at the nearest knight.

But she never made it.

She didn't see the bolas until it had whipped itself around her wings, pinning them together and sending her into free fall. A simple rope with two weights bound on its ends, it was a weapon more effective than any bolt or spear.

Ellie fell with a scream frozen on her lips. Tumbling head over heels, she was helpless to slow herself. Her wings were too tightly bound by the bolas.

The young knight who'd thrown it leveled his crossbow, intent on finishing her off. But then Zain appeared between them, yelling to draw the knight's attention to himself. Ellie lost sight of them both in her tumble through the sky.

Desperately, her wings fought against the rope, but it was no use. She hurtled toward the ground and certain death.

"Ellie!"

She felt something solid slam into her, knocking the wind from her lungs.

"Corion!"

The prince held her tight as his wings flared, attempting to slow them both. But strong as he was, he couldn't carry her for long. They spiraled to the ground, crashing through the brittle branches of the trees and landing roughly in a heap.

"Get it off, get it off!" Ellie wheezed.

He winced, nursing a bruised shoulder, but fumbled with the bolas until it fell free. Ellie's wings burst open. She checked for any serious injury before she felt reassured.

"Zain—" she started, but a thump interrupted her.

Whirling, she saw a body crumpled a short distance away, and her heart dropped.

She sprinted toward it, but it was Corion who reached it first. He rolled it over—and let out a cry.

"It's not him!" he said, relief palpable in his tone.

"It nearly was," said a voice.

They both turned to see Zain fluttering down behind them, his face white. With another wordless shout, Corion ran to fling his arms around the Hawk.

"His name is—was—Zephyr," said Zain dully. "He was in my training squadron back in Thelantis."

Ellie looked down at the body. It was the Goldwing who'd lassoed her wings. His side was sliced open, and his eyes stared sightlessly at the sky. With a grimace, she knelt and closed them. Zain was trembling, staring at the young knight as if he *wanted* him to get up and attack them all over again. Ellie thought that if a hundred gargols attacked at that moment, Zain would not have noticed.

"I didn't mean to . . . I only wanted to stop him hurting *you*, Ellie." Tears welled in his eyes. "And now he's . . . because I . . ."

Corion put his hand on Zain's shoulder, watching him with concern. "Ellie's safe because of you. You defended your friend, and that's what counts."

Zain just shook his head, his face fixed in a tear-streaked grimace. He looked away from the knight, then stumbled a few steps away before emptying his stomach onto the snowy ground.

"We have to help the others," Ellie said gently, spreading her wings and crouching in preparation for takeoff.

Zain turned around, his shoulders slumped. "Ellie, no. It's too late."

"We can cause a distraction or—"

"You don't understand." He stared at her, his eyes hollow. "There's no one left to save."

Ellie straightened, her wings sagging. "What?"

"They're dead. All of them."

"Gussie and Twig!"

"They flew off before the fighting really started," he reminded her. "They're probably the only ones who got away, except us."

She nodded, still sick with dread. "Brennec—"

"They shot him three times. I saw it. He was dead before he fell."

"They . . . they can't be gone." She stared at Zain as if he were a stranger. "They were just—they were just *alive*."

He nodded, his face crumpling. "The Goldwings slaughtered them."

Horror struck her more coldly than any winter wind. Corion had to pull on her arm to get her to move.

"We can't stay here," he said. "They'll come after us."

"The—the others," she stammered. "Their family, we left them—"

"They're safer if we don't lead the Goldwings to them," said Corion gently. "They'll kill anyone seen with us, Ellie."

She heard him, but the words didn't penetrate. She was still too dazed to comprehend. The world around her swam like a dream, the rocks and trees suddenly seeming insubstantial as smoke.

They slaughtered them.

Brennec and the cynical Warbler woman and all the others whose names she hadn't even learned. And Brennec's nephew—skies above, he wasn't more than seven or eight years old. He'd be shivering and cold in the rock warren, wondering when his uncle would return for him. Who would tell him? Who would take care of him?

Not Ellie. Ellie couldn't take care of anyone. Corion had said it— even association with her was a death sentence.

You are nothing.

You can do nothing.

Nothing but bring pain and disaster, it seemed.

"Then . . ." She drew a deep breath. "Then I'll lead the Goldwings away from them. *Far* away."

Corion stared for a moment, before slowly nodding. "*We* will lead them away. No, don't argue with me. I'm coming with you. Maybe I'm not a prince anymore"—his lips twisted, as if he was still trying to come to terms with his sudden drop in status—"but I still have responsibilities to the people of the Clandoms. We'll lead the knights away."

"Well, you're not leaving *me* behind," Zain said, squaring his shoulders.

"We're tired and injured," Ellie pointed out. "They'll likely catch us in the end."

Corion nodded again. "I know. Unless we fly now, sneak away while we can."

Biting her lip, Ellie glanced through the trees in the direction of the people they'd left on the ground, most of them unable to fly at all. The Goldwings would find them with barely any searching, and they'd be helpless in the knight's hands.

"No," she said firmly. "Let's make this count."

Corion grinned, looking a bit maniacal. "It would be my honor, Ellie Meadows, to fly with you a little longer."

"Yeah, a real honor," Zain added, rolling his eyes, but not entirely masking his fear. His face was still drained of color, and he looked five years older than he had that morning. "My mother always warned me you'd be the death of me."

Smiling back ruefully, Ellie launched into the air, with Corion and Zain a wingspan below her.

They rose above the treetops and began shouting for all they were worth. The Stoneslayer and his men had fanned out, sweeping the sky, but now they turned like dogs catching a fox's scent. With a roar, the general sent his troop soaring toward them.

"Let's go!" Ellie shouted.

The three of them dove toward the ground, spiraling and twisting through the branches, before spreading wings and bolting through the lower trunks.

Goldwings dropped through the trees behind them, cloaks fluttering like ghostly shrouds.

"*Fly!*" Zain shouted.

Ellie couldn't think, could barely speak. But flight was action, and that was what she needed right now—to *move*, or else she was dead where she stood.

They took off, soaring as quickly as the trees allowed, zigzagging desperately. Ellie's shorter wings became her advantage and she pulled ahead, able to navigate the trunks more easily. She pressed for speed, flying through branches that scraped and bruised her skin. Just because she'd wanted the Goldwings to chase her didn't mean she wanted to be *caught*, however slim their chances of escape were now. With luck, they'd lead the knights miles away from the others, giving them plenty of time to slip away.

She didn't see the trap until it was too late.

The net was woven with white cord, making it nearly invisible, and she struck it at full force. Seconds later, Zain and Corion crashed into her, unable to slow themselves in time to avoid collision. The net, held between four Goldwings hidden in the trees, closed around them.

Immediately, Ellie grabbed a cord and began gnawing on it, in a wild attempt to tear it open. But it was no use; the fibers held. She was tangled with Corion and Zain, their wings crushed and bent painfully, their limbs folded at awkward angles. Struggling only made it worse.

The net was lowered to the ground, with more Goldwings flocking to grab hold. As they set them down, the Stoneslayer landed gracefully, his hands folded behind his back. The three of them lay in a heap, panting and shivering, and he stared balefully down.

"Sir," said another knight, landing beside him. "Do we . . . only take the prince captive?"

"*Former* prince," the Stoneslayer corrected him. He seemed to weigh this, studying Ellie and Zain coldly.

Ellie stopped breathing. Her body went absolutely still as she waited to hear what the general would say.

"No," the Stoneslayer said at last. "The Sparrow has become something of a folk hero among the low clans. Better to let them see justice done than to let them make a martyr of her. As for our treasonous Hawk here . . . let him suffer in Thelantis, in front of all the Goldwings, as a display of what happens when His Majesty's own turn against him."

The Goldwing nodded, and the net was cut free. Ellie exhaled shakily, her legs going limp. A knight had to haul her upright and hold her there; her knees shook too badly to support her.

"The Sparrows!" she said. "My clan! Did you . . . did you take their wings? Answer me!"

He flipped a dismissive hand, ignoring the question. "Silence her."

Ellie's eyes bulged as they tied a strip of wool over her mouth. Shackles were produced and clamped around their wrists, while their wings were bound with ropes. Ellie thought she might make a run for it anyway, until Goldwings took up position on either side of her, holding ropes they tied to her shackles and wings. As long as they were holding the other ends, she had no chance of escape.

She exchanged despairing looks with Corion and Zain, but they were kept apart, unable to speak or make any plans for breaking free. Even if they could, Ellie didn't know what she'd say. Her mind was as exhausted and beaten as her body. She couldn't even fathom an escape attempt, much less spring one.

The knights spent an hour recouping from the battle and retrieving their traveling gear, which they'd stowed before the ambush. They'd taken a few minor injuries, but mostly they laughed about how easy the fight had been, and how quickly it had ended. Only one had been lost—the one called Zephyr. They retrieved his body and wrapped it to transport home, but even the young recruit's death didn't seem to dampen their spirits.

Ellie watched them and wavered between nausea and fury, that they could take such amusement in the deaths of two dozen innocent people, people who were only trying to save their loved ones. But the

Goldwings spoke of them as if they were rabbits they'd speared in a hunt. It made Ellie burn with hatred. She saw Zain and Corion listening with equal rage, as helpless as she was to do anything about it.

Finally, the knights were ready to move out. They unbound the prisoners' wings and removed the gags, but left their hands tied. They kept firm grips on the rope tethers they'd bound to each. Then they took off, flying north for the capital. It was an awkward affair for Ellie, trying to fly without the use of her hands to balance, and with the Goldwings pulling her along by the ropes. They refused to slow down for her, and laughed when she cried out in pain, the ropes yanking her arms nearly out of their sockets.

When they stopped that night to camp, the storm had passed, leaving in its wake a wintry stillness, as if the air itself had frozen solid. The clouds remained, dense and low, promising snow to come.

The Goldwings built a fire and spread blankets. They didn't bother to set a watch. There was no one to challenge them and they knew it.

Ellie, Zain, and Corion were tied together, wings bound, close enough to finally talk. They'd been given no blankets and were left to shiver against one another.

"I'm sorry," Zain said first, in a rush, as if he'd been waiting all day to spit out the words. "I failed to protect you, Your Highness."

Corion sighed. "I'm not a prince anymore, Zain. You swore your oath to protect the royal family, which . . . I'm not, anymore."

Zain stared at him. "You think I've followed you all this time because of some stupid oath?"

They gazed at each other in a way that made Ellie blush, and she looked aside.

"You're still a prince," said Zain. "Whatever he might say or do— *you're* the one I'll follow."

With a little smile, Corion shifted nearer to the knight and laid his head on his shoulder. "I know," he whispered. "I just wanted to hear you say it."

Feeling suddenly lonely, Ellie pulled her wings around her and thought of Nox, and wondered if he was lonely too. Was he still flying for the horizon, or had he found some safe place to land? Did he miss her? Would he ever know what had happened to her? Were Twig and Gussie safe, or had they been found in the forest and . . . She couldn't finish that thought.

Her mind started to wander then to Thelantis and what would happen when they arrived there, but it was too painful. She wrenched her thoughts away and stared at the fire. The knights had placed the three of them just outside the reach of its warmth, and she was sure that had been intentional.

"Poor Brennec," she whispered. "All of them. How can the Goldwings be so heartless? How can the king?"

Corion sighed, stirring again. "I thought . . . for too long, I thought he was just misunderstood. That he was trying to do the right thing for everyone. I wanted to make excuses for him, to defend him against his critics. But after today . . . No, not just today. After he tried to execute three kids—that's when I should have done something. I waited too long, and look how many people have suffered because of it."

"You couldn't have stopped him," Zain insisted.

"I could have tried. At the very least, I could have tried."

"When it came down to it, you did the right thing," Zain said. "You're a better person than he could ever be."

"What good is it to be better," said Corion, "when I'm completely useless? Don't you get it? He's won. There might have been a chance . . . if the Phoenix were here, if people saw him rise against the king . . . but he's not and he won't."

Ellie hung her head. Nox might have made a difference—*the flame to light a great fire.* She knew the prophecy was about Nox leading the way back to Tirelas. Just as it was about her destiny, her responsibility, to help him do it. But she'd lost him, even before he'd flown away.

Now she and the Clandoms would pay for it.

CHAPTER TWENTY-SEVEN
· NOX ·

With a groan, Nox rolled his head. He was lying on something hard and cold, and his arm burned where the gargol had bitten him. Thoughts bubbled and burst in his mind, struggling to form. Slowly, his memory returned, and with it, a pit of dread in his stomach.

If he wasn't dead . . . where was he?

For a moment, he tried to imagine he was back in his little attic room in Thelantis, and that the gargol attack in Thraille had been a dream. He imagined it with all his strength, as if that might make it true. As if when he opened his eyes, he might see Twig hovering over him, telling him the Talon had a new job for them.

Instead, he saw gargols.

All around him, they leered and snarled, numbering in the dozens. He grimaced and peeled himself up, propped on his elbow. At least his limbs all seemed intact enough, albeit bruised and scraped. He spread his wings experimentally, to see if he could scare them off with their fire, only to find they'd been chained to the rock slab he was lying on. His hands were free, though. He felt his pocket, only to find it empty.

The firestone was gone.

Breathing hard, Nox looked around until he spotted him: the man among the gargols, made of the same smooth marble as Icara. He had a smooth face and long stone robes that scraped over the ground. In his left hand he carried a staff that had to have been wood once, but now was stone too. A gnarled, petrified branch at its top curled around a dark amber stone—an earthstone, Nox realized. It looked just like the one in Icara's earring, only much larger.

"Demetrace," he muttered.

The man walked to him, his skystone gaze unblinking. He looked down on Nox expressionlessly and said, "Phoenix."

"What do you want from me?" Nox asked. "Why didn't your monsters just kill me?"

"I had to see you for myself. To know if it was true: if the Phoenix line lived on."

"Yeah, well, you don't have much to worry about, then. I'm the last of us, or so I'm told. Garion and the Eagles did your work for you."

Nox wondered if the sorcerer knew who Garion was, or cared, or if he had any feelings at all. He looked as capable of emotion as his gargols.

Demetrace leaned closer, his skystone eyes like blue fire.

"No . . ." he murmured. "You're not a full-fledged Phoenix after all. Your eyes give it away. You haven't completed your transformation, boy."

Nox's heart skipped a beat. "I— What?"

"Pathetic." The sorcerer leaned back again, a cold smile touching his lips.

"Look, I get it," Nox said, babbling now as Demetrace merely gazed at him. "I'm not supposed to be sneaking around your islands. So, I'm sorry, okay? I promise to never ever do it again. For real. I am dying to—" He winced at the poor choice of words. "I really would love to stay on the ground and never come back. So if that's all right by you, I can just . . . go. Right?"

He attempted a grin.

Demetrace stared at him for so long Nox wondered if the man had truly turned into a statue. But then he shifted, lifting his chin slightly. "Come, and see what becomes of trespassers."

He flicked a hand, and the chains around Nox's wings crumbled.

Whoa. The guy really did have control over stone.

Nox burst up at once, his feathers flaring as he tried to lash out with fire. But as usual, the flames only sputtered on his wings. He cursed inwardly.

Demetrace did not look impressed. He turned and walked away, as if expecting Nox to follow.

Nox did, helpless. The gargols hemmed him in on all sides; it wasn't as if he'd get far even if he tried.

Demetrace led him down a set of shallow steps and through more ruins. They passed open courtyards and broken arches. Nox supposed the place had been pretty grand in its heyday. Now it was nothing more than a jumble of perches for the many gargols that stalked his every move. He felt like a beetle struggling in a web, a hundred hungry spiders waiting to snap him up.

They were in Cyrith, he was fairly sure. He could see the other islands drifting in the distance, and he could hear the low groan of the chains tethering them together. Was Icara nearby? Would she help him? But then, he didn't see what she could do against so many gargols and her father too. Besides, after the way they'd parted, he didn't think she'd be in the mood to save his life.

Demetrace took Nox into what must have been a garden once; tangled shrubs and vines clotted the space, surrounded on all sides by crumbling cloisters. The center had been cleared around an array of statues. *Winged* statues, life-size and disturbingly realistic.

Nox gulped as he approached the first. It was a woman doubled over, hands raised to protect her face, her wings curled as if in mid-takeoff.

His throat knotted as he bent to look at her expression of horror.

"They're, um, very nice statues," he said hoarsely.

"Trespassers," said Demetrace flatly.

Nox sighed. "I was worried you might say that."

All these people had been like him once—unlucky fools caught flying too high. And Demetrace had turned them to stone just like his daughter, only without the life left in them.

He looked at the next statue, and blinked. "Is that . . . the Hunter?"

Stepping closer, he saw the resemblance was too strong to be mistaken. The man had clearly died in agony, trying to take off, but he never made it. Shuddering, Nox tried to imagine him weeks ago, when he'd nearly carved Nox's eyes out with a knife. Even then, Nox couldn't make himself feel better about the man's horrible end.

"You killed them all," he whispered.

Demetrace didn't even flinch. "It wasn't the stone that killed them. It was the loneliness. That will turn a heart to stone faster than any magic."

"They . . . they were *alive* in there, after you turned them?" Nox felt sick. How long had the Hunter been trapped in that stone skin before he faded away? Had he been aware of his surroundings or just . . . lost in the dark, completely, terribly alone?

Nox looked down at the ground, unable to stomach looking at any other statues. But from the corner of his eye, he spied a small terrace overlooking a much larger garden, and he couldn't resist walking toward it. The gargols tracked him, creeping along the rooftops above, while Demetrace trailed behind.

With a gasp, Nox looked down on hundreds—*thousands*—of grisly statues arranged in neat rows across a field of dead, brittle grass. All the people who'd disappeared over centuries, the missing, the lost loved ones of so many families . . .

"You're a monster," he breathed. He whirled to face Demetrace. "You can't stop all of us. The Skyborn are remembering this place. They're going to return sooner or later, and your gargols won't be enough to stop them!"

Before he could make a move, Demetrace's hand shot out, curling into a claw in the air. The earthstone on his staff began to shine brighter.

Nox's feet suddenly went numb. He twisted in place, unable to shift them. Terror clogged his throat. It was as if he'd been trapped in drying mud, but looking down, he saw the truth was far worse.

Stone crept over his shoes, up his ankles. It flowed like honey up his legs. Even his clothes were stiffening into rock. He choked on a scream and wrenched himself, but couldn't pull free.

"They will fail," said Demetrace calmly. "Because they will all be dead."

"What?" Nox whispered, freezing.

"I gave your people mercy once. I will not grant it twice." His gaze flicked over Nox, to the sky beyond.

A massive island hung there, buoyed on skystones the size of hills. But something was *moving* across the face of the glowing rock. Nox squinted, trying to get a batter look.

Gargols.

They were chipping away at the skystones, and before Nox's eyes, a large piece of one broke away and drifted off into empty sky. The gargols continued on. They chipped and hacked with their stone claws and even their teeth.

"What are they doing?" Nox asked.

"What do you *think* happens when you remove all the skystones from an island?"

Nox's gaze slid back to Demetrace. "It . . . falls?"

He nodded once.

"Why would you . . . ?" Nox's mind raced ahead of his tongue, putting it together. "You're going to drop it. On purpose. Where?"

Demetrace didn't answer, only smiled—and that smile was the single most terrifying thing Nox had ever seen in his life.

"Where?" Nox screamed.

With a flick of his hand, Demetrace resumed his magic, turning Nox to stone. Nox thrashed and fought uselessly. He beat his wings, but no matter how he tried, again the fire failed him.

"WHERE?" Nox bellowed as his chest and neck went gray. His hands stiffened, outstretched. He tried to yell it again, but then his jaw locked; his vision darkened. The sound of hardening stone filled his ears.

Then—a whisper in his ear.

"I will drop it on your greatest city," said Demetrace. "In a matter of hours, Thelantis will be crushed, and then my gargols will follow. Your warriors will fall, and the clans behind them. The Skyborn will cease to exist, and my beloved Isalora will finally be avenged."

Nox couldn't even scream. He was buried alive in a coffin of stone, robbed of all senses, drained of all hope.

CHAPTER TWENTY-EIGHT
· ELLIE ·

They were an hour's journey from Thelantis and what would be, Ellie was sure, her final fate. There would be no escape this time. King Garion wouldn't hesitate to render his judgment and have it carried out—he just wanted to be sure as many people saw it as possible.

She tried not to think about it, instead imagining Linden and wondering how her clan was faring. Skies, had they kept their wings or not? The Stoneslayer still ignored her questions about them. Shuddering, she tried picturing Nox in some far-off corner of the world, probably napping and not thinking of her at all. She hoped Gussie and Twig were all right, that the king would be satisfied with capturing Ellie and forget all about them.

But it was hard to feel hopeful the closer they got to Thelantis. They'd reached Bluebriar Forest the day earlier, the trees bare and brittle below.

The Goldwings were edgy and impatient, eager to get home after their long mission of killing innocent people and capturing kids half their size. They skipped lunch and flew through the day, ignoring Ellie's exhaustion and dragging her along behind; her wings ached from trying to keep up.

And to think, just months ago she'd been a breath away from being one of them.

The rush and whisper of wings filled the cold air. Everyone was exhausted, too tired to converse. Ellie flew in a daze, staring dully down at the mesmerizing flow of the forest below.

Then, out of nowhere, a cloud of glittering blue smoke burst in the air just ahead of the Stoneslayer. Goldwings scattered, shouting in confusion.

"We're under attack!" a knight yelled.

Ellie bit back a gasp, a jolt of adrenaline shooting through her wings.

Gussie!

That smoke could have had only one source—but her excitement was quickly followed by a rush of dread.

If Gussie and Twig had somehow learned of Ellie's capture and launched a rescue attempt, then they were fools. There was no way they could take on a whole squadron of knights. They'd just be captured or killed.

Ellie panicked as the Stoneslayer dispatched his knights to scour the woods below, weapons drawn. If Gussie had been meaning to get their attention, she had it.

No, no, no, Ellie groaned inwardly. *Get out of there, Gus! Get Twig away!*

Half the Goldwings vanished into the trees, while the rest waited above, bristling with spears and crossbows. Ellie hovered between her two guards, nibbling her lip and exchanging anxious looks with Zain and Corion.

Five minutes passed, and none of the knights returned to report back.

The Stoneslayer snarled. "You!" he snapped, pointing at an Osprey clanner. "Get down there and see what's going on, then return at once."

The man nodded and dove, but minutes passed, and he didn't return either.

With a sharp curse, the Stoneslayer ordered the rest of the squadron to dive, leading them himself. Only Ellie, Corion, and Zain were left behind, with five guards—two for each boy, one for Ellie. The knights descended into the trees, and the sky fell silent.

Five minutes.

Ten.

There was no word, no sign from the knights below. The five guards looked nervously at one another, then at their prisoners.

"What do we do?" asked the one holding Ellie's rope. "Go on to the city?"

"And report what?" returned another. "That we *lost* the general and the rest of the squadron in the woods and were too afraid to go looking for them?"

"Let's give it another ten minutes. Could be they're still searching."

But they didn't need ten minutes.

Because seconds later, a swarm of people burst up through the treetops below, on a flurry of coppery-brown wings.

Ellie gaped.

Sparrow clan.

She'd recognize her people anywhere. There was Chief Donhal, in the lead with a pitchfork, followed by several of Ellie's cousins, the cook from the Home for Lost Sparrows, all of them familiar faces—and yet she'd never seen them like this. They were angry, determined, even . . . *warriorlike*. And they were all still in full possession of their wings.

The Stoneslayer hadn't shorn them off after all.

"Chief!" she shouted. "Watch out!"

With a wild yell, Donhal did a barrel roll, evading a Goldwing's arrow.

The knights dropped the rope tethers to instead reach for their swords, but it was too late. Scores of Sparrows converged on them, swinging farming tools, staffs, sticks—Ellie saw one of her distant cousins brandishing a large knitting needle, which she jabbed into the leg of the knight who'd been guarding Ellie. He howled and pinwheeled away.

"Skies above!" Ellie gasped.

The Goldwings fled, bruised and bewildered, in the direction of the city, and half the Sparrows took off after them.

"That's it, you scabby cowards!" Donhal roared, his wings spread to their fullest as he waved his pitchfork. "Flee! Flee the wrath of the Sparrow!"

He was red-faced from exertion, his eyes wild. The other Sparrows swooped and rolled all around, shouting and cheering as they routed the knights.

Ellie could not stop staring.

"What are you gawping at, girl?" Donhal said. "Get down before they come back with reinforcements!"

She landed on the forest floor, her legs wobbly with exhaustion. Zain and Corion dropped beside her.

They looked at one another, still shocked, then began to laugh. Ellie laughed so hard she began to cry, and then she was sobbing, reeling with relief. Someone untied her hands and asked her if she was hurt, but she couldn't even answer.

When she finally got control of herself, she looked around to see her clan around her, grave-faced. She hiccuped, then spotted Mother Rosemarie.

Old instincts kicked in; Ellie froze, immediately feeling guilty. She braced herself for the inevitable lecture.

But none came.

Instead, Mother Rosemarie strode to her, wrapped her up in her strong arms, and squeezed her till she squeaked.

"You're alive," she breathed. "Ellie Meadows, you're *alive*."

Ellie tried to answer, but could only give a strangled groan.

Mother Rosemarie finally released her and stepped back, her face flushed from flying. She had been carrying a sharpened hoe as a weapon, which she'd dropped to hug Ellie.

"You were right, child," she said. "All those months ago, in the king's palace, you were right to stand up to him. We see it now. He sent his knights to Linden to . . . Well." She stopped to raise an eyebrow. "You already know about that, of course. You were there."

Ellie's mouth dropped open. "You . . . saw me?"

"Who do you think brained that lout of a knight so you could escape?"

Ellie remembered the rock that had been thrown at just the right moment, distracting a Goldwing so that she could escape Linden. "That was *you*?"

Mother Rosemarie grinned, then sobered again. "After you flew off, our sense kicked in and we fought off the knights. Nobody takes our wings from us. *Nobody*."

The Sparrows had fought back?

A feeling like sunrise expanded in Ellie's chest—relief and shock and pride. Looking at the other Sparrows, she could see how much they'd changed since that terrible day in Linden. Their eyes were bright, their jaws set, their wings ready to fly at any moment. These were not the sleepy, meek farmers she'd known all her life. And to think that she'd felt guilty about abandoning them, wondering what she could have done to save her clan.

As it turned out, they'd saved themselves. Her only regret now was that she hadn't been there to see it. What a fight it must have been—the whole of the Sparrow clan rising up against the Goldwings.

She wiped away a tear and smiled at Mother Rosemarie.

"Thanks for rescuing me, again," Ellie said.

She nodded. "A few Goldwing scouts will have reached the city by now, so the king will have warning of our approach. We should move quickly."

"Move quickly *where*?" Ellie looked around, flabbergasted. "What in the skies are you all doing here? And what happened to the Stoneslayer?"

"The who?"

"Big, scary general? Lots of gold on his armor?"

"I saw that one," said another Sparrow. "He got winged by Chief Donhal but scrambled off into the woods."

Ellie winced. She didn't like the idea of the Stoneslayer being out there still, getting up to more dirty tricks.

"We got most of the others," Mother Rosemarie said. "They're sleeping off a strong dose of bronze root powder. It was easy enough to drug them, thanks to Gussie here."

Ellie whirled until she spotted the Falcon, who stepped shyly forward. Twig hung behind her, grinning.

"I, uh . . ." Gussie scuffed a foot, looking uncertain. "I reconfigured my smoke bombs to hold powdered bronze root. Turns out that's a pretty effective way to knock out a squadron of knights. It was tricky, though. I had to find a chemical agent to bond with—"

Ellie ran to Gussie and flung her arms around the Falcon. The girl tensed, as if shocked, then slowly hugged Ellie back.

"I'm sorry," Ellie whispered. "I should have forgiven you earlier. You were in an impossible position."

"No, *I'm* sorry," Gussie replied. "I betrayed you and you have every right to—"

"Shh," said Ellie. "It's over now. We're a team again. We're . . . we're clan."

She pulled away, and the two girls stared at each other for a moment.

"Yeah." A slow smile spread across Gussie's face. "Yeah, we are."

Twig jumped in then, hugging them both. He chattered away about the scuffle with the knights, which sounded like it had ended rather quickly, with the Sparrows ambushing them from the treetops and filling the air with enough bronze root powder to knock out a pack of lions.

"So what *are* you all doing here?" Ellie asked. "How'd you end up with the Sparrow clan?"

"Not just the Sparrows," said a voice.

Ellie looked around until she saw the speaker—Mayor Davina of Linden, from Oriole clan.

"The king attacked *my* town," said the mayor. "And the Sparrows are part of that town. Every family in Linden—except for those cowardly high clanners—is ready to put a stop to the king's madness. We knew it was just a matter of time before Garion sent a bigger force to our doorsteps."

"We met your clan two days ago, purely by luck," said Gussie. "Turned out we were headed in the same direction—Thelantis. Twig and I figured the knights would take you there. When we learned the Sparrows' plan, we decided to help out in hopes we'd find a way to rescue you."

"Any friends of Ellie's are welcome to travel with us," said Chief Donhal. "As for the king, he's gone mad. And just as it is the clans who make the king, so must the clans *unmake* any king who abuses his power."

"You're . . . going to Thelantis to depose King Garion?" Ellie's eyes nearly popped out of her head. She looked around at her clan, her kinsmen, the humble farmers and oil makers, and saw them in a wholly new light.

"We may be low clan," said Mother Rosemarie, "but we are not beneath anyone. I think . . . perhaps we had forgotten that, for a while. It's a lucky thing we had someone to make us remember."

Ellie blinked until she realized she was talking about *her*. "What did *I* do?"

"You won the Race of Ascension," said Mother Rosemarie, as if that were obvious. "You proved the skies belong to us as much as anyone. I'm sorry for my part in trying to hold you back, Ellie. You were right—we Sparrows are no lesser than any other clan. We should fight for our place in the sky too. It was our home once, as much as anyone else's."

"Tirelas," breathed Ellie. "You believe in it?"

"Well," said Chief Donhal. "We heard the rumors supposedly being spread by a certain Sparrow. Not that we believed them, at first. They are pretty wild tales, young lady."

"Did you really paint yourself gray to blend in with the gargols so you could sneak past them?" asked one of her cousins, a freckled kid barely older than a fledgling. "Then break off one's arm and use it as a sword to battle your way through thirty more?"

She blinked. "Huh?"

"Anyway," said Mother Rosemarie, "all that changed the night we saw *him*."

"Him?"

"The Phoenix," said the mayor.

Ellie stared at her. "You saw No—you saw the Phoenix?"

"Bright as a torch in the night, soaring so quickly we nearly missed him."

"What way was he headed?" Ellie grabbed her arm. "Was he okay? Did he look hurt? Did he land or talk to anyone?"

"So it's true?" asked Mother Rosemarie. "We heard he was a friend of yours. We sent a few of our fastest fliers to follow him, but he lost them within minutes."

Nox was alive, or had been not long ago.

Ellie didn't realize how scared she'd been for him until she felt the cool relief seeping through her body. "So you're really going to try and dethrone the king?"

Mother Rosemarie nodded. "We sent messengers to clans far and wide the day after the knights tried to take our wings. The other chiefs will meet us in Thelantis. The king might attack us alone, but he wouldn't dare wage war on *all* the clans. We will demand he step aside . . . or be *made* to."

"Speaking of which," said the chief, "we'd better hurry and get to it. If the king sends his army out, we might never even make it inside the walls."

They seemed sure of their plan, but Ellie wasn't. She looked to Gussie and Twig, both of whom shrugged. Around them, the Sparrows gathered their satchels and weapons and, under Chief Donhal and Mayor Davina's orders, started marching toward the city. They were a ragged band, but Ellie could feel their determination like a buzz in the air.

"Maybe this is the best way," said Gussie as they walked through the trees. The Sparrows had decided to make their final approach on foot, so as not to give the Goldwings any easy targets in the open sky. "Maybe it's the *only* way. At least someone's doing something."

"Let the adults fix things for once," added Twig. He fed an acorn to Lirri.

Ellie blew out a breath but said nothing. She was proud of her clan, and didn't doubt they were doing the right thing.

She just hoped it would be enough against the strength of the Eagle king.

All too soon, they stepped out of the trees and found the gates of Thelantis waiting ahead, beneath a sky dark with clouds.

CHAPTER TWENTY-NINE
· NOX ·

Nox's mind drifted, untethered from his body. He had lost all feeling in his limbs, his body, his face. He saw nothing, heard nothing, breathed no air. He was left only with panic and terror, and for a while—it could have been minutes or hours—he struggled to keep his grip on sanity.

Was he dying?

Or would he be trapped in here forever, a fate worse than death?

Were his insides turning to stone too? Would anyone ever know what had happened to him?

Panic scraped at his mind like a rabid animal fighting against its cage. It shredded his thoughts, gnashing its fangs, seeking escape from the darkness. He was locked in with it, helpless, drowning in the black.

Let me out let me out let me out!

But there was no *out*, and there was no one to hear his silent screams.

A part of Nox wanted to laugh bitterly. He'd finally gotten his wish—he was completely, eternally *alone*.

Delirium set in. His mind bounced from place to place; he was asleep in the wilderness, and any minute Ellie would wake him. He was curled up in the cargo hold of the ship that was carrying them to the southern jungles, and the memory of his mother's death was still fresh and sharp in his mind.

Then he was in Thelantis.

He walked its familiar streets and alleys, moving from shadow to shadow, toward some unknown destination. The familiar patterns of the city helped calm his mind, giving him solid ground on which to gather himself. He drew on every memory of home he had, adding details to his imaginings: the scent of bread baking, the rattle of harnesses on donkeys as they drew carts to the market, the hum of voices and rush of wings.

His panic stopped rampaging through his mind; it cowered, panting and exhausted, as the memories of his home soothed it like a gentle voice.

He lost himself in the reverie, meditating on the smallest things: the way the sunlight reflected on puddles in the street, turning them to gold. The slow rustle of laundry hung between buildings. Dust rising in lazy puffs from the sweep's brooms.

Calm settled over Nox. He felt as if time had stopped, and he hung in suspension between heartbeats.

He might have drifted like that forever, as insubstantial as a dandelion seed floating through the Thelantine streets.

But then, like a thunderclap, he saw an island the size of a mountain dropping from the sky, crushing the city and every person in it, to dust.

Just like that, the panic returned.

Nox thrashed and screamed inwardly, trying to remember what Demetrace had said. *A matter of hours . . .*

They would have no warning, no chance to save themselves. The clouds would hide the island until it was too late.

And Nox, the only person with any chance of warning them, was a stone statue hidden in the ruins in the sky—utterly helpless.

In his mind's map of Thelantis, he saw people appear, stepping out of doorways, leaning from windows, gathering in the street. They stared at him, hollow-eyed and pleading, or accusingly and with disgust. All his life he'd done everything he could to *avoid* being noticed. It had been the only way to survive. But even in his own mind, he couldn't make them look away. He'd lost control of his imagination; it played of its own accord, mocking him with the terrible pantomime.

He saw the thieves he'd once run with, the kind baker's apprentice who'd left day-old bread out for him and the other street kids, the guard who'd once caught him picking pockets when he was only eight and who'd pretended to look the other way long enough for Nox to flee. He saw Winster and Borge, the tavern keeps who'd always been friendly to him, warning him when the Talon had been in a bad mood so he could stay away. He saw faces he'd passed every day, but whose names he'd never learned. And all of them stared back, knowing their deaths were imminent, knowing only Nox could save them.

Stop! he cried in his mind. *Don't look at me—I can't help you! I'm not what you think I am. I've already failed. Why me? Why does it have to fall on me?*

He ran through the streets, but around every corner there were more of them, waiting, staring, pleading.

Nox felt pressed on all sides, as if the air were squeezing him, crushing him as inexorably as the stone wall in the Phoenix clan's riddle chamber.

The maze of Thelantine streets turned in his mind; like a panicked rat he ran onward, trying to take flight, only to find his wings had turned to stone.

Finally, he came to the great central plaza, and there he found Ellie, Gussie, and Twig.

They stared at him in silence, their wings folded, holding hands with one another.

No.

No, they couldn't be in Thelantis. It was only his imagination. They were far, far away, surely—surely! They knew better than to return to that city.

But dread blossomed in Nox's chest.

This wasn't his imagination anymore. He'd lost control of what he was seeing, and no matter how hard he tried, he couldn't shut out the vision.

He thought suddenly of the Restless Order, the reclusive folk who'd once sheltered him and his friends in the Aeries Mountains.

It is through meditation, one of the Order had told him, after he'd once asked why they sat still so long, staring at nothing, *that we seek visions of the future—and our path home.*

Certainty dropped into his mind like a pebble into a still pond, sending out ripples that shook his entire being.

This was no dream, no reverie.

This was true, the kind of vision the Restless Order spent their lives seeking. They tried to escape their bodies through meditation. Nox had been *forced* out of his—into a future he knew, with unshakable surety, would soon come to pass.

Ellie and Gussie and Twig were in Thelantis. He knew it as well as he knew the sun was hot and the moon cold. They were in Thelantis, and in hours, they would die with everyone else when Demetrace dropped his island out of the sky.

Unless Nox reached them first.

The image of Thelantis dissolved, as if affirming he'd understood the vision. He pushed his thoughts in all directions, probing the black, straining for any sense of feeling in his body. But all he found was darkness, limitless and indifferent.

How did he escape a prison he couldn't see or feel?

How did he fight back when his only weapons were his thoughts?

If only he could control his Phoenix fire and turn it against the stone around him . . . but Nox wasn't a full Phoenix yet. Demetrace had said so, and despite the man being a stone-hearted murderer, Nox had a feeling he was telling the truth. How had he put it? *Your eyes give it away. You haven't completed your transformation.*

Words sparked in Nox's memory—the riddle on the floor, the Phoenix test.

> *The truth will shine in golden eyes,*
> *From ash alone may a Phoenix rise.*

Was that what the Phoenix test had really been? Some kind of final step in the transformation process? Ellie had started it with her madcap arson on the beach, but was there more to it?

Then came a whisper, his own voice murmuring in his mind's ear:

If there were, would you do it? Or would you run away, like you always do?

He'd never asked to be a Phoenix. Never wanted it. He still didn't want it.

But Nox knew that wasn't enough anymore. It wasn't reason enough to keep fighting the truth—that maybe he wasn't who he thought he was, and that maybe he was capable of more than he'd ever dreamed.

Maybe he was even capable of stopping Demetrace from destroying Thelantis and everyone he loved.

Nox grasped for the riddle in the stone chamber, trying to piece the words back together, the instructions he'd not understood—or perhaps had chosen not to understand.

Wings of light, heart of flame,
Face your shadow, speak its name.

Dread seeped through him, followed by a cold spear-thrust of understanding.

Face your shadow.

He thought of snarls in the dark, of a beast curled in his chest, waiting.

No, it couldn't mean that. *Surely* not that. Not the monster that brought destruction, the thing that had hurt Ellie and started so many fires. It waited inside him still, always at the edge of his consciousness, breathing its hot breath down his neck.

You're still fighting it, he could hear Ellie saying. *Stop fighting it. I trust you.*

Her voice was so clear in his head it was as if she were whispering into his ear.

Isn't it time you trusted yourself, Nox?

The thought sent a shiver of heat through his mind.

No, he didn't trust himself. He wasn't sure he ever would. But one thing was certain. One thing he knew to be true above all else:

He trusted Ellie.

He struggled against his fear, which urged him to fight the monster back, to press it down as he had been doing ever since he woke on that beach.

The fireproof boy, afraid of fire.

But not this time.

This time he had to be stronger.

Cold with terror, Nox reached through the darkness, not for escape, not for daylight . . . but for the creature of shadow and flame. Even since he'd learned of its existence, he had avoided it, feared it, held it at bay.

Now, for the first time, he reached for it.

And at once, it was there.

Shifting flames, swirling and mingling with shadow. It rose to meet him, its growl vibrating through his being. He could sense its ravenous hunger. Feeling like prey, he resisted the urge to pull back. His thoughts quested nearer to it, trembling, until his whole attention was focused on it for the first time.

It breathed, and a hot wind swept through Nox's mind. In it, he saw flashes of memory: Ellie screaming in pain as his fire burned her, the moment he'd realized Gussie had betrayed them, Twig lying on a bed with his wings shorn off, his mother dying in his arms, his father's last smile . . .

The monster wasn't just fire. It was fear, and shame, and regret, and anger. It was everything about himself he hated most, the sum of every mistake he had ever made.

The monster was himself.

Face your shadow, speak its name.

He didn't have to do this. He could drive it back like he always had, pushing it down and making it small.

But that wouldn't help Ellie or anyone else.

This is who I am.

I am a Phoenix.

Pulling together every scrap of courage he had, he faced the creature.

"I know you," he said. "Your name is Tannox Corvain. You're me and I am you."

With a roar like a wildfire sweeping through dry grass, the creature rushed at him. It swept through his mind and fused to his thoughts. It shot through his being, an all-consuming fire.

He let it burn until the last of his fear and rage and longing had burned away, and only the fire remained. Light filled Nox from end to end; not a corner of his mind was left in shadow. Every part of him was laid bare to those white flames, every ugly and beautiful and shameful and noble thought. Every regret. Every triumph. Every weakness. The creature he'd so feared was himself, but now that he faced it, *embraced* it . . .

He realized it didn't want to destroy him at all.

It only wanted to be free of the cage he'd put it in—the cage he'd put *himself* in.

Ellie's words rang through him: *That thing inside you is your power. Let it burn. Let it burn!*

He pressed and strained and reached, stretching himself in all directions until, suddenly, he felt his fingertips—immobilized in stone, cold and hard.

He kept pushing as the roaring inferno swelled deep inside him. He didn't fight the heat. He let it grow, let it roar. He opened every pathway in his mind so it could flourish. He held nothing back. His surrender was total.

His fire wasn't born in his wings. It was born in his heart, which no cursed magic could contain.

And Nox's heart had never burned hotter.

A scream echoed through Nox's mind—until it burst through his stone lips, ripped from his stone lungs.

And on his stone cheek, a crack appeared.

All at once, the stone shattered, and in a great burst of flames, Nox fell to his knees, gasping in air. Cold daylight burned his eyes. He choked and coughed, blinking away dust from the shattered rock.

When his vision cleared, he stared, stupefied.

Fire swirled around him in a great vortex, sweeping up stray leaves and burning them to ash. He knelt, shoulders hunched and hands shaking, as the flames whooshed upward and around, almost playful. Then, with a rush like ocean waves, the fire settled in the air in front of him. It condensed, taking for the briefest of moments an animal-like shape. A snout extended, a tongue of flame tasted the air, and two eyes of gold regarded Nox.

"H-hello," Nox stammered.

With a shimmer of flames, the fire swept over him and then vanished.

Nox pressed a hand to his chest and found it hot. When he shut his eyes, he could sense the fire there, coiled and watchful.

Mind wheeling, he breathed in slowly and waited for his pulse to settle.

The gray sky shone above him. All around, leaves crackled and danced over the ancient stone courtyard. He was alone; there was no sign of Demetrace or the gargols, so he assumed they'd gone to finish their work of dropping an island on Thelantis.

He didn't have much time.

Shutting his eyes, he reached inward one last time. His fire was still there, a flame burning steadfastly. He had only to think of it, and warmth rushed through his body, flared in his feathers, nuzzled his fingers affectionately.

He wondered that he had ever been afraid of it.

With a deep breath, Nox opened his eyes and stood, spreading his wings.

He had no idea how far it was to Thelantis. He could only hope he wasn't too late.

CHAPTER THIRTY
· ELLIE ·

Cardinal and Jay. Starling and Thrush.

From all across the Clandoms, they had come.

Robin and Finch. Weaver and Hummingbird . . .

The crowd in front of Thelantis's gates had grown to the size of an army. Dozens of clans were represented, each sending a hundred or more people. They were all armed too, albeit most carried wood-cutting axes, pitchforks, and other tools, rather than actual weapons. The chiefs gathered at the head of the throng, where they conferred in low voices. The city gates were shut, the guards atop the walls watching the clans with scorn.

Ellie stood near Chief Donhal as he shouted up at them. To his right and left stood the chiefs of the Dove and Owl clans.

"Open the gates, boys!" the chief bellowed.

The guards exchanged looks but didn't move.

"You won't stop us getting in, not unless you plan to shoot us all between the three of you."

Then a familiar Goldwing appeared, soaring to the top of the gates, where he landed roughly beside the guards. Ellie noticed he was nursing an injured wing.

"The Stoneslayer," she growled.

The general said something to the guards, and a moment later, the gate began to grind open.

"We don't want trouble," said Donhal. "We just want to speak to the king."

"Set foot through these gates," the Stoneslayer called down, "and you declare treason!"

"Oh, we mean to declare things," Donhal called back. "But we'll do it to His Majesty's face, if you don't mind."

The Stoneslayer sneered, then flew off into the city.

The chiefs led the way through the gates.

The walk through Thelantis was quiet—*too* quiet, in Ellie's opinion. She saw some faces peering through shutters, but when she looked, they quickly vanished. A few doors slammed shut, but otherwise there was little sign of the city's residents. The air was tight and thin, making it feel as if she couldn't quite catch her breath.

Where were the guards? The Goldwings?

They had to know about the crowd marching through their streets. She couldn't believe they'd fled.

A few minutes later, she found out.

King Garion stood in full battle regalia in the central plaza, where Ellie had nearly been hanged weeks ago. His armor was polished white to match the knights', and from his shoulders hung a long red cloak. His great tawny wings lifted and spread, feathers stretched to their fullest length. He looked magnificent, especially with the armored crown on his brow, shaped to both protect him and to announce his royalty, with a large ruby gleaming in its center. He braced his hands on a naked sword, its point balanced on the stones beneath his feet.

Behind him spread the guards, the Goldwings, and the army. Several hundred high clanners all together, each of them armed and armored.

They waited in total silence.

From the corner of her eye, Ellie saw nervous looks being

exchanged between the chiefs and their retinues. Their numbers were greater by about four times, but their weapons seemed paltry compared with the force that waited for them.

The low clanners came to a halt at last, Chief Donhal in the lead.

He stepped forward, with the chiefs of the Dove, Finch, and Gull clans beside him.

"Garion," he called out, "don't make trouble. The chiefs make the king, and by law, we can demand your abdication. You stand accused of crimes against the Sparrow clan."

"And against the Gulls!" called the Gull chief. "My cousin Brennec was slaughtered by your Goldwing dogs!"

Donhal lifted his chin. "Garion, by the right of the clans, we demand— *Oof!*"

With a hiss and a *thunk*, a bolt fired from an unseen crossbow buried itself in the center of Donhal's chest.

He looked down in astonishment, then up at Garion. Then he toppled, dead before he hit the paving stones.

Ellie's heart stopped. She stared at the fallen chief, spread just a step in front of her, and felt the ground tilting under her feet.

Garion looked over the clans, his expression severe. No one dared move or speak.

"*I,*" he pronounced slowly, "am king. *I* bow to no chief, no clan, *none. I* will have your fealty and obedience, or you will be eradicated for the traitorous rats you are."

He waited, perhaps for the clans to fall to their knees and beg for mercy, but no one did. The faces around Ellie looked ill, terrified even, but they held firm. Still, with Donhal fallen, they seemed confused about who was in charge.

Seemingly emboldened by their hesitation, Garion lowered his wings a little, his expression turning to a smirk. "Is that it, then? You came armed only with words and feeble, outdated laws? Pathetic. Where is your leader? Where is your *Phoenix*?"

The chiefs shifted, eyes sliding away, uncertainty weakening them. Ellie felt it like a changing wind. They were losing their resolve.

"Well?" bellowed Garion. "Where is he? Where is your savior from the sky? Your fire-winged prince? WHERE IS HE?" He spread his wings and launched upward, hovering over them. The wind stirred by his feathers washed over Ellie and the low clans. "You want my throne, *boy*?" he shouted into the sky. "Then come! Let's see you claim it!"

Ellie shut her eyes.

If they gave in now, they'd never have another chance to rise up. This was it. This was the final moment, where they fought . . . or they faded away. This was, she realized, the day they determined whether the Skyborn kept their wings or not. Whether through wingrot or the king's blade, they would become earthbound forever.

Someone had to do *something*.

Nox wasn't here. Maybe he'd never return. She'd waited as long as she could for him to save them. All these months, she'd believed in destiny, believed she'd seen the path ahead so clearly—Nox becoming the Phoenix, returning to stop the king and then to lead the Clandoms back into the sky where they belonged. That was what all the signs and prophecies had been pointing to, wasn't it?

But over the past weeks, she'd realized the truth: Nobody was coming to save them.

"What about you, Corion?" The king picked out his son among the low clans; it wasn't hard to do. Corion stood a head above most of them. "Will you really throw everything away for these traitors?" He held out a hand. "Come to me now, boy. Come now, and all will be forgiven. We will make peace in our kingdom together."

Corion's gaze widened. The people around him drew back, and it seemed every eye was fixed on the prince.

He looked at Zain, who stared steadily back, waiting on Corion's choice. If the prince took his father's offer, would Zain follow?

"I will stay where I am, Father," the prince said at last.

The king went red, spit flying from his lips as he roared, "Do you know what you are doing, you fool boy?"

"Of course." He glanced at Ellie. "I'm choosing a side."

"Fools!" Garion shouted. "All of you are fools! You are *nothing*!"

Ellie's head snapped up.

You are nothing.

You can do nothing.

Oh, Ellie was *sick* of those words. They'd been biting at her for weeks, worming their way through her thoughts, poisoning her.

Nothing? *Nothing?*

She had won the Race of Ascension.

She had escaped the king's prison not once but twice.

She had flown into the gargols' city and out again.

She had discovered the cure for wingrot and the truth about her people's history.

That was not *nothing*.

That was everything they'd said was impossible. But she had *done it*.

Ellie stepped forward. She walked past Donhal's body and stood alone before the king and all his soldiers.

Garion laughed. "Little Lilly Meadows, I should have guessed. So this is who the mighty chiefs of the Clandoms have sent to lead them: a *little girl*."

"My name is Ellie," she said. "And I don't lead anyone. I'm not a soldier, or a knight, or a hero. But I know a coward when I see one. I'm looking at one right now."

A whisper of shock rippled through the chiefs and soldiers alike.

"Shut up," said the king, his face reddening with fury. "You will pay for that, girl."

Looking at him, Ellie realized how small he was inside. However wide his wings, however bright his armor, he was as easy to rankle as a common bully.

"You could have been great," she yelled. "You could have listened to me months ago, when I told you about the skystones. You could have listened when we told everyone about Tirelas. *You* could have led us back to the sky, to drive out the gargols and take back our true home. That was your job—to save your people. But you didn't, so now we have to do it ourselves."

"You have nothing," spat the king, sweeping his wings forward. His draft whipped her hair and ruffled her feathers, but she didn't flinch. "You have no leader, no Phoenix. It was all a lie, wasn't it? There *is no* Phoenix, or else he is dead. All the Phoenixes are gone, do you hear? *I* wiped them out. *I* am the only king!"

He raised his sword, and that must have been the signal his soldiers were waiting for. Because all at once, they rushed forward.

The clans broke. They couldn't stand against that force. But when they turned to flee, they found the sky behind them suddenly blocked—by the high clans.

The Ospreys, Hawks, Falcons, and other high clans had sneaked into the city, or had been waiting all this while. They rose up, trained from birth to fight, while their relatives in armor pressed from the other side.

The low clans had no choice but to fight for their lives.

"Stay low!" shouted Ellie. "They have the advantage in the air!"

Her words were passed on, and the low clans managed to scrap together some kind of organization. They broke off in groups, using the awnings and roofs around them for cover, engaging with the high clanners on the ground. Even so, their farm tools and kitchen knives were poor weapons against swords and spears.

Ellie was pressed into a doorway with Corion and Twig by a pair of guards. Corion fought one with his long knife, while Ellie and Twig took on the other. She jabbed her attacker in the gut with her staff, and Twig stretched out his arm, allowing Lirri to run down it and leap onto the man's head. She scratched and bit, and while the guard screamed and tried to brush her off, Ellie landed an arcing blow on his ear. He crumpled, unconscious, and Lirri leaped back onto Twig.

"Nice one!" Twig said, grinning.

Then he gasped, as a spear pushed through his side and was withdrawn again.

"NO!" Ellie screamed.

She dropped to her knees, catching Twig as he fell. His eyes were wide and startled, fixed on hers.

The Stoneslayer loomed over them, breathing hard. *"Finally,"* he hissed. "I've wanted to crush you brats for—"

A wild, ear-piercing screech cut him short as Lirri leaped from Twig's pocket.

The little creature flew through the air, landing claws-first on the Stoneslayer's face. He howled and stumbled back, trying to pull Lirri off.

Ellie sobbed, pulling Twig to her chest and trying to stanch the wound in his side with her hand. His blood ran down her arm and pooled on the cobblestones.

"Twig," she whispered. "It'll be all right. Please, *please!*"

Hearing a wild cry, she looked up to see Lirri leaping back to Twig, her teeth clamped over something small, round, and bloody.

"MY EYE!" roared the Stoneslayer, holding a hand to his mangled face. "I'LL SKIN THAT ANIMAL! I'LL—"

He was cut short as a strange sound filled the street. A tangle of barks, hisses, and yowls rose from all around, growing louder until it drowned out every other noise. Corion stood over Ellie and Twig, looking bewildered. Those fighting around them paused, weapons frozen in midair, to gape at the flood of animals pouring out of the cracks and crevices of Thelantis. Dogs and rats, cats and lizards, they flowed in a furry, fanged river that swept toward the Stoneslayer.

With a scream, he started to stumble away, but only made it a few steps before the animals swarmed over him.

He fell without a sound, terror in his one remaining eye. Ellie bent over Twig, holding him tight as the animals dragged the general into an alley, yipping and howling, biting and tearing.

Then the creatures, and the Stoneslayer, were gone.

"Twig," Ellie whispered, cradling his face. "Twig?"

He stared at her, his eyelashes trembling, but didn't speak.

"Ellie?" She heard Gussie's voice behind her. "What—what happened?"

"Gussie! He needs help!" Ellie screamed. "What do we do?"

The Falcon's face had gone gray and tight. Tears streamed down her cheeks. "I don't know," she whispered.

With a long, low cry, Ellie pushed her face into Twig's chest, her hand still pressed to the wound in his side. Nothing in her healer's apprenticeship had prepared her for an injury like this.

At that moment, two high clan guards landed on the street in front of them. She had no choice but to lower Twig to the ground, so she could help Gussie defend against their attack. The guards drove her farther and farther from Twig. She clenched her teeth, holding back tears, wishing she could just scoop him up and fly far away.

Low clanners dropped all around, wounded or dead. Few of the high clanners fell. The king's plan was clear: His people were driving the chiefs into the plaza again, where they'd be easy pickings.

Ellie fought ferociously, using every technique the Restless Order had taught her. Jab to the head, whirl, swipe the feet, stab the gut. She found herself face-to-face with a young Goldwing, an Eagle who looked suspiciously familiar. She was pretty sure he'd tried to murder her in the Race of Ascension.

"Sparrow!" he howled, and then she *knew* he recognized her. "I'll finish what I should have—"

Ellie thwacked him between the eyes. He blinked at her, startled, before dropping hard onto his bottom.

She hated this.

She felt every inch the child she was, no longer a warrior, no longer anything but afraid and heartbroken. In the fray, she'd been driven from Twig's side, and had lost sight of him. She didn't even care about winning anymore. She just wanted it to *end*.

The battle was over not much later. The low clans' ranks were decimated, the streets littered with the fallen. The remaining chiefs and their people were herded into the plaza. The Goldwings laughed and rained down insults, having expended almost no effort at all against them. Half the king's forces had hung back, their strength unneeded.

All at once, the fighting stopped.

The king landed, his fist upraised in an order to call off his troops. They formed a tight circle around the low clanners, grinning and confident.

King Garion's eyes probed the plaza until he picked out Ellie and Corion. With a gesture, he sent several knights forward to seize them. Exhausted and bruised, they put up no fight.

Ellie's knees hit the ground hard in front of Garion, just as a gentle rain began to fall. The cobblestones darkened as they grew slick with water. Ellie kept her head up, but her mind swirled. She was sick with dread. She hoped the king would just get it over with quickly.

Tears stung Ellie's eyes. She glanced at Corion, who gave her a sad, weak smile.

"We gave it a shot, anyway," he said.

His father slapped him. *"Fool!"*

Corion reeled. He dropped his face, his damp hair hanging over his eyes, his shoulders trembling. Ellie started to reach out to the prince, only to find the king's sword at her throat.

"This is *your* doing," he snarled. "You corrupted my son. You destroyed my family. And for that, I will make your suffering long. *Bow.*"

She swallowed but didn't lower her head.

"I said *bow!*" he roared.

The rain pattered and the clouds darkened. Ellie didn't bow.

The king crouched over her, so she couldn't look away. Despite his armor and crown, up close, his face was haggard. These months had drained him, leaving his eyes sunken, his skin sagging. Even his hair seemed thinner and grayer.

"You've lost everything," he said. "Your clan, your home, your friends, your freedom. There's nothing left for you. Nothing but this: *I win.*"

She raised her gaze, staring at the sky.

"He's still out there," whispered Ellie.

"What?"

"The Phoenix." She tried to swallow the knot of fear in her throat but it bobbed up again. "He's out there, and you can't do anything about that. He's alive and he's everything you fear."

"If that were true, he would be here now." The king swiped a hand through the air, indicating the obvious. "Face it, girl. No one defies me and lives for long. So. If you have any final words, speak them now."

"Watch the skies," Ellie replied softly, still gazing at the clouds. She began to smile.

The king groaned. "Unoriginal. Now—"

He was cut short as all across the square, gasps rose, and then the words spread. Voice by voice, they began to call out, the low clans lifting their gazes.

"Watch the skies."

"Watch the skies!"

"*Watch the skies!*"

"Stop!" said the king. "Shut up, all of you! You've lost, do you hear me? *You've lost!*"

Ellie raised one finger to the sky. "Have we, Garion? *Watch the skies.*"

All her life, she had heard those words spoken in warning—watch for clouds, watch for gargols, watch for death. But for the first time, repeated by a hundred voices . . . those words were spoken out of wonder and hope.

Garion finally looked up, and his knights followed his gaze. The guards did too, then the high clanners, then everyone in the city was looking up, as out of the clouds, a figure dropped.

Someone small, swift, and ablaze with fire.

CHAPTER THIRTY-ONE
· NOX ·

Nox dove toward Thelantis, rain stinging his face, his fiery wings angled for maximum speed.

He'd been so afraid he would be too late. He'd flown as fast as his new wings could go, dodging lightning bolts, tumbling through peals of thunder. Gargol screeches echoed around him, but he couldn't tell whether they were hunting him or preparing for their assault on the clans. Of Demetrace, he'd seen no sign, but he knew the sorcerer was close to carrying out his terrible plan.

He had to reach Thelantis before that happened.

Wind rushed past Nox, whistling in his ears as he dove. When the clouds finally parted and he saw the city below, he didn't slow down. Instead, he angled for the ground like an arrow, aiming for the heart of Thelantis.

He saw a crowd in the central plaza and at first thought there might be some festival going on. Hundreds of people were packed into the area, dressed in browns and grays, ringed by white-armored Goldwings.

Then he saw the glint of swords.

Dropping from above, Nox flared his wings, feathers stretched wide to slow his descent. His flames danced and curled away, bright against the dark clouds above.

He gaped at the scene below him, where hundreds of knights and soldiers had hemmed in a small group of low clanners. They looked up as Nox hovered over their heads, their faces stunned, afraid, and . . . hopeful. *Hopeful?* What was going on here? Why would they—

Then he saw her.

Kneeling at Garion's feet, with the king's sword at her throat, was Ellie.

Fury rushed through Nox; he felt his wings grow hotter, the flames jumping in response to his anger.

"GARION!" he roared.

The king lowered his sword, his shock lasting only a moment before he masked it in cold rage. Lifting his blade, he pointed it at Nox.

"Kill him!" he shouted.

A score of bolts shot from crossbows, all aimed at Nox.

Instinctively, he flapped his wings and sent a wave of hot wind rolling outward; it easily turned aside the bolts, and they fell back to the ground with a clatter.

The knights who'd fired looked at the king uncertainly.

Nox didn't have time for this.

"Listen to me!" he shouted. "You all must leave the city—*now*! Any minute, a rock the size of a mountain will fall on Thelantis!"

He saw Ellie's eyes go wide, and she glanced at the boy kneeling beside her. Was that Corion, the crown prince? How had they ended up together?

No, there was no time for questions. Nox shook his head, pointing at the sky. "Garion, I'm not your enemy. I swear, all I want is for you to believe me. You *cannot* stay in the city!"

They heard him. Eyes turned upward, but there was little there to prove Nox's words. The thick, dark clouds completely hid the weakening island from view. Obscured as it was, they wouldn't see it plummeting until it was too late.

"Liar!" Garion took to the sky, his teeth bared and blade in hand. "Kill the Phoenix! Knights, to me!"

Goldwings launched upward in a flurry of wings and swords. Taking advantage of the moment, the trapped low clanners—Ellie among them—jumped up and began fighting the remaining soldiers on the ground. The air soon boiled with ferocious activity.

Nox groaned. They were wasting time they did not have.

Skies! If they wouldn't believe him, he would just have to *show* them.

Rising higher, with the king and all his Goldwings speeding toward him, Nox closed his eyes. He reached for the fire within him and found it waiting and ready, docile as a puppy. Calling to it, he opened his eyes.

Then he whipped his wings with all his might.

A wave of fire rolled forth. Flames rushed outward hungrily, growing in strength as they spread through the sky. A pup no longer, the fire burned through the clouds like a pack of wolves, the air hissing as the heat met the moisture in the air, turning it to steam. For a moment, everything went white—he couldn't see beyond his own hand.

Then, in seconds, the steam dissipated and the sky over Thelantis burned bright, blue, and clear—with the exception of the sky island hanging just overhead. The underside, once bulging with lighter-than-air skystone, was now riddled with gaping holes where the gargols had pried the skystone loose. Only a few chunks remained, and gargols scrabbled over these, frantically hacking. Another large piece came loose and floated away. With a groan that shook the sky, the island sank lower.

The battle below froze as every person, low clan and high, looked up.

The king and his knights flared their wings, nearly reversing in the air.

"Do you see it now?" Nox shouted.

Chaos and terror broke out below. A mixture of low clanners and soldiers fled at once, flying toward the city walls and the sky beyond. A few knights looked like they wanted to follow but resisted and looked to their king.

Garion's eyes went from Nox to the island and back again. Indecision played out on his features. He seemed to grapple with two desires—killing Nox or responding to this new threat.

It was no surprise to Nox when the king finally roared, "It's a trick! The Phoenix thinks to steal my throne with lies and deceit! *Kill. Him!*"

But the knights didn't move.

Still hovering in place, they looked from the island down to the city, and then at one another.

"Our families are down there," said a Hawk clanner. "What if it's true?"

"What if?" Nox couldn't believe his ears. "It's right there! You can see it's true!"

With a splintering crack, another slab of skystone broke free of the island's underside and went tumbling through the air, floating high into the blue until it was lost to sight. The island dropped visibly before stabilizing again, but several large rocks hurtled toward the ground, smashing onto the streets. Paving stones splintered to bits, and pieces went spinning wildly, smashing windows or punching through walls.

That, at last, convinced everyone.

The knights broke, diving back to the city.

"We have to get everyone out!" one said. "Sound the bells!"

They scattered across Thelantis, and in moments, the alarms rang across the city—not the measured ringing to warn of a gargol attack but frantic, ceaseless clanging that rattled the streets. Shutters flew open; heads poked out of doors.

Nox sagged with relief, but not for long.

Garion charged him.

With a yelp, Nox turned a backflip, narrowly avoiding the spear the king hurled his way. Then he shot upward, winging toward the island. It was sinking lower and lower, and only a few skystones still held it aloft. When those were gone—which he guessed would be in minutes—the island would fall.

He flew as fast as his wings would take him, but looking back, he saw the king was closing in. Nox cursed and pushed himself harder. He wanted to be down on the ground, helping clear the city. He wanted to make sure Ellie and Twig were all right.

Instead, he flew for his life, panic stabbing through his heart, fury prickling his skin like a rash.

This was so *stupid*! They needed every minute to evacuate the city. Nox had to end this here and now, before the king's vendetta cost even more lives.

Nox turned a looping barrel roll, changing directions in a blink to face Garion. The king pulled up in surprise, then glowered.

"I'll cut off your wings the same as I did the last Phoenix I found, boy," he growled. "Then I'll hang you like I hung your worthless father! *I* am the only king here! There is only *me*!"

The last Phoenix?

Did he mean Tanra, Nox's grandmother?

Fury and flames rolled off Nox in hot waves, but he fought to control his anger. As much as he hated Garion, the man wasn't worth fighting. There were people who needed Nox, people who matteed far more, and he intended to reach them. He had no more time to waste on this mad king.

"That's your mistake, Garion!" he shouted. "You're so worried about your throne on the ground, you've forgotten the most important law of the skies."

The king's face twisted. "What law? There is no law but mine!"

Nox's eyes flickered beyond the king to the cliffs under the island—where hundreds of gargols clung to the rock like bats. They blended into the dark stone, almost invisible except for their glowing blue eyes. They watched him and Garion hungrily, their dark wings twitching.

"Spread your wings in skies of blue," Nox said, his voice so soft he wasn't sure the king could even hear him. "But skies of gray are death to you."

Garion, sneering, raised his sword. "*That* child's drivel? I'll have your head—"

His voice was drowned out by the sudden roar of stone wings as all at once, the gargols dropped from the cliffs and took flight.

The king turned, going rigid with shock as the wave of gargols bore down on him, a black wave of death.

Garion turned, locked eyes with Nox for a heartbeat—and then he vanished, swallowed up by the screaming, snarling horde.

Nox didn't wait to meet the same fate.

He closed his wings and let himself fall.

Slowly, he wheeled until his head was pointing toward the ground, his body stretched long and taut. His heart seemed to stop beating altogether. The wind howled past him, and the sound of the gargol horde filled his ears.

He reached Thelantis only a few wingbeats ahead of the monsters.

People were still stumbling out of their homes, bewildered by the clanging alarms. Knights and low clanners, who'd been trying their best to slaughter one another minutes ago, now worked side by side to sweep the streets, desperate to find every last person and tell them to flee.

Then the gargols began dropping from above, targeting anyone they could get their claws on. Screams began rising across Thelantis.

Desperately, Nox flew up and down the streets. The city was growing darker by the second as the island descended, blocking more and more of the sun. Soon, it was as dark as night. In the confusion and chaos, Nox had only his memory of the streets to guide him. But if there was anything he knew, it was the maze of Thelantis.

"Ellie!" he yelled. "Twig!"

He called their names over and over, and whenever he saw someone's face in a window, he stopped only to yell, *"Get out of the city! Go now!"*

Where were his friends?

He aimed for the central plaza, where he'd seen them last. But when he turned a corner, he nearly crashed into a large, lizard-like gargol.

Shouting, he threw himself aside, tumbling into a wall and landing hard on the street. The gargol roared, intent on a family that had been trying to escape their house. The family now cowered under a flimsy wooden awning.

"HEY!" Nox shouted, drawing the creature's attention.

When it turned, he thrust his wings, and just as he'd done in the wheat field weeks ago, he sent a torrent of fire washing over the gargol. It shuddered, screeched, and then shattered into a thousand stone pieces.

"Th-thank you!" called out the father.

"Go quickly!" Nox said. "Take anyone you can find and *go*!"

They took flight, and Nox continued on.

He finally found her near the city's center, knocking on the windows of a large building, telling the people hiding inside that they had to come out.

"ELLIE!"

He flew toward her and as she turned, they collided in a massive hug, tumbling to the street. Nox quelled the flames on his wings just in time.

Ellie cried out and squeezed him back. She was a wreck; he noted the wounds on her wrists where she'd been recently shackled, and the newly healed burns on her arm that had been his doing. Her clothes were torn and her face was scraped up, but she was alive.

"Nox!" She pulled back at last, and gripped his sleeves. "Where have you *been*? Your wings—you learned how to put out the fire? Why are your clothes all burned? And the island up there! What—"

"I'll tell you everything later! We have to get out of here!"

"Your eyes! What happened to you?"

"My what?"

Ellie stared, lifting a hand and almost touching his cheek. "Your eyes, Nox. They're . . . *golden*."

He blinked, then shook his head. "There's no time! I'll explain later!"

A shadow raced over them; a gargol was hunting above. He pulled Ellie under a doorway, just as Gussie landed nearby. She was as ragged as Ellie, her hair frizzing and her face streaked with dirt and scrapes. Her long Falcon wings dragged tiredly as she folded them.

"So. You really are a Phoenix," she whispered, her eyes wide. "I would love to study—"

"You!" Nox flared his wings, flames hissing.

"Whoa, easy!" Ellie said. "She's with us again. Long story, but you can trust her."

Nox eyed Gussie as he closed his wings. "How can you be sure?"

"Because Twig . . ." Ellie stopped.

"Where *is* Twig?"

"I lost him in the streets. He—he's hurt pretty bad. I don't know if . . ."

"We have to find him, and fast. There's a horde of gargols attacking the city and that island could come crashing down any minute. Demetrace is determined to wipe us all out."

"Demetrace?" echoed Ellie.

"He's a sorcerer," Nox said in a rush. "From Tirelas. He's, like, a thousand years old and made of stone. Oh, and he created the gargols and is still up there, controlling them."

Ellie's eyes widened. "The stone man! I saw him—"

"I know." That felt like ages ago, when they'd flown into the storm over the Crag—all in a failed attempt to save Nox's mother. Ellie had told him she'd seen a stone man up there, but he hadn't quite believed her. Once again, she'd been right and him wrong. "Ellie, even if we get everyone out of the city—"

"The gargols will hunt us to extinction," she finished, catching on.

He nodded. "I don't know what to do," he confessed.

Ellie looked up, toward the sky festering with gargols, knights, and fleeing families. "This Demetrace—he's up there? And he controls the gargols?"

Nox nodded.

Her eyes turned hard, and she raised the knife from her belt. "Then let's pay him a visit."

CHAPTER THIRTY-TWO
· ELLIE ·

"**Y**ou don't understand!" said Nox, trailing Ellie through the streets. They dodged gargols as they waited for a clear shot at the sky, but the air was thick with the monsters. "He's a *sorcerer*! He can turn people into stone!"

Ellie glanced over her shoulder. "If he controls the gargols, then he's the only one who can call them off, right?"

"But—"

"*Nowhere* is safe, Nox! People can't take shelter in Thelantis with that island about to slam into the ground, and they can't fly to safety outside the city with an army of gargols waiting to strike! We have to make this sorcerer stop the attack!"

They slipped through a covered alley and ran into familiar faces on the other side.

"Corion!" Ellie cried. "Zain!"

The prince and the knight were ushering an elderly couple out of their home, directing them toward the city gates. They turned at Ellie's shout.

"Ellie!" Corion's eyes flickered to Nox. "Whoa. Your wings really *are* on fire."

"We have to get up there," said Ellie, pointing to the island hanging above. "Apparently all of this is the work of a thousand-year-old sorcerer, and he's still up there controlling the gargols."

Corion blinked, looked as if he had a hundred questions crowding his throat, but then he tossed his hands in the air. "Right. Thousand-year-old sorcerer, why not? You go deal with *that*, and I'll work on clearing the city and keeping watch, in case my father shows up."

Nox shook his head slowly. "He . . . uh, won't be coming back. I'm sorry. I saw him fall."

Corion swallowed, his face pale. "He chose his path," he whispered, hoarse. Silently, Zain put a hand on his shoulder and squeezed, and Corion leaned into him on shaky legs.

"You're king in Thelantis now," Ellie said, meeting Corion's eyes. "So act like one. Get these people out of here, and we'll deal with what's-his-name."

"*Demetrace,*" offered Nox.

Corion shook his head, straightening, though she could see how much effort it cost him. Skies, had it only been that morning that she, Corion, and Zain had woken up as captives in a Goldwing camp? They were all beyond exhausted. "I'm disinherited, remember? I'm no king, or even a prince . . . but this is still my city. We'll evacuate as many as we can. Go, Ellie. Watch the skies."

"You too." Her gaze shifted to Zain and she impulsively limped to him and threw her arms around his neck.

"Stay safe," she whispered. "And find . . . Twig for me, please."

She'd almost said *find Twig's body*. Skies, he had to be all right. He *had* to be. But she'd seen the spear thrust into his side. She'd seen how much blood he lost.

Zain hugged her just as tightly. She could feel that he was afraid too. "I'll do my best."

Stepping back, she wiped away a tear and laughed. "We've ended up a long way from Linden, huh?"

Zain gave her a weak smile. "Just like you always said we would. If

I know anything, it's that Ellie Meadows can be trusted. You'll save us, Ellie. You will."

She gave him a grateful look, though she was not at all sure she deserved his trust. Ellie had no idea what to do next, only that if they had any hope at all, it lay in the sky above.

As one, she, Nox, and Gussie launched off the ground, while below, Corion and Zain went back to their task.

But no matter which direction they flew, a gargol appeared to block the way. They were forced again and again to seek cover in the street, unable to break through to clear skies. The gargols tended to stick together in packs of three or four—too many for them to take on.

"We'll never make it out of the city!" Gussie shouted as they hovered above a row of warehouses. "Much less to Tirelas!"

"We have to try!" Ellie replied.

Nox glanced back, as if about to say something, but then his eyes grew wide and flames roared across his wings. *"Watch out!"*

He dove, pushing Ellie out of the path of a huge wolflike gargol just before it could crunch her skull with its massive jaws. She flipped one way, Nox the other, and the gargol sped through the gap between them.

Nox snapped his wings, sending a torrent of flames spiraling at the gargol, but this one moved faster than any Ellie had ever seen. It rolled out of the fire's path, shrieking as the flames cracked the tip of its wing.

Then it charged again, right for Ellie.

Caught off balance, she had no time to think. Nox fought to close the distance, but he wouldn't reach her in time.

The gargol's scream filled her ears.

Then, out of nowhere—a streak of shining white.

Ellie gasped as a figure split the sky between her and the monster, brandishing a shining spear. Golden hair flowed on the wind; a white cape rippled like a banner.

And it was like Ellie was a fledgling again, fluttering over the sunflower fields. She *knew* that hair. She knew that spear. She'd lived this moment before.

"Aglassine!" she breathed.

The Goldwing captain—*former* captain, Ellie recalled—took on the gargol without hesitation, driving her spear at its eyes. The creature howled and swatted at her, and she swooped nimbly out of its path. Then she jabbed at it again, keeping its attention on her and away from the kids.

"Over here, ugly!" Aglassine taunted. "That's it! Just try and get a bite of *me!*"

Last Ellie had heard, Aglassine had been imprisoned for disobeying the king's orders to cut off the Sparrow clan's wings. Had she been freed, or had she escaped? Ellie supposed it didn't matter. The captain had not turned out to be the hero Ellie had idolized all her life, but here she was nonetheless, saving Ellie once again.

"Let's fly!" Gussie urged, catching up to her.

Ellie nodded, but still hesitated. Aglassine would need their help, surely.

"Ellie!" Nox waved above her. "Now's our chance!"

"Go, little Sparrow!" Aglassine shouted through clenched teeth. Her spear was a blur, blocking the gargol's attacks, but the creature was driving her backward through the sky. The knight's wings beat frantically, feathers flying as she struggled against her foe. "I will hold it off while you— *Agh!*"

Ellie cried out as the gargol finally broke through Aglassine's defenses and raked its claws over her wing.

The feathers crumpled, and the captain began to fall.

"NO!" Ellie dove, catching Aglassine's hand. But the knight was too heavy for her to lift. Still, she beat her wings with all her strength.

"Let me go!" Aglassine said. Her broken wing hung in useless tatters, and her sweaty hand began to slip from Ellie's. "You and your Phoenix—you have to save the clans! *Go!* I'm not worth saving, not after all the evil I did for Garion!"

"You saved me!" Ellie shouted. "Remember? A little Sparrow girl in Linden, years ago? I can't let you fall!"

Aglassine's eyes widened. "Linden . . . Yes, I remember you."

Ellie had to concentrate fully on keeping a grip on the knight's sweaty hand. Above her, she heard Nox shout, and felt a flush of heat from his wings. A great cracking sound split the air, and then pieces of the gargol rained all around Ellie and Aglassine.

Nox had shattered it.

"Gussie! Nox!" she yelled. "Help me!"

Out of the corner of her eye, she could see them racing toward her.

But Aglassine's hand slipped further in hers.

"Remember me as I was that day," the captain whispered. A tear shone in her eye. "A true knight. Please, Sparrow. Forgive—"

Her hand slipped, and Aglassine fell.

Ellie dove again, but a sudden side wind caught her wings and bowled her over, pushing her farther from the knight. Gussie and Nox caught up to her, but they were too late.

Aglassine fell without a sound, her eyes closing before she hit the ground.

"No," Ellie whispered. "*No.*"

How much more could she lose today? How many more would fall?

"Ellie, we have to go!" Gussie said. "You can't save her now!"

"But maybe we can still save everyone else," Nox added.

Ellie nodded, swallowing hard. Aglassine's death was another thing she would just have to put aside until the battle was over.

They flew upward, the knight's sacrifice clearing their way just enough so that they could rise above Thelantis and the gargols ravaging the streets.

Ellie felt the weight of the island above pressing down on her. Its shadow darkened the city below, where gargols dove and attacked. Screams mingled with the monster's screeches.

Twig was down there, all alone. She'd left him lying on the stones, bleeding, maybe even dying.

No, she couldn't imagine the worst.

The best thing she could do to help Twig now was to stop this battle.

Wings up, Ellie, she ordered herself, repeating Twig's own words to her not so long ago. Scrubbing at her tears, she lifted her gaze, and the three of them raced higher and higher.

"Follow me," Nox said.

His wings lit the way. He'd grown into them since she'd last seen him. He flew with confidence and skill. She longed to know what he'd been doing all this time, and where he'd learned that trick to burn away the clouds. But all the questions in her head suddenly seemed small and unimportant. She felt almost shy around Nox; he was so different now, so sure of himself and so ready to . . . *lead*.

This was the Nox she'd been waiting for.

This was the Nox she'd believed in.

Never in her life had she been so glad to see someone as the moment Nox dropped from the sky. At first, she had thought it was her imagination, conjuring him up out of sheer desperation. But then everyone else had seen him too, and her hope had been reflected in their eyes.

Nox led them up and over a mountain of cloud. Behind it, a

group of islands hovered together, joined by chains. Ellie gasped in recognition—she'd seen this place before, floating above the island prison where Nox's mother had died.

"Cyrith," Nox said. "The old capital of Tirelas."

Ruins were heaped on each of the islands, covered in green vines and cool mist. Ellie saw wide avenues, crumbling markets, empty pools, and overgrown gardens. This place was like *five* Thelantises all tethered together, each drifting silently in the cold sky. The black windows of the broken towers seemed to watch them as they flew.

The chaotic battle below felt miles and miles away. With no gargols in sight, the place was eerily quiet. *Too* quiet. The hairs on Ellie's arms rose.

"It's beautiful," Gussie breathed.

Nox tilted, leading them higher, to one of the smaller islands. "That's where I saw Demetrace last. Let's start there."

They touched down in a stone courtyard filled with statues. Only when Ellie looked closer, she realized they were a little too lifelike to just be stone. Horrified, she look at Nox.

"What is this place?" She circled one of the statues, her stomach churning. It was shaped like a woman, her clothing old-fashioned. She was stretched tall, one hand reaching for the sky, while her eyes looked over her shoulder in terror.

"These aren't just statues, are they?" she whispered.

He nodded, grimacing. "Whatever you do, don't stop moving. Don't give him a clear shot at you or he'll turn you to stone. Got it?"

Gussie and Ellie nodded.

"So what's the plan?" asked Gussie. "How do we beat a guy who can turn us to stone?"

"I . . . have an idea," said Nox. "Sort of. See, Demetrace has this staff with an earthstone on it."

"Earthstone?" echoed Gussie.

"Right. Apparently there are types of magic other than skystones. Firestones, for example. Or earthstones."

He led them toward a terrace overlooking rows upon rows of more petrified figures. Ellie felt ill.

"You know how the skystones make Twig's ability stronger?" Nox said. "Earthstones do the same for Demetrace. It's what he used to create the gargols and to make himself immortal by turning himself to stone. And it's how he . . . did all that." He looked down grimly at the statues.

"How do you know all this?" Ellie asked.

"Some of it I figured out. The rest, Icara told me."

"Icara?"

"Oh, right. She's . . . Demetrace's daughter."

"His *daughter*?" Ellie prickled. "You've been away all this time because you were hanging out with an evil sorcerer's *daughter*?"

"She's not like him!" he protested. "Well . . . sort of. She's not exactly on our side either, but— Look, that's not important. What *is* is that I saw Demetrace's earthstone, on his staff. If we can smash it or something, maybe it'll weaken him enough that we'll stand a chance."

Now that, Ellie understood.

"Great," she said. "So now we just need a plan to—"

She was interrupted by an explosion of stone to their left, as an enormous bull-headed gargol crashed into the courtyard, bellowing in rage. A dozen more flew behind it, intent on the trio.

"Scatter!" Ellie yelled. "Nox—find the sorcerer! We'll lead the gargols away!"

"But—"

There was no time to argue with him. She'd already taken off, and he was forced to do the same as the bull-headed gargol charged.

Ellie lost sight of Nox and Gussie as she shot through the ruins on a flurry of wings. She dove through archways, sped through tunnels, and turned hairpin corners, trying to keep ahead of the gargols pursuing her. Staying low in the streets at least gave her some cover. The gargols, too big to flit through the narrow paths, instead crashed through whatever walls stood in their way. Cyrith echoed with the cacophony of shattering stone.

This is it, Ellie thought.

This was the battle where they won—or lost—everything.

CHAPTER THIRTY-THREE
· NOX ·

Nox flew erratically through Cyrith, dodging gargols. He found the spot where he'd woken up after being captured by Demetrace, but there was no sign of the sorcerer there. He struggled to think where the man might have gone.

A shadow flickered over him. Nox turned just as a pair of panther-like gargols attacked out of the sky above. One dove and nearly crushed him. Nox fell on his back and frantically whipped his wings forward, but he didn't have enough momentum. The fire sizzled uselessly in the air. The second gargol landed behind Nox, trapping him.

Then a pop of smoke down the street drew the creatures' attention.

"Gussie!" he shouted.

"*Go*, Nox!" The Falcon stood on a rooftop, holding her crossbow and arming it with another powder capsule.

Her distraction was enough for him to slip away, and seeing her on the rooftop had sparked an idea in his mind.

If *he* were a vindictive madman orchestrating all this chaos, he'd want a good view of it.

Lifting into the air, Nox looked around until he spotted the tallest tower in Cyrith, a ruin on the far side of the island.

He sped toward it.

Another gargol hurtled toward him, screeching. This time, Nox was prepared, and he didn't even slow as he spun in the air, sending a wave of fire rolling over the creature. It screamed as it shattered, the pieces raining down on the city and smashing through tiled rooftops. Nox flew through the spot where it had been, dodging flying chunks of its stone body.

As he approached the tower, he saw flashes of light from the highest balcony—bursts of gold and yellow, the same shades as he'd seen swirling in Icara's earthstone earring.

He'd guessed right.

There, high above at the tower's peak, stood the ancient sorcerer, brandishing his staff. In response to the gesture, a dozen more gargols rose from the sky below and spread across Cyrith.

Demetrace knew they were in the city, Nox realized, and he was setting his creatures on them like hounds running down foxes.

Several gargols spotted Nox and charged his way. He slowed, feathers flaring, as his heart dropped into his stomach. He couldn't possibly take on that many at once. He'd never reach Demetrace in time.

All he could do was stare helplessly as the monsters swarmed toward him.

Then, suddenly, the sky filled with wings.

Nox reeled in confusion as dozens of people rushed around him, racing to meet the gargols. Feathers of every shade and shape flashed by, and the air echoed with shouts. Sunlight gleamed on spearpoints and long, curving bows, and as he turned in midair, Nox saw even more people swooping in behind him. It was like being caught in a swirling storm of leaves, the sound of feathers like the breaking of ocean waves.

"Hey, Nox!"

He whirled, spotting a bright splash of colorful feathers. *"Tariel?"*

The Macaw girl grinned and twirled her spear. "You didn't think us Macaws would miss the fun?"

"What are you—*how*?"

It wasn't just the Macaws he saw; there were Quetzal clanners too, and Kingfishers and Toucans and, howling and whooping, twirling fiery torches, the bright-pink-feathered Flamingo clan.

"What are you *doing* here?" Nox asked.

"After everyone in the south heard about Tirelas," Tariel explained, "we decided to send a delegation to your Eagle king, to propose a pact to retake the sky islands. Only we show up to find you lot with a mountain hanging over your heads and gargols carving up your sky. Anyway, met your prince—Corion, now *there's* a face a girl could—"

"Tariel, now's not the time!"

"Right. Anyway. To battle!" She crowed and swooped toward the fray, where the southern clans were spreading massive nets in the air, trying to throw them over the gargols.

An older woman intercepted Tariel, grabbing her arm. Nox's eyes widened as he recognized the chief of the Macaws.

"Tariel! What did we tell you?!" the chief said in exasperation. "Stay on the *ground*! I swore to your grandmother I wouldn't let you—"

A roar like thunder shook Cyrith. He saw one tower, already half-caved in, actually topple under that onslaught of sound. His teeth vibrated with it; his hands clapped over his ears of their own accord. If the noise of the Southern clans' arrival had been like a breaking wave, this noise was like a mountain collapsing on top of him.

All around the island, the sky turned black as gargols rose from every side. Hundreds, *thousands* of them, thick as a swarm of bees, hovered on wings that sent wind gusting through the streets.

The blood drained from Nox's face.

Demetrace must have recalled his entire horde.

The southern clans quailed in uncertainty, now finding themselves outnumbered.

"Chief!" Nox called, and the Macaw leader turned to him. "I have to get to that tower! If I can stop that man, maybe we can end this for good!"

She glanced up at the spire, then nodded, her face grim. "We'll make a path."

Ellie

A monkey-faced gargol dropped onto the street in front of Ellie, smashing the paving stones. Ellie toppled backward, wings fluttering in an effort to keep herself upright.

She was cut off from every side. Gargols above, ahead, and behind.

Helpless, Ellie pressed against a stone wall, panting hard. This was it. She couldn't fight, couldn't fly—the only question was which gargol would reach her first.

The one with the monkey face lunged, screeching.

Ellie didn't hesitate. She leaped for it, swinging her staff with all her might. Sliding right up to its head, she began whacking its snout.

"I—am—so—tired—of—*gargols*!" she roared.

The creature seemed more confused than anything. It retreated, blinking, then stretched open its jaws in an ear-shattering screech. Ellie snarled and jammed her stave in its mouth, pinning it open. While it thrashed and howled, she took flight, winging away as fast as she could go.

Above, a rush of wings drew her eye, and she looked up to see a flood of people filling the air. Macaws, Quetzals, Flamingos—the southern clans!

Where had *they* come from?

Whatever the case, Ellie had never been so relieved in her life. But just as quickly, she saw the horde of gargols amassing against them— skies, there had to be *thousands* of the creatures—and realized they were still vastly outnumbered.

Taking to the air, she spotted Nox, wings flaming as he shot through the sky. The southern clans were forming a tight formation around him, armed with spears and nets.

Ellie followed Nox's line of direction to the high tower behind her—and the stone man on its balcony.

Demetrace.

She recognized him at once; just like the first time she'd seen him, he was waving his staff around, commanding the gargols from on high.

The sky shook with the screams of the southern clans and the roars of the gargols as they battled. It sounded like a massacre. It would *be* a massacre, if they didn't find a way to stop it. The monsters were simply too many to fight.

Nox *had* to be right about this plan. If he wasn't, none of them would leave Tirelas alive.

She reached the tower's base and hesitated, then spotted a doorway at the very bottom. Diving through it, Ellie flew up a spiraling staircase. It was so dark she could barely see where she was going, but at least this way, she couldn't be spotted by gargols. She'd have the element of surprise—but that would be her only advantage.

Had Nox made it through the gargols? Would he reach the tower in time?

She had no way of knowing. She could only fly and hope.

Nox

This was no battle.

This was carnage.

The southern clanners fell like rain, injured or worse. They couldn't make a dent in the gargol horde. The creatures swarmed like ants, growing in number with every passing second, while the clans desperately tried to carve a path through their ranks. Macaw clanners flew around Nox, sweeping their great fishing nets through the air. The nets could slow a gargol, but only briefly, until the creature tore through the fibers with its claws and teeth.

Nox wouldn't make it. Even if he thought he could, the southern clanners would be wiped out just trying to clear his way.

He looked around, desperate for inspiration, but all he saw were gargols diving, slashing, scattering the southern clans. Beyond them, the storm clouds churned and thundered, lightning pulsing in their swollen gray bellies. For a moment, his mind went blank, overwhelmed by the chaos, by the death and pain all around.

Then the southern clans' protective formation broke.

Gargols rushed to Nox. He rolled and swooped, flying for his life. He didn't make it a dozen wingspans before a stone claw caught him hard against his chest, throwing him through the air. He slammed into a wall and slid to the ground, winded.

For a moment he sat there, stunned and seeing stars, unable to move. He struggled to regain his sight, his breath, while the world spun around him. Dimly, he heard screams above, southern clanners calling to one another, or crying out in pain. It felt like the end of world. It might well have been.

Then, seeing a flash of movement to his right, he whirled—and froze.

"Icara!"

She was crouched in an alley, watching him.

Nox regarded her cautiously, unsure which side she was on. "Did you tell him where I was?" he asked. "Are you the reason he caught me in Thraille?"

She scowled. "If you're going to throw around accusations, I'll just leave."

"No! Wait. I—I need your help."

"You think I'll fight my own father?"

"I'm sorry, Icara. But he's going to kill thousands of people. He's—"

She waved a hand until he stopped talking. "I came to give you this."

Nox stared as she took something from her pocket and held it out, her stone fingers uncurling one by one.

There, glowing on her palm like a burning ember, was the firestone.

Nox's eyes popped. "*You* had it?"

"I got to you before my father did, after his gargols grabbed you. I couldn't free you, because there were too many of his monsters around. But I did get this."

His gaze lifted to her face. "It didn't change you back to your old self? You're still . . ."

She touched her fingers to her marble cheek, then said softly, "I never tried."

"Why not?"

She swallowed, her fingertips tapping on the hard surface of the firestone. "Because if I used it, it would be destroyed. And it's the only one we have."

"What about your plan? Being alive again?"

She looked down, the fine, pale fringe of her marble eyelashes glowing faintly in the light of her skystone eyes. "Like someone told me recently . . . it's more important to be alive in *here*."

Her marble fingers came to rest delicately over her heart. Nox's lips parted, but he couldn't find the right words to say.

Suddenly, she thrust the firestone out. "Take it. Before I change my mind."

"Icara . . ."

"*Take it.* You won't be able to beat him without it. He's strong, much stronger than me or any gargol. But with this? You might have a chance."

"What do I do with it?"

She shrugged. "I don't know. But it's got to be good for something. Earthstone enhances my father's Legacy, makes it a hundred times stronger. Maybe this one does the same for yours."

"What about you?"

"You're running out of time, Phoenix."

He nodded and took off, watching her slip back into the shadows.

Turning on his wingtip, Nox flew for the tower, clutching the firestone to his chest.

Corion

Never in his life had the prince of the Eagles run so hard, for so long. He'd knocked on what seemed hundreds of doors, shouted at countless people to fly for their lives, and dragged more than a few out himself when they'd not believed him. But every time they saw the island hanging in the sky above Thelantis, they snapped into action, taking their families and fleeing.

Finally, Corion found himself back where he'd started, in the great city square, having completed the sweep of the southwestern district. Zain had finished his own circuit, and they stared at each other, panting and exhausted.

Then Corion stumbled toward the knight and collapsed into him, shaking as he pressed his face into Zain's shoulder.

"There's not enough time! We'll never get them all out!"

"We have to go, Corion," Zain said. "You can't save everyone. That thing could come crashing down any second!"

The island was so low that it entirely blotted out the sky. He could see the gargols chipping away at the last of the great skystones. Once they freed it, the island would fall. Anyone still in the city would be crushed. The Goldwings who'd flown at the gargols, to try and stop them from cutting the skystone loose, all lay scattered in the streets like broken toys. They'd been easily rebuffed by the monsters. Far more Goldwings had fled altogether, grabbing only their own families and leaving the rest of the city to its fate. A scattering of low clanners had remained to help, but Thelantis was vast, and there were dozens more houses to be checked.

The task seemed impossibly huge for one prince and his knight.

"Corion!" called a voice.

The prince lifted his head, eyes wide. "Mother? Diantha?"

His family landed, flanked by a handful of their most loyal attendants. His mother looked as regal as ever, amazingly, but his sister was clearly terrified, her hair undone and one of her shoes lost. Seeing how few protected them, Corion felt a rush of fury. Where were all the guards, the warriors of the Eagles, Hawks, and other high clans? The ones who were supposed to protect the queen and princess? Cowards! They'd been surrounded by cowards all this time!

The queen frowned. "Your father—"

"He's dead." Corion's voice was flat. "Which makes Diantha here the queen."

His mother took a step back, her hand pressing to her chest as she took in this news. It took her a moment to collect herself. Then she shook her head. "He drew up the papers, but he never finished signing them. I think . . . he hoped you might . . . It doesn't matter now. You're not disinherited, Corion. *You* are king."

Corion blinked at her, as she and her attendants dropped to their knees. Zain followed, his face pale.

"What are you *doing*?" Corion roared. "Get up, get up! You think anyone cares about kings or crowns right now?" He lifted his mother by her elbow. "Get out of the city as fast as you can. I'll join you after I've made sure everyone has evacuated."

"Come with us, Corion!" his mother wailed, gripping his arms. "You'll die here!"

"If I *am* the king, I have a responsibility to these people. So go, and let me do it."

"You can't save the whole city on your own! You may be a king, Corion, but you're also a child."

"He's not on his own, Your Majesty," said Zain, his voice wavering a bit; Corion wondered if the Hawk had ever addressed the queen directly before. "I will stay with him, no matter what."

Corion smiled, taking hold of the knight's hand. Zain's grip alone fueled him with strength he didn't think he'd had. "We're losing time. Let's go."

Taking flight again, he and Zain wheeled over the city and shot toward the next district. He could only hope his mother would act with more sense than his father had and flee while she could.

As for himself . . . whether he was a king or a prince or a disinherited pauper, it didn't matter now. Only the job at hand mattered, and the lives still in need of saving.

But even with Zain at his side, he knew they'd never finish sweeping the city in time.

A deep, aching groan, like the shifting of continents, shuddered in the sky. Corion looked up, sickened, to see the skystone slip. It was nearly free. The island sank lower.

At any moment, the entire thing would plummet.

"Corion . . ." Zain gave him a wide-eyed look.

"I know. I saw it."

"No, not that. *Them.*" The knight pointed.

Corion looked down to see the streets suddenly filling with people. Clanners of every feather were landing and running from door to door, frantically pulling people out of their homes.

"Who are they?" Corion stared, bewildered. The strangers were all dressed similarly, in blue and white. He dove for the nearest one, a tall Swan clanner his own age.

"Hey!" he shouted, just as the Swan was about to knock on another door. "What it this? Who are you?"

The boy nodded, then tapped on the door with the hooked staff he carried. "Restless Order," he said breathlessly. "Here to help. I'm Charlo."

"The Restless . . . !" Corion had heard many rumors of the hermetic group but had never seen one for himself. His father had dismissed them as fanatics and mystics, harmless if irritating. "The Eagles drove your kind into hiding. Why would you help us?"

"We're Restless, not heartless. And we're wasting time."

That was true. Corion reached out and briefly squeezed the Swan's shoulder. "Thank you. I mean it—*thank you.*"

The boy nodded, then knocked again on the door, eliciting a frightened "Hello?" from inside.

Leaving him to it, Corion and Zain flew toward the upper city.

"They'll handle the lower districts," Corion said. "We should head to the upper."

Zain nodded. "I'm right behind you."

Despite the arrival of the Restless, Corion's heart squeezed as he glanced up at the island.

"No matter what, Zain?" he asked in a voice much smaller and more uncertain than the one he'd used with his mother. "You promise?"

Zain gave him a smile that was just as weak, but his tone didn't waver when he replied. "No matter what."

Nox

The firestone burned in Nox's hands. As it flared brighter, so did his wings.

Before, when he'd held it, he'd been uncertain, his heart and mind divided. His path unsure.

But now, guided by instinct, or perhaps the ghostly memories of his Phoenix ancestors, he knew exactly what he needed to do, and why.

The only question left was whether he would succeed.

He rose on flaming feathers, scorching the air around him. Heat shimmered off his skin. As he lifted higher, above the rooftops of Cyrith, he saw the gargols arrayed before him, gathering until they were thick as a cloud, still battling the dwindling forces of the southern clans. Beyond them—Demetrace's tower.

Nox looked around until he spotted the Macaw clan chief.

"Tell your people to get down!" he yelled. "All of them—now!"

He worried that she wouldn't understand—skies, *he* barely understood his sudden certainty—but something in his voice must have convinced her, because she took one look at him and nodded. Then she raised a horn and blew into it three times.

At once, the Macaws dove for the ground. The other southern clans, seeing this, looked confused but followed suit. In moments, they'd all retreated into the ruins, leaving the sky filled with gargols.

The chief gave Nox a salute, then dove after them.

Nox inhaled, deep, deeper, his knuckles whitening as his hands tightened on the firestone. Something inside him sang to the stone, and the stone answered. The light within it began to condense into fine, glowing tendrils that threaded through the air and wrapped around Nox. He pulled it in, let it gather in the center of his chest, where it burned hotter and brighter, until he could see his own ribs silhouetted beneath his skin.

Suddenly, the firestone cracked and went dark. It had nothing left to give; all its energy bundled in a tight, scorching knot between his lungs. His hands opened, letting the drained stone fall. When it hit the street below, it cracked into a dozen pieces.

Nox exhaled slowly.

Flames began to curl around his fingers. They shivered in the air around him, swirling, whirling, growing bigger and brighter, until he was entirely encased in a spinning vortex of fire. He curled up, wings spread wide and stiff as sails, the heat alone enough to hold him in the air.

Out, out, Nox breathed, releasing more of the firestone's power. He heard a roar, and realized it came from his own throat. His mouth was stretched wide, his hands in fists. He wasn't sure how he was doing it, but he let instinct guide him, the way it had told him to burn away the storm concealing the falling island.

The way it had broken him free of his stone prison, and before that, guided him back to Thraille.

The way it had made him look into the eyes of a Sparrow girl, months ago, and decide to trust her.

At last, out of breath, Nox flung himself wide, arms and legs and wings spread, with a final resounding shout.

His fire rushed outward, consuming the air, hissing and lashing. Like a flood, it pushed away everything in its path—knocking over towers, snapping trees, and sending the gargols careening. The monsters tumbled and screeched, helpless against the tidal wave of flames. The smallest of them cracked and shattered, while the others were flung far into the sky—clearing the path to Demetrace.

Nox shot forward on flaming wings, straight and true as an arrow.

He closed the distance in seconds, smashing into the sorcerer before Demetrace could raise a hand.

They hit the hard floor of the tower balcony and rolled. Then Nox sprang up again, looking for the staff with its earthstone shining atop it, only to be backhanded across the face by Demetrace's stone hand.

He crumpled, head ringing, tasting blood on his lips. Sparks burst in his vision. He fought to rise again, but stumbled. He spotted the staff, just by his foot. All he had to do was reach it and—

Then Demetrace was on him.

With all the weight of his marble body, the sorcerer pressed his knee into Nox's abdomen, pinning him down. Then his hands wrapped around Nox's throat.

Nox choked, eyes wide. He stared at the cold stone face above him, unable to even speak. Demetrace squeezed tighter and tighter, a cruel smile curling in the corners of his lips.

"The last Phoenix," he hissed. "How sweet vengeance tastes, even after all this time. Look at me, boy! I want to see your fire go out."

Nox struggled in vain. There was nothing he could do against that grip. All the power he'd drawn out of the firestone was gone, spent washing away the gargols. Even now, the creatures were amassing again, gathering around the tower to watch him die.

In the end, he'd done nothing to stop them or their maker.

He had failed again.

His eyes began to roll, his vision blackening. He glanced around one last time, tears in his eyes, desperate . . .

And then he saw her.

Ellie.

Where had she come from? How had she gotten past the gargols?

Fly! he wanted to scream. *Get away from here! Save yourself!*

She stood behind the sorcerer, eyes wide, looking around for something to fight with. Nox's eyes widened as she bent and picked up the staff.

The gargols spotted her. They began to screech, rushing in on a flurry of stone wings, claws outstretched to grab the Sparrow.

Nox's heart stopped.

Then Ellie swung the staff at Demetrace's head.

The earthstone burst against the sorcerer's marble skull, shards flying in all directions. The power contained within it rushed outward in a great wind that smelled of stone and soil and clay, the scents of earth. The howling gale of magic roared around the tower, then burst outward, sending a shock wave rolling across the dome of the sky. Clouds rippled and disintegrated in its path; even the sun seemed to darken for a moment.

When it was gone, everything went still.

Nox and Ellie, Demetrace, the horde of gargols—all hung in the suspension between heartbeats, waiting.

Then a crack splintered over Demetrace's face.

Slowly, it spread, webbing over his torso, his wings, his hands. A look of horror dawned on the sorcerer's face. His skystone eyes met Nox's, looking suddenly afraid.

"Icara," he breathed.

Then he shattered into a million pieces.

CHAPTER THIRTY-FOUR
· NOX ·

Nox took Ellie's hand and climbed unsteadily to his feet. Bits and pieces of Demetrace crunched underfoot; he grimaced and tried to step around them.

"Blazin' skies!" Ellie gasped. "Did you see—I just—*did you see what I just did*?"

"Yeah," rasped Nox, his voice a thin hiss. He put a hand to his bruised throat. "You just brained a thousand-year-old sorcerer."

"Served him right," Ellie said. But she looked just as rattled as he felt. "He was going to throttle you."

"He *did* throttle me," groaned Nox. Speaking wasn't worth the pain, he decided. So instead, he threw his arms around Ellie. She was shaking but unharmed, to his relief.

"What happened to *not being the hugging type*?" she laughed. But she hugged him back just as fiercely, her tears damp on his shoulder. "We did it, Nox. We did it."

He couldn't make himself believe this was real. That *she* was real, even with his cheek pressed against her hair. She smelled of sunflower oil and dust and sky.

Then Nox realized how long he was letting this hug last, and his face went hotter than his wings.

"Wait!" he said hoarsely, pulling back. "The gargols!"

They whirled, Ellie holding the remains of Demetrace's staff defensively—but the sight that greeted them struck them both speechless.

All around the tower, and far into the depths of the sky, there was not a gargol to be seen.

Instead, there were . . .

"Animals?" Ellie's voice pitched upward in disbelief.

Not just animals. *Winged* animals.

In every spot where a vicious, raging gargol had hovered, now there floated boars, horses, wolves, dogs, leopards, creatures Nox didn't even have names for. And every one of them was fitted with its own pair of wings.

"What in the skies . . ." Ellie whispered. "Twig was right."

"Twig?"

"He said the gargols weren't evil at all, that they were *made* into monsters . . ." Tears welled in her eyes. "Nox, these must be the native animals of Tirelas. They're winged, just like us."

"Twig will *love* this!" Nox laughed.

Ellie tensed beside him but said nothing.

The animals seemed to be just realizing that they'd been freed of their enchantments. The sky filled with a cacophony of roars, yowls, trumpets, and screeches. The shocked and disoriented creatures began flapping in all directions, trying to get away. Ellie and Nox leaned over the balcony's stone rail and watched them disperse, laughing at their expressions of bewilderment.

"There they go!" Ellie cried. "Can you believe we were just flying for our lives from *that*?" She pointed at a snorting winged pig as it careened this way and that, its white wings clumsily bearing it off into the blue.

"You did this," Nox said. "You smashed Demetrace's earthstone—it was the source of all his power. The minute it broke, everything he transformed . . ." His heart stopped. His eyes widened. "Icara."

Without another word, Nox climbed over the rail and leaped into the sky, spreading his wings. He heard Ellie shout, but didn't slow.

Where had he seen Icara last? He tried to remember the alley she'd been hiding in. Zigzagging, nearly getting clobbered by a panicking winged bull, he finally spotted it.

Nox dove, landing with a little hop-skip. "Icara! *Icara!*"

At first, he thought she was gone. The alley was filled only with old rubble.

Then the rubble moved. "*Nox.*"

He rushed to Icara's side as Ellie landed in the mouth of the alley. The stone girl was lying curled up, her marble form covered in splinters and cracks. As he watched, a section of her shoulder turned to dust and flaked away. She held her comb tightly in her hands, as if it were the only thing still keeping her alive.

"Tell me how to stop it!" Nox said. "Tell me how to save you!"

She only looked at him, her skystone eyes flickering. "You can't."

"Did you know? Did you know if I shattered the earthstone, you would . . . ?"

"A thousand years is long enough," she whispered. "It's okay, Nox. It's okay."

"There must be something I can do!"

She gave a gravelly laugh. "It's funny . . . after a thousand years of living, I finally feel . . . *alive.*"

Nox cried out as Icara began to crumble in his hands, marble to dust. Her skystone eyes faded and fell, clattering dully on the ground. In moments, she was gone. He was left holding only her beloved comb.

"I'm sorry," Ellie whispered. "She . . . must have been important to you."

Nox swallowed. Rising to his feet, he stared at the dust already dispersing onto the breeze, a pale stream twisting into the sky.

"She was the last of her kind," he said. "Just like me."

They stood a moment longer in silence, then Ellie gently took his hand.

"Come on," she said. "Let's check on the others."

They flew across Cyrith, until they found where the southern clans had gathered in an ancient amphitheater to gape at the swarms of animals winging overhead.

"Ellie! Nox!"

Tariel of the Macaws came bounding to them.

"We won!" she cried. "I mean, I'm still not totally sure *how* or *why* we won, but hey! Gargols are nice now! Who knew? I saw one change right in front of me, y'know. It's like the stone just sorta melted away. Weird, right? Gade is not going to believe it when I tell him. Oh, did I tell you? We're engaged! Me and Gade! I mean, sure, he said no when I asked him, but he'll come around. His sisters are totally in, anyway. Well, I guess that makes them *my* sisters now—"

"Tariel," Ellie said wearily, but still smiling.

"Right! Sorry! Shutting up!" She grinned.

"Have you seen Gussie?" Ellie asked. "Skies, I hope she's—"

Nox tapped her shoulder, then pointed.

Gussie was walking down the steps at the far side of the amphitheater, looking weary and bruised. She was limping, using a sword as a crutch. When she saw them, she raised a hand in greeting, but despite their victory, she wasn't smiling.

Then a small, furry head poked out of her pocket.

"Lirri? Why is Lirri . . . ?" Nox's stomach dropped. He turned to Ellie. *"Where is Twig?"*

Ellie

Thelantis was gone.

They stood in a field just south of the city, surrounded by thousands of other people. The air was utterly silent. No one spoke, no one moved. They simply stared, and Ellie stared with them.

Where the great capital had been, there now rested a mountain. The island had fallen at last, crushing everything below. It lay at an angle, its rocky roots against Mount Garond, the ruins atop it a towering heap of rubble.

"We won," Ellie whispered.

But it didn't feel like victory.

Next to her, Nox was silent. He hadn't spoken a word since she'd told him how they'd left Twig, broken and bleeding in the street, but his emotions were clear in his feathers; for the first time that she'd seen, their fire had gone out completely.

A flutter of wings drew their attention. They turned to see Corion and Zain land on the grass behind them. The pair were covered in dust and scratches, exhaustion making them seem years older. The prince leaned on the knight, though Zain looked in danger of collapsing himself.

"We got them out," Corion said, looking relieved. "We got them all out, thanks to your friends."

"Our friends?"

He gestured and Ellie turned to see a crowd of familiar faces, all dressed in blue and white and carrying lockstaves. The Restless Order! And there was the Swan boy, Charlo, who'd taught her how to use her own stave. She let out a cry of surprise and ran to greet him.

"What are you all doing here?" she asked.

"I had a vision of the sky falling," said Charlo gravely.

"Really?"

The boy scoffed. "No. We saw *that*." He pointed to the fallen island. "It was kind of hard to miss. Lots of us have family in Thelantis. We couldn't sit on our mountain and just watch them die." His eyes went round as he stared at Nox. "Nice wings, Crow."

"It's Phoenix now," Nox said.

Ellie's eyes began to tear up again. "Charlo, we left Twig . . ."

"We found him." Charlo's face turned somber. "We brought him out, but then the animals came out of nowhere. They wouldn't let us get close. He's . . ."

Charlo pointed toward the edge of the forest, where a crowd of animals had gathered around a small, still form. Wolves and deer, squirrels and mice, and, lurking in the forest's gloom, the great shaggy outline of a mossbear. A group of clanners had gathered to stare at them, hanging back at a safe distance.

Nox, Ellie, and Gussie went to Twig's side. The creatures around him stared but did not challenge them. One of the wolves tossed its head back and howled mournfully. Ellie stood stiff, tears running down her cheeks.

"Is he . . . ?" She couldn't finish the question.

Nox dropped to his knees beside Twig. The boy was curled up and motionless, his skin drained of color. Gently, Nox put a hand on Twig's shoulder.

Ellie stopped breathing. Her ribs seemed to tighten around her heart. They'd battled so long, given everything they had, only to lose . . .

Softly, Twig's eyes fluttered open.

"N-Nox?" he whispered.

The relief in Ellie's chest broke like water from a dam. She sank down beside Nox. Twig was in bad shape, and clearly in pain, but he was alive.

How?

Ellie looked him over until she saw it: the dent in his metal wings. They hadn't stopped the spear's point completely, but the mechanical feathers must have dulled the blow just enough to save Twig's life. His wound had stopped bleeding, thanks to a bandage someone had wrapped around him, though he would clearly have a long road ahead to full recovery.

"Your invention saved him, Gussie," Ellie said, turning to the Falcon girl. "*You* saved him."

Gussie was staring, eyes wide, at the bent pieces of metal. Then her lips began to tremble, and her eyes flooded with tears. Something seemed to rush out of her as her shoulders lowered and her wings dropped to the ground. She knelt beside Twig and pressed her face into his shoulder, while he looked around in confusion.

Ellie had forgiven Gussie for her betrayal days ago.

But she realized that it wasn't until this moment that Gussie finally forgave herself.

CHAPTER THIRTY-FIVE
· ELLIE ·

"You know," Ellie said, "I think you tried to take a bite out of me once."

She squinted against the sun, watching a winged cat stretching on a tree limb high above her. It was hard to believe that the small, lithe creature with its tabby feathers was older than Thelantis—or that it had once been a raging gargol.

All across Tirelas, the animals had returned to their dens and thickets, burrows and fields. Ellie never got tired of seeing a deer suddenly burst into flight when she startled it from its hiding spot.

She wasn't sure how the animals had survived the breaking of Demetrace's power, when the sorcerer and his daughter, Icara, had not. A council of scholars had been formed to study the remnants of the earthstone, as well as the firestone Nox had told them about. Last she'd heard, their going theory was that Demetrace's gargol enchantment hadn't affected the animals as fundamentally as the one he'd used on himself and Icara. Their true natures had remained unchanged—which Gussie said could explain why Twig was able to communicate with them.

Maybe it was true, maybe not. There was still so much they didn't know about the things Nox called "origin stones" or the magic they held. All Ellie cared about was that there were no gargols left.

The sky was safe at last.

The islands of the Sparrow clan were lush with forests and hills. It had taken her weeks to find them, exploring the newly freed skies with Nox. After Thelantis had fallen, there had been thousands of people left homeless.

Luckily, the sky above was full of homes.

For the last two months, they'd sent out search parties to every corner of the sky, to chart the islands and reunite the clans with their ancestral homes. Just last week, Ellie had led the dazed, slightly nervous Dove clan to their sunny archipelago, where she'd helped little Mally and her mother choose a spot to build their house.

And yesterday, at last, she'd found the Sparrow islands.

She had felt the connection to the place even before she found the clan crest—a sunflower, of course—carved into an ancient stone hearth. It just felt *right*, these forests and meadows, the gentle mountains where the clouds continually poured rain. Water tumbled in streams and waterfalls down to the plains where, even after centuries, sunflowers still grew, dropped their seeds, and grew again.

"Does it feel like home?" Nox asked.

They were walking along the edge of one of the villages. Mother Rosemarie directed the clan's efforts to clear out the overgrowth, pulling weeds and vines off the stone remains of their ancestors' houses so they could begin rebuilding.

"I'm not sure . . . but if there's one thing I know, it's that home is more than just a place," Ellie said. "We were one of the last clans to find our ancestral islands, you know. I was starting to think we'd never find them."

"Ellie Meadows, give up?" Nox scoffed. His wings were warm; she could feel their heat like the pleasant glow of a campfire, but only a few small flames shimmered on his feathers. He could call on his fire or suppress it at will now, a thing that still filled her with relief whenever she thought about his first disastrous days as a Phoenix. As he walked, he held a small comb in his hands, absently running his thumb over its bristles. She wondered at that; he didn't talk about Icara much, but he seemed to think of her often.

"I did, though," she said quietly. She lifted her hand to touch the fragile wings of a moonmoth perched on a branch. It shivered at her touch and fluttered away.

"Huh?"

"I gave up, Nox. When the Goldwings had us surrounded in Thelantis . . . I stopped believing. Just for a moment. Then *you* showed up and saved us all."

Ellie took a few more steps but realized Nox had stopped. She raised her eyebrows, turning to look at him. "What?" she asked.

"I didn't save you."

"Of course you did. You showed up in the nick of—"

"Ellie." He gave her an odd look, as if she were missing the point on purpose. "*You* were the reason the southern clans showed up. The reason the Sparrows stood up against the king. You were the reason Corion turned against his father, and the reason the Restless Order was here to help."

She stared, looking confused. "But—"

"Icara told me your clan's Legacy was planting seeds. Whatever they planted, grew. And you've been planting seeds for months, Ellie—in the southern jungles, with the Restless Order, among the Sparrows, the whole of the Clandoms . . . in *me*. And when the time came, all those seeds sprouted. You think all these people came together at the right time just by chance?" He shook his head. "It was you, Ellie. It was all you."

"Nervous?" Gussie asked.

Ellie nodded, jittery. "Aren't you?"

"I'm not the one they're all waiting for."

"Thanks for the reminder. And for doing this. I wasn't sure . . . Well, you're so busy these days, with much more important clients than me."

She glanced up at the new sign over Gussie's workshop door, which was in the central district of Cyrith.

AGUSTINA BEREL, INVENTOR, it read.

Businesses and shops were opening up all over the Tirelan capital, as fast as the ruins could be cleaned out, roofed, and made usable again. After Demetrace had dropped one of the ancient city's islands on Thelantis, eleven had remained in the archipelago, and they were quickly filling up with new residents.

The sky was full of wings now, and not all of them were made of feathers. Gussie's workshop was busy from dawn till dusk, as her team of apprentices helped her craft metal-and-skystone wings by the dozen. Everyone who'd lost their flight to wingrot was being given a pair, funded by the king's treasury. Ellie had heard the word *ironwings* thrown around lately, not in mockery but in awe, and there was talk of setting up a special race just for those who wore them. She was sure most of that talk was being generated by the ironwings' first member—Twig.

Gussie nodded. In the last months, she'd grown even taller. Now Ellie barely came to her shoulder.

"Your order is ready," she said. "Here."

She handed Ellie a shining new lockstave. Based on the Restless Order's original design, Gussie had added a few elements of her own. Ellie opened a little compartment and laughed in delight as a mechanical spring popped out and produced a small flame.

"An igniter!"

"One of my first inventions," Gussie said, eyeing it appraisingly. "And still one of the most useful. Not *all* of us can be walking torches."

"Speaking of Nox, I should get going. Are you coming?"

"Wouldn't miss it." She grinned and elbowed Ellie. "Let's pick up Twig on the way."

They looked for him on an overgrown island just west of Cyrith. It had recently become infested with a pack of winged wolves, now freed from their gargol stone skins. A band of Osprey hunters had decided to clear them out and set off with traps and nets. When Twig had heard, he'd flown there first and warned the wolves, resulting in a two-day standoff that ended with the hunters retreating in exasperation.

Now "Skywolf Island" had become Twig's personal domain, where he was gathering quite a collection of winged animals. No one was brave enough to challenge him on it, not when he had several dozen furry, toothed sidekicks to back him up—not to mention one fiery-winged Phoenix.

Still, even Ellie felt nervous when she landed on the small island. The trees had grown thick over the ruins that lay there, so it was more forest than city. Howls and yips sounded from its shadowy depths.

"Twig!" she called. "Are you—"

"Watch out!" Gussie warned.

Ellie jumped when a pair of yellow eyes suddenly gleamed at her from the dark underbrush. A shaggy wolf lumbered out, stretching its gray wings and showing its teeth.

Then Twig stepped out of the trees, and the fierce animal immediately went docile. It rolled over, begging for a belly scratch. Laughing, Twig obliged.

"It's okay, Fuzzbutt," he said to the wolf. "No more hunters will come to bother *us*, nope!"

From his breast pocket, Lirri glared at the wolf, planting a paw on Twig's shoulder as if to say, *Mine!*

"Hey, Gussie! Hey, Ellie!" Twig said.

"Hey, Twig." Gussie eyed Fuzzbutt warily. "You coming to Ellie's thing?"

"Oh, right! Sorry, I was busy convincing the wolves to let Stripeybutt move onto the island. They don't want to give up any more territory, but I explained it's only fair until we can find him a more permanent home."

"Stripeybutt?" Ellie echoed.

Gussie sighed, scrubbing her face with her hand. "Do we even wanna know?"

Twig grinned. "I found a winged *tiger*! I'll introduce you later. Oh! And I want your help making a list of all the animals up here. You know, the wolves said there are winged horses off to the east. I—"

"*Twig,*" Gussie moaned.

"Oh. Right. Ellie's thing! Give me just one minute." He let out a sharp whistle.

A moment later, another, smaller kid swooped out of the trees to land beside Twig. He folded his own mechanical wings—Gussie's latest model—and snapped a salute. The metal and cloth of his wings had been painted in Gull clan colors.

"Yes, sir!"

Ellie felt a touch of sadness when she recognized Brayden. His uncle Brennec had been one of the brave souls killed by Goldwings on the quest to retrieve skystones. He'd never returned, and Brayden's wings, like so many others, had succumbed to wingrot as a result. Gussie had insisted on first providing ironwings to every one of the people who'd lost a loved one on that terrible winter day, before anyone else.

Ellie wasn't sure how Brayden had fallen in with Twig, but the little Gull clanner was taking his new duties as a warden of Skywolf Island very seriously.

"Keep an eye on Fuzzbutt and the others while I'm gone," Twig ordered.

Brayden nodded and let the wolf nuzzle his hand. "You got it, sir!"

With that settled, Twig, Ellie, and Gussie took flight.

Ellie kept a close eye on Twig, watching for any sign that the wound in his side was bothering him. The spear had left a scar, but otherwise, he'd healed well. Still, the Macaw doctor who had tended him insisted he keep flying to a minimum for a few months—and that he should bathe more often. Ellie thought she'd heard the woman use the phrase *public health menace*.

Twig, of course, had ignored both orders.

The day was cold but bright, and the trio soaked up the sun's rays as they followed the giant chains to the archipelago's center. Teams of Skyborn worked to scrub the links, clearing off centuries of rust. The polished metal now shone as if it had just been forged.

The enormous palace at the heart of Cyrith thronged with representatives of every clan, from Sparrows to Hawks to Macaws. A great celebration was underway. Music filled the air, and Flamingo clanners performed a fire dance on the palace steps. Hummingbird clanners flitted all around with long, colorful ribbons tied to their ankles, filling the sky with color and confetti.

Ellie landed outside the great throne room. "Where is he? He's supposed to be here."

Gussie rolled her eyes. "You know he hates attention. He'll slip in at the last minute."

"I guess some things never change."

Sure enough, it wasn't until the doors to the throne room were opening and the blast of trumpets sounded inside that Nox finally deigned to appear.

He landed beside her so suddenly that she yelped.

"Nox!" Ellie swatted his shoulder. "You're late."

"But I'm here." He grinned impishly. "Nervous?"

"Why does everyone keep asking me that?" She smoothed back her hair, hoping the warrior's knot she'd tied it in hadn't come too undone. "You know, it could be *you* sitting on one of those big thrones."

"Ha! Not a chance. I'm no king, Ellie. Can you imagine the messes I'd make?"

"I think I can." She laughed.

"All right, no more stalling." He gave her a light push through the doors, and Ellie stumbled into the grandest room in Tirelas.

It put even Garion's old throne room to shame. Parts of it were still being reconstructed, but it was hardly noticeable under the garlands of flowers and ribbons. Today, the room thronged with the chiefs of every clan, a veritable rainbow of feathers gathered under the enormous latticed dome. But outnumbering all the rest were the Sparrow clan—jostling and whispering, fluttering up to sit on the many high ledges the ancient Skyborn had installed, presumably, for just such occasions. Mother Rosemarie—no, now she was *Chief* Rosemarie, Ellie reminded herself—greeted Ellie with a kiss on her forehead, then thumbed a smear of sunflower oil on each of her cheeks. It was the traditional Sparrow blessing.

"Ellie Meadows," she said warmly, clasping Ellie's hands between hers, "you have made your clan very proud."

Ellie flushed, then looked down in surprise. Chief Rosemarie had pressed a golden shield into her grasp.

"What . . . what is it?"

Tarnished and faded, it was clearly a relic of old Tirelas, though someone had given it a good scrub. It depicted swords crossed over a sunflower, a variation of the Sparrow clan crest Ellie had never before seen.

"We found it on the Sparrow Isles," said the chief. "Ellie . . . it's proof that long ago, Sparrows were warriors just like everyone else. But then, I suppose I don't need to tell you that."

Ellie looked up at the old woman, then gave her a tight hug.

"Thank you. For everything."

The six tall thrones sat empty. Already the clans were arguing over who would sit there, and for how long. They only thing they'd agreed on was that the six monarchs would not come from the same clan—something Nox had insisted on, surprisingly. It was the one contribution he'd made at the great clan moot held to discuss the governance of Tirelas.

"No one clan should rule all the others," he'd said. "That's something the Phoenixes got wrong too."

For now, there was only one king in Tirelas, and instead of sitting, he stood in the center of the circle, waiting for Ellie with a huge smile.

"Hello, Ellie," said King Corion.

Not everyone had been happy about seeing an Eagle in a crown, after everything Garion had inflicted on the Clandoms. Corion himself had been the first to decline the title. But then the stories of his deeds during the Fall of Thelantis had spread. Dozens told of how the prince had personally saved their lives, staying until the last possible second to ensure his people's safety. Their testimonies had been enough to push the reluctant Corion onto one of the Tirelan thrones, and in the weeks since, he'd been as gracious and kind a leader as his father had been cruel and selfish.

Ellie didn't doubt that the earnest young Eagle would soon win over even his loudest critics.

"Hello, Your Majesty." She shot a glance at Zain, who stood behind Corion as a member of the new king's personal guard. He grinned back.

Corion raised his hands until everyone fell quiet. He was dressed in a white shirt and trousers, with a deep red vest trimmed in gold and the Eagle clan crest embroidered on the chest.

"People of Tirelas," he said in an impressively booming voice. "Today we celebrate our return home, the unification of the free clans, and the end of the wingrot plague and the gargol wars. Today, we honor someone at the heart of our homecoming, the brave Sparrow whose actions and courage are the reason we all stand here."

Turning back to Ellie, he said in a softer voice, just for her, "Your greatest strength was never in your wings, Ellie. It was in your heart. It was your belief in all of us, even we'd stopped believing in ourselves. Who would have thought the faith of one small Sparrow could save a world?"

She looked down, blushing. "You weren't too bad either, Your Majesty."

Grinning, he whispered, "This is the part where you kneel."

"Oh, right." She dropped to one knee.

"It's my great honor as a king of Tirelas," said Corion, "to knight you, Ellie Meadows, as the first of the new Goldwings. Under your wings, may we all fly free."

Zain handed Corion a patch—golden wings, same as the old Goldwings once wore. The new crest, however, also showed a spiral in a triangle, the symbol of Tirelas. The king gave it to Ellie. She accepted it with trembling hands.

"Fly, Sir Ellie of the Sparrows, and watch the skies."

"Watch the skies!" shouted the Sparrow clan and the gathered chiefs.

Unable to keep the smile off her face, Ellie burst upward to take a celebratory flight around the throne hall. She wheeled three times along the dome's walls, while everyone below cheered and tossed flowers. Turning in a final acrobatic loop, she landed beside Nox, back by the doors. Others were already lining up to be knighted, and a great many of them were low clanners just like Ellie, looking excited and nervous. They'd each been chosen for their bravery in the battle of Thelantis or the battle of Tirelas that had followed. When most of the knights had fled, these were the ones who'd remained and fought to the end, showing bravery that far outspanned their wings.

Ellie exchanged looks with a few of them—Tariel of the Macaws, with her spear in her hand, waved wildly. Charlo of the Restless Order, his lockstave swinging at his side, gave her a broad grin. Even Tauna of the Falcons, who'd once looked down on Ellie, now gave her a small, respectful smile, which Ellie returned. Tauna had been knighted before, but the council of chiefs had decreed all offices held on the ground were now void. Only a few of the old Goldwings would be knighted again; many wouldn't even show their faces, not after they'd abandoned Thelantis in its hour of need. The high clans were in disarray and disgrace; it would be a long, long time before the other clans trusted them again.

And eventually, there would *be* no high or low clans in Tirelas.

Instead all would fly as equals. At least, that was their hope. The road ahead would be rocky, Ellie suspected. Clans were already jostling for power, for a seat near the ruling council, for a bigger piece of the sky.

But they'd figure out the rules of their new world together, and everyone would be given the chance to leave their mark in the clouds.

Ellie believed that with her whole heart.

"Well?" Nox grinned. "How does it feel?"

She knew he meant the new golden patch shining on her chest. But instead of replying right away, Ellie looked around at the sky full of wings, the city rising anew from the clouds, the smiles on the people all around her, and Gussie and Nox and Corion and Zain and her whole clan gathered together.

At last she said, "It feels good to be home."

THE CLANS OF
SKYBORN

*The Clandoms and surrounding lands are home to many scores
of clans, each with its own unique identity and heritage.
Here are a few found in Phoenix Flight.*

SWALLOW

CLAN SEAT: White Quarry

CLAN TYPE: Low

WING DESCRIPTION: Dark blue feathers with pale or tawny undersides, tapered to points. Highly maneuverable and suited for endurance flying.

WINGSPAN: Short

TRADITIONAL OCCUPATIONS: Stone masons, sculptors, artisans

KNOWN FOR: Their skill in working with stone, clay, and mud; most of the greatest sculptors come from Swallow Clan. Nobles and royalty often commission their work.

WOODPECKER

CLAN SEAT: Delven

CLAN TYPE: Low

WING DESCRIPTION: Dark feathers with bold white patterns, either in solid stripes or evenly distributed dots. Rounded in shape, highly suited for vertical flight and soaring.

WINGSPAN: Medium

Traditional Occupations: Loggers, woodcarvers, carpenters
Known for: Their skill in working with wood and trees, supplying the majority of the lumber used in the Clandoms. Red hair is common among this clan, and they are known to be boisterous singers.

ROBIN

Clan Seat: Robinsgate
Clan Type: Low
Wing Description: Dull gray on both sides, with some lightening on the tips of the feathers. Long and rounded in shape.
Wingspan: Medium
Traditional Occupations: Farmers
Known for: The largest clan, and most widely distributed. They supply most of the grain produced in the Clandoms.

FINCH

Clan Seat: Finchton
Clan Type: Low
Wing Description: Pale brown to gray, with some white streaking and slightly lighter undersides. Rounded and short, ideal for fluttering short distances and rapid takeoffs.
Wingspan: Short
Traditional Occupations: Farmers, tea growers
Known for: Producing a range of highly sought-after dandelion teas

OWL

CLAN SEAT: Nightglen

CLAN TYPE: Low

WING DESCRIPTION: Wildly varied, but always large and round. Most commonly, wings are brown with black stripes and white undersides, though the northern branches of the clan feature wings that are snowy white on both sides.

WINGSPAN: Medium to Long

TRADITIONAL OCCUPATIONS: Scholars, inventors, historians, administrators

KNOWN FOR: Not quite a low clan, due to their wingspans and proximity to the high clan nobility, Owls are often seen as a category of their own. They run the universities in the Clandoms and oversee most academic matters. There are always a few Owls in residence at any high clan court, to handle administration and research.

OSPREY

CLAN SEAT: Lake Pandion

CLAN TYPE: High

WING DESCRIPTION: Dark brown with golden highlights and white undersides flecked with brown. Wings arch in flight. Powerful wings suited for steep, fast dives and long-distance flight, particularly over large bodies of water.

WINGSPAN: Long

Traditional Occupations: Warriors, nobles, naval officers

Known for: Controlling the seas around the Clandoms. Most of the soldiers in the king's navy are Ospreys, and they represent nearly all the naval high command.

HUMMINGBIRD

Clan Seat: Troila

Clan Type: Low

Wing Description: Iridescent green or blue, with long and sharply tapered feathers suited for extremely high speeds over short distances. They are the only clan whose wings do not have an alula joint.

Wingspan: Short

Traditional occupations: Couriers, messengers

Known for: Being the fastest clan alive. A hummingbird can outpace even a high clanner over a short distance, though they tire quickly. Their wings beat so rapidly they produce a musical, "humming" drone. One of the smallest clans in terms of stature, they are nevertheless quick-tempered and swift to pick fights, even against those much larger than they are.

PHOENIX

Clan Seat: Cyrith

Clan Type: High

Wing Description: Iridescent and luminous, appearing to change between metallic shades of gold. Wide and powerful, suited for high soaring and long-distance flying. Feathers are unnaturally hot, capable of producing smokeless flames when agitated.

WINGSPAN: Long to Very Long

TRADITIONAL OCCUPATIONS: Monarchs, judges, warriors

KNOWN FOR: Ruling the sky islands of Tirelas for thousands of years, until their fall to the gargols led to their destruction and the exile of all the Clans

ABOUT THE AUTHOR

Jessica Khoury is the author of many books for young readers, including *Last of Her Name*, *The Mystwick School of Musicraft*, the Corpus Trilogy, and *The Forbidden Wish*. In addition to writing, she is an artistic mapmaker and spends far too much time scribbling tiny mountains and trees for fictional worlds. She lives in Greenville, South Carolina, with her husband, daughters, and sassy husky, Katara. Find her online at jessicakhoury.com.